PAXON CHUTE

*A Novel about Life and Other Funny
Things in the Texas Hill Country*

Keith Cartlidge

KS Connected Publishing

Paxon Chute: A Novel about Life and Other Funny
Things in the Texas Hill Country

www.paxonchute.com

KS

KS Connected Publishing
PO Box 1234
Keller, Texas 76244

This book is a work of fiction. Names, characters, places, and
incidents are either products of the author's imagination or are used
fictitiously. Any resemblance to actual events or locales or persons,
living or dead, is entirely coincidental.

Scripture quotations taken from the New American Standard Bible®,
Copyright © 1960, 1962, 1963, 1968, 1971, 1972, 1973, 1975, 1977,
1995 by The Lockman Foundation. Used by permission.
(www.Lockman.org)

Set in Garamond

ISBN: 978-0-9916101-1-2

To Stacey
Who believed from the beginning
in what is now before you

TABLE OF CONTENTS

———

———

CHAPTER ONE

A distinct scraping sound came from behind the stack of boulders in the playground. Edgar turned away from the river and listened.

"Shovels." He checked his watch and frowned, then trotted towards the noise.

Rounding the large pile of smooth rocks Edgar came upon two middle-aged men furiously digging a hole. "Hey!" he yelled.

The taller of the two men straightened up and spun around, slinging a shovelful of dirt onto the boots of his companion.

"Come on now. We've got rules posted about this." Edgar pointed at a nearby wooden sign with yellow lettering.

The tall man squinted and slowly read aloud, "Welcome to Nickel Rock Park—"

Edgar interrupted him. "Not that part, down at the bottom. And you," he spoke to the shorter man who continued working, "stop that right now."

The taller man squinted harder. "No digging allowed."

"So we've confirmed you can read that sign from the exact spot where you are standing at this very moment, digging. What have you got to say for yourselves?"

The shorter man leaned on his shovel. "Just who are you, anyway?"

"I'm the head park ranger here." Edgar indicated the patch on his uniform.

"Well now, head park ranger, if there's no digging allowed then why'd they sell us a tip sheet on where to find the treasure?"

Edgar frowned. "Where'd you get a tip sheet?"

"Up at George's Goods." The man jerked his head in the direction of the town square.

"Ward." Edgar glanced at the square. "He was told to pull those from his shelves."

The tall man spoke up. "It wasn't on a shelf. He had to go in the back to fetch us one. Very hush-hush he said, and guaranteed to improve our chances."

"I swear that man lives his whole life inside a loophole," Edgar muttered to himself. "Listen, guys, he's not supposed to sell those sheets anymore. Don't you think that if there was any useful information on them someone would have found this mythical treasure already?"

The short man kicked at the pile of dirt. "Not the way he told it to us."

"I bet." Edgar chuckled. "Since you gentlemen don't look familiar I'm going to assume I've never caught you doing anything like this before, and I'll let you off with a warning. Now get this filled in right away."

The two men slowly poked their shovels at the dirt but almost nothing went back into the hole.

Edgar unclipped the radio hanging from his belt. "Eggman calling River Rat, over."

The radio beeped and a voice answered, "River Rat here."

"Where are you? I've got a couple of diggers filling in their hole but I have a childbirth class starting in a few minutes. Beth will go nuts if I'm late again."

"I'm all the way upstream."

"Dang it. I can't leave until they finish."

After a brief pause the voice spoke again. "It's just a hole, Edgar. It'll keep, one way or another."

"Never mind, I'll make sure they get this done before I go. Eggman out." Edgar clipped the radio back onto his belt and frowned at the men. "Seriously, guys? Get moving. You were both digging like fiends a minute ago so I know you've got it in you."

The short man leaned on his shovel again. "It was more excitin' before you showed up."

"Here." Edgar reached out his hand. "Give me that."

Edgar took the shovel and attacked the mound of dirt as both men stood watching. Five minutes later he smoothed it out and stomped it down.

"Don't let me catch you doing this again." Edgar returned the shovel. Wiping the sweat and dust from his face he checked his watch. "Shoot!" He sprinted up the riverbank and over to the town square.

* * *

Edgar, breathing heavily, slowly closed the classroom door. He crept onto the exercise mat where his wife lay on her back with her knees propped up on pillows.

She opened her eyes. "Kinda hard to sneak in when there's only the two of us in class."

Nurse Irene whirled around from the chalkboard. "Ah, there you are, Edgar. We were just reviewing the signs of labor, which are on the sheet I gave to Beth. You'll want to keep that handy 'cause your baby is comin' real soon. So what we're doing now is relaxing. Beth, if anything comes to mind that prevents you from relaxing, I want you to share it with Edgar." Irene sat down at the desk near the chalkboard and opened a file folder. "While you two do that I'll catch up on some paperwork."

Beth took a deep breath in through her nose and puffed her cheeks as she exhaled through her mouth. "Okay, this isn't going to work until I know why you were late again."

"Sorry," Edgar spoke quietly, "but on my way out of the park there were these treasure hunters digging a huge hole…"

"Someone slogging around digging holes in the park is no excuse. That goes on all the time."

He swallowed. "But it was right there in the playground so I couldn't leave until it was filled in."

"This is not helping me." Beth breathed deeply. "And anyway, how can I relax when we don't even have a name yet?"

"Oh good grief." Edgar grabbed a clump of his hair. "I knew that would be next."

"Last night you said I was a weirdo."

Irene looked up from her paperwork, her eyes narrowed and she shook her head. "Hmmm."

"That's not what I said. I only said you had some weird issues that made it harder for us to decide."

"Oh." Beth closed her eyes again. "That's better. A little. But it's not my issue, we have issues to overcome because of you, Mr. Rerd. I'm still not used to the stares I get when I say your name."

Edgar frowned. "You mean our name. And you knew what you were getting into from the first night Marlon introduced us."

Beth took hold of the edge of the mat and pulled, slowly working her way onto her side. "I know, of course I know. Don't forget I started going by Beth so I could marry you."

"I never thought Liz Rerd was all that bad."

"You still don't hear that it sounds like lizard? That's exactly the kind of thing I'm trying to avoid, the kind of mistakes your parents made."

"What's that supposed to mean?"

"Okay, so they had a difficult task, no doubt, but some

combinations are worse than others. Like your sister, Verda Rerd. It's like they couldn't get enough of Rerd, so they scrambled the letters around then swapped in a V."

"No." Edgar shook his head. "It's because Dad believed they were in Mexico when Verda was conceived."

"And then there's your older brother. Just because your Dad had been reading up on presidential history, he picked Grover Rerd? Seriously? Who does that to a kid? The only thing worse than that is your biblical younger brother, Japheth Rerd."

"Dad felt very close to the Lord after being struck by lightning."

"I know, but there are lots of other options in the Bible. What's wrong with John? And the initials for all of you are just as bad. Verda Consuela Rerd is a VCR, Japheth Abram Rerd is a jar, Grover Roosevelt Rerd is an angry grrr!" She growled and waved her fists in the air.

Irene set her pen down. "Remember, we're trying to relax during this time."

"Okay, I'll try." Beth took a slow breath. "And your initials are E-A-R."

"Really," Edgar sighed, "it's not a big deal and hardly anyone even knows that anyway."

"Think about your name." Beth pointed at him. "It ends with an 'r' which doesn't give any kind of separation. It all flows together into Edgarrerd. The first name really needs to end with a distinct sound to give it a chance."

"When I was little they called me Ed." He slid a pillow between her knees.

"I know, but Ed Rerd sounds like someone struggling to say Edward."

"Wow." Edgar paused. "Okay, so you want it to stand out. How about Tom? That has a good powerful anchor on the end."

"Tom? Let's see…" Beth lay still for a moment. "No! People sometimes switch the first letters around by accident, which makes Rom Terd."

"That's ridiculous. Who does that? And who would care?"

"I'll tell you who. The announcer at homecoming my junior year. He fumbled around and introduced our queen as Wamela Piggs, and Pamela cared. She cared a lot."

Edgar raised his eyebrows. "I do believe she would. Look, you're still not relaxing. Maybe you're upset because I was late. I really am sorry. It's just everyone's going crazy over some new rumor about Molly's treasure. Oh, and Marlon called. He's coming back to town and has some fantastic venture he says will be a great opportunity for us. It's going to have to be better than anything he's come up with before."

"Thanks for the apology, and please stop talking about all that other stuff. I can't think." Beth fluffed up the pillow under her head. "Name, Edgar. We need a name."

Irene stood up. "Okay, this does not appear to be working for you two. Again. Let's practice your breathing technique instead. Go ahead and sit up, Beth. Edgar, get closer, look her right in the eyes, and breathe for her, coaching her. Remember, in through your nose and think 'ree.' The exhale is longer and slower, out your mouth and you're going to say 'laaax.' Re-lax, nice and calm. We'll work it for ninety seconds, so go ahead and start."

Edgar breathed in and Beth matched his pattern.

"Laaax," they both spoke on the exhale.

Then Edgar snickered. "I feel like an idiot every time we do this."

Beth continued breathing, louder and louder.

"Oh, sorry. I'll try to be serious." Edgar resumed the technique.

"That's good, Beth." Irene walked over to the mat. "You're really concentrating. Okay, you can stop now."

Edgar stopped but Beth kept going, and with increasing intensity. "Laaaaax!"

Irene knelt down. "You're not practicing, are you, honey?"

Beth shook her head.

"Well what do you know about that." Irene smiled. "And all of us right here in the hospital like we knew what we were doing. Let's check our time and see if they keep coming."

After another long exhale Beth shook her head. "I can't be in labor, we haven't picked a name yet."

* * *

Beth lay in the hospital bed clutching the rail and shouting, "LAAAAAAAAAAAAXXX!"

The wide-eyed Edgar stood beside her bed, very still. His mouth hung open but no coaching sounds came out.

Nurse Irene walked briskly past the open doorway and glanced inside the room. Without missing a beat she pivoted smartly and came in to check on her patient. Brushing past the immobilized Edgar she took Beth's hand and helped her regain focus.

Irene spoke quietly. "Reeeee...laaaaaaaxx. There you go, that's good. Slow your breathing."

A few seconds later Beth let go of the rail and sank back onto the mattress. After resting for a bit she tugged on her hospital gown, trying to get it straightened out. "I feel like a bloated cow."

"A cow?" Irene checked the drip on the IV bag. "Honey, you are not a cow." She looked over her shoulder and glared at Edgar.

He held up his hands. "She said it, not me."

"Well, your job is to convince her she's wrong, Edgar." Irene studied the printout from the monitor. "Your contractions are about five minutes apart so try and rest in between. Remember, if anything is bothering you be sure to let Edgar know."

Beth glanced at Edgar and her brow furrowed. "You said I had to make up my mind about the name before the baby's born."

Irene shook her head as she left the room.

"I didn't say that, Irene," Edgar called out to the retreating nurse, then turned to his wife. "I just thought it would help you relax if we settled on a name. Right now all I'm worried about is you and the baby, that you'll both be okay." He sat on the bed and leaned over to place his ear on her belly.

"You're so sweet." Beth laid her hand on his head. "I think the perfect name just came to me, but can I surprise you?"

Edgar sat up. "Um, I guess that—"

"Ooooh!" Beth's entire body stiffened with another contraction.

Edgar called out for Irene and started to stand but Beth clawed at the front of his shirt and dragged him down until their noses almost touched. He tried to pull back a little but she easily overpowered him.

"LAAAAAAAAAAXXX!" Beth exhaled through clenched teeth, sweat beading up on her reddened face.

* * *

Clyde Rerd sat atop an old Montgomery Ward lawn tractor, cutting the grass, when his cell phone rang. He struggled to get the phone out of the front pocket of his overalls. Pushing back his feed store ball cap, he yelled into the phone, "Clyde's mowing service."

"It's Edgar, Dad. What's all that noise?"

"I'm cuttin' the grass."

"Should you be doing that?"

"It's better than pacing around in the waiting room."

"No, I mean, should you be driving the mower while you're talking on the phone?"

"Can I get a baby update first, and the safety briefing afterwards?"

"Yeah, you became a granddad about fifteen minutes ago! Beth and the baby are both fine."

"That's outstanding!" Clyde slapped his thigh. "Does this baby have a name?"

"Beth's picked one out but I still don't know what she's decided. It's got me a little worried. Anyway, I can't wait for you to see him."

"I'm on my way over right now." Clyde pocketed his phone without disconnecting the call.

Clyde drove off the lawn and onto the driveway. Reaching the end of the drive he turned right onto the grassy shoulder of the two lane country road, slid the throttle from half turtle to full rabbit, and pointed the square orange hood towards town. As he picked up speed the empty utility trailer in tow began to hop and bounce around.

The road meandered through the Texas Hill Country, roughly paralleling the path of the Cobb River. Dark green trees covered most of the landscape except for the open meadows along the river. Clyde approached a big wooden sign on the side of the road that read "Welcome to Paxon Chute! Population 1,787."

The town got its name in part from a trapper, George Paxon, who happened upon a stretch of the Cobb River flowing over smooth rock formations. The rock channeled the river into a series of natural water slides, or chutes, as George called them. He built a home by the river, and the numerous friends and acquaintances he brought to the area eventually led to the establishment in 1869 of the little town of Paxon Chute.

Clyde drove right between the two thick posts holding up the welcome sign and ducked so he didn't hit his head.

Halfway through his journey the mower deck beneath his feet sucked up a stray shoe. The distracted Clyde had failed to notice the tidily mowed mile-long strip of grass behind him. A terrific whanging and thumping shook the whole rig as the mower blades did their best to mulch the shoe to shreds. Clyde stared into the distance as he felt around for the lever to disengage the power to the mower. He pulled absently on the lever and the dismembered shoe dropped down out of the mower and back onto the roadside to await its next adventure. Clyde smiled and motored on, humming an impromptu tune.

Clyde entered town and turned onto Side Street. A police cruiser, lights flashing, pulled up behind the mower. Clyde kept going, having no rearview mirror to see this new development. The siren blipped a few times, and the startled Clyde turned around to discover his escort. Both vehicles came to a halt in the middle of the street.

Police Chief Aaron Turner got out of the cruiser and walked up to the mower, studying the rig as he approached. "Clyde, what are you doin'?"

"Hello, Aaron. I'm going to see my new grandson." Clyde pointed his thumb in the direction of the hospital.

"Well congratulations, that's splendid news!" Aaron laughed and they shook hands. "Say now Clyde, I've got to talk with you about this little outfit of yours." He looked it over again. "You see, I've got a bunch of firewood I need to haul over to my woodshed, and my big gate is busted so I can't get my truck back there. But this should fit nicely through my small gate. Can I borrow it next Saturday?"

"Any time, just come get it if I'm not there. The key's always in it."

"Thanks. Sorry to startle you with the siren." Aaron walked back to his car and shouted, "Congratulations again!"

Clyde started the engine and waved goodbye.

He turned into the hospital parking lot and drove up over

the curb, stopping the mower on the immaculate grass near the front door.

Ned Sloan, the groundskeeper, poked his head up from one of the flower beds. "I didn't think that sounded like my Grass Thrasher."

Clyde slid off the seat. "Sure, Ned, rub it in. Every gardener in the county knows their mower can't compare to your Thrasher."

"What's that old thing doing on my lawn?" Ned pointed his pruning shears at Clyde's tractor.

"It's a mower, this is where it belongs."

Ned laughed. "All right, I guess. But it better not leak oil on my grass."

Clyde entered the two-story hospital building and asked for Beth's room number at the front desk. Up on the second floor, he opened the door to her room and a woman inside greeted him immediately. Penelope Anne Paine-Owens, Beth's mother, and the bearer of the only hyphenated name in Cobb County, stood halfway between the door and the foot of the bed.

"Hello, Clyde." Her voice filled the room. "I arrived here myself only a few moments ago. We received a call from Edgar as I was in the middle of my weekly massage from Dejmina. She's so wonderful, she sets up her little table right in my bedroom. Anyway, as soon as I heard it was Edgar on the phone, do you know what I said?" She hesitated ever so briefly, then continued. "I said, 'Elizabeth is in labor, isn't she!' Somehow I just knew. We can't always pick a convenient time for things to happen, can we? And I said to my husband, 'Richard, dear, I'm not quite ready to leave the house.' Even after Dejmina finished my massage I still had to do my hair and put my makeup on and get dressed. I knew my little girl to be in good hands here at the hospital." Her face pulled back into a smile and she reached out to pat the footboard of the bed. "And I believe that it's extremely important to take care of yourself on a big day like this, don't you agree?

"Besides," she continued, "it takes me a little while to be this presentable, ha ha ha." Her forced laughter rang out as she bent her knees slightly and threw her arms up in the air. "And of course Richard needed to pick up this outfit I'm wearing from the cleaners. Doesn't it look fabulous on me?" The pattern of orange and yellow abstract lines and shapes resembled a cubist movement painting.

Penelope Anne paused to inhale and Clyde managed to wedge in a reply. "I suppose it would be awkward to disagree."

"Thank you!" Penelope Anne blurted. "So you see I couldn't get here any earlier—"

"Excuse me Penelope Anne." Clyde walked past her to the hospital bed. "Is there a new baby here, or am I in the wrong room?"

Beth lay in the bed resting. Her eyes were a little glazed over.

"Hello Beth, I'm so proud of you." Clyde bent over and kissed her on the cheek. "How are you sweetie?"

"Hi, Dad. I'm wonderfully tired."

Penelope Anne flinched. "Now, Elizabeth, Clyde is your father-in-law. We all know who your real father is."

Clyde glanced around the room. "Where's the baby who shall be nameless?"

Penelope Anne flinched again. "Really, Elizabeth, you could tell your own mother the name you've picked out."

"Everyone will know soon enough, but not until I have a chance to show Edgar the birth certificate. Dad, they're working the baby over down at the nursery, why don't you go see him? Edgar and Mom are there too."

"I'll do that. You get some rest now, Beth. Penelope Anne, I'm sure I'll hear from you soon."

"Richard is here, he's already visited the baby. You see,

I've got him out watching the car." Penelope Anne gestured towards the window with both hands. "The last time we went to the market I didn't have him watch it. When we came out, someone had parked their grubby work truck very, very close to my side of the car. They left no way for me to get in. Richard had to back the car out, stop it in traffic, then get out of the car so he could come around and open my door. It was terribly inconvenient for me, so today I insisted Richard stay with the car—"

"I'm sure he's endeavoring to persevere," Clyde called out over his shoulder as he left the room.

* * *

Edgar and his mother, Ruth, stood in the nursery watching Nurse Amy take the baby's vital signs.

"Isn't this nice, Edgar?" Ruth patted her son on the arm. "Amy's like family, she was that close with Verda when all you kids were little."

Edgar cleared his throat. "Nice? I remember the two of them ganging up on me for their wedgie attacks."

"I'm so sorry, Edgar." Amy giggled. "I'd forgotten all about that."

The baby cried steadily but without conviction as Amy worked on him, his eyes scrunched up and his face a reddish-purple color. He lay on a blue disposable pad and Amy used a pen to mark a line on the pad at the top of his head. She then extended his leg and made another mark for his foot. Unwrapping a sterile measuring tape, she checked the distance between the two marks.

"Eighteen and a quarter inches. He's beautiful, Edgar." Amy smiled at him.

Edgar cringed when Amy measured his son's elongated head. He moved closer to his mother and spoke quietly. "Are you sure he's gonna be all right? I didn't expect him to be so…"

"That's all normal, sweetie. You just haven't been around very many newborns."

"I guess I expected him to look more like me, or Beth."

"Nonsense, he has Beth's eyes, and I can see hints of your rascally grin."

Edgar leaned to one side and tilted his head, checking the baby over from various angles. "I don't feel like I thought I would. I expected to be all puffed up with pride, or something…"

"Don't you worry about that." Amy smiled at him again. "A lot of people have that experience, especially with their first one. It's a lot for your mind to take in all at once."

Ruth giggled when Amy pushed on the ball of the baby's foot and his tiny toes grappled her finger. She took hold of both his hands, pulled his arms up in the air and let them go. He startled and cried much more emphatically.

"Hey, what are you doing, Amy?" Edgar stepped closer to his son. "Are you going to give him a wedgie next?"

"It's okay, I'm checking his reflexes."

Edgar raised his head up, closed his eyes, and inhaled deeply. He breathed out through his mouth.

"Well what do we have here!" Clyde walked into the nursery and bent over the clear acrylic crib to get a peek at his grandson. "What a fine looking young man." Taking out his handkerchief he wiped his eyes and blew his nose, then folded the white cloth and returned it to his back pocket with the smooth efficiency of a lifelong practice.

Clyde wrapped his arms around Edgar. "I'm so proud of you, son, you and Beth both. I'm just tickled to death."

"Thanks, Dad. I can't believe he's here, that I'm a father."

"Shoot, you were born to be a dad, and this child here will know it and be thankful for it every day of his long and blessed life." He turned to Ruth. "And hello there, you." Clyde hugged his wife, lifting her off the floor a few inches.

"Ooh!" Ruth gasped and then laughed.

Clyde turned back to his son. "I stopped by to see your lovely wife on my way in. She appeared a bit strained, but I'm not sure whether that's from giving birth or visiting with her mother."

"Clyde!" Ruth swatted his arm. "You're terrible."

Amy poked the baby's heel to check his blood sugar, and the mild, mumbling cry he had been chewing on gave way to full-throttle screaming.

Edgar's shoulders tensed and he held his breath as Amy worked to get a drop of blood onto the test strip. When she applied a bandage to the baby's heel, Edgar finally exhaled. "Before, when Beth was pregnant, it seemed like there was still time to get ready. Now I feel like the pause button has been released." He scratched his head.

"Things will settle down for you. With the baby, with your finances, everything." Ruth nodded. "It'll all be okay."

"Aw, Mom, now I'm thinking about money again." Edgar scratched his head with both hands.

Clyde laughed. "You got fleas? You're gonna scratch a bald spot to match your baby."

Ruth smoothed out Edgar's rumpled hair. "I'm only trying to help."

"I know. But it's so hard to trust that everything will work out. The big things are good, I guess. Beth and the baby are both healthy."

"Amen to that." Clyde directed his gaze at the ceiling. "It's good to remember what's most important."

Edgar continued. "But it seems like there's always something new waiting to stress me out. With Beth not getting a paycheck now, our money is so tight every month I just can't figure out the figures so they work. We're down to seventy-three dollars in our checking account right now and there's tons of bills due."

"You know your mother and I, not to mention a whole host of other people in this town, would never let you go without."

"I know, and I appreciate that. But still." Edgar walked over to a window that provided a view of the town square and the river. A flash of sunlight drew his eye to a man walking slowly along the riverbank, hunched over a shiny metal detector. A woman with a pickaxe followed. "Maybe I should try to find Molly's treasure, except that would make me like them, crawling around looking for something that doesn't even exist."

Molly Hardwick, a wealthy socialite from back East, married George Paxon not long after the founding of the town. She died thirteen years later and, according to local history, that's when George started making references to Molly's treasure. George lived a miserly existence for fifteen years after Molly's passing then died without a will or any heirs. No trace of the couple's considerable wealth had ever been found and their general store, George's Goods, was auctioned off on the courthouse steps to pay outstanding expenses against the estate. Over a century of treasure hunters had believed the grief-stricken George went a bit crazy at the end of his life and hid his fortune somewhere around Paxon Chute.

Edgar watched through the window as the man with the metal detector stopped and pointed at the ground. The woman swung her pickaxe in a wiggly arc and the man bolted out of the way. She drove the point deep into the soil.

"That'll be another hole for me to fill. What a destructive waste of time. Still, I guess I'd dig a thousand holes if I thought it would actually help." Edgar drew in a deep breath.

Clyde placed his hand on Edgar's shoulder. "That's right, breathe in, and breathe out. Things will get better, unless they get worse. But regular breathing is definitely important if you want to stay in the game."

Edgar sighed and looked down at the flowers blooming in the neatly landscaped hospital grounds. A rain cloud passing overhead grayed out the sun. The soft, staccato plopping of the first raindrops quickly escalated into the mild din of a steady summer shower.

Clyde turned his ear towards the window. "That'll be soaking the seat on my tractor, but I don't mind gettin' a little wet, helps me give up the illusion of control over life." He reached up with his right hand and rubbed his chest, just above the heart.

"Yeah Dad, I know. I've got webbed feet from that spring break we spent building a fence in a monsoon."

Clyde laughed. "I don't recall it being all that bad."

"Thirty-six inches in eight days, that's a whole yard of rain. It was like trying to dig postholes in the middle of a lake."

"The soft ground sure made it easy to set those posts deep. That fence is still strong as Fort Knox."

Ruth cleared her throat. "You two weathermen are missing the first bath over here."

Amy finished rinsing the baby. After wrapping him in a blanket and combing his fuzzy hair she laid him back under a radiant heater to warm up.

Edgar ran his finger across the palm of his son, who in turn grabbed onto his father's thumb. The baby's pale, perfectly formed fingers and flawless skin contrasted sharply with Edgar's weathered hand.

The rain stopped a few minutes later. Edgar looked out the window, staring into the dark turmoil of the departing cloud.

Clyde took a quick glance out the window, but in a different direction. He turned to Ruth. "You look like you swallowed a rainbow."

She chuckled. "What in the world does that mean?"

"Well, I guess I don't rightly know, but I just saw one and that's what you remind me of." Clyde kissed her cheek then whispered, "I love you, Granny Rerd."

* * *

Beth was alone and resting in her room when Amy wheeled in the crib. Edgar followed close behind, his eyes fixed on their swaddled baby.

"Hello there, little mother. Here is your beautiful child." Amy gently picked up the baby and laid him in Beth's arms. "I'll leave you three alone so you can get acquainted. Give me a holler if you need anything." She closed the door quietly on her way out.

"Our first baby," Beth murmured. "Still kinda hard to believe."

"Speaking of getting better acquainted, when are you going to tell me his name?"

"Take a look and see." Beth pointed at the birth certificate lying on her bedside tray. "It's the best name I know."

Edgar laughed. "Well this is a surprise. Edgar Allan Rerd Junior. I love it."

Beth gazed into their baby's hazy blue eyes. "Even the initials are perfect. I've got to have two EARs, don't I, Junior?"

Turning to wipe his eyes on his shirtsleeve, Edgar looked out the window where a wiggly pickaxe once again swung through the air down by the river. He scratched his head.

CHAPTER TWO

Clyde drove out of the hospital parking lot on his tractor and waved at Richard, who leaned against a severely polished Lincoln Continental. "Richard! Come with me to the Bull, if you can break away from sentry duty. I'm just going to have the one drink."

Richard shrugged his shoulders and waved his hands in the direction of the car.

Two blocks down on the town square Clyde pulled into a curbside parking spot in front of the local watering hole, The Snorting Bull. He turned the key and the clattering engine slowly wound down into silence. Clyde dismounted his slightly rusty steed and entered the bar.

The two stories of windows that filled the entire front of the building provided an unobstructed view of the river, where the water churned endlessly through the most adventurous section of the chutes. Inside, the natural lighting created shadowy areas reminiscent of a time before electric lights reigned over every waking hour.

On that slow Tuesday afternoon three customers were sitting at the bar along the back wall of the high-ceilinged room. To the left sat Clyde's younger brother, Drew Rerd, and next to him Wilbur Dunlop, the local postman. Tom Walker, frequently affixed to the establishment as solidly as the beer taps, finished out the trio. Behind the bar Eloy Chibitty, owner of The Snorting Bull, deftly scraped the salt off a mini pretzel before eating it.

"Sideward!" Tom shouted at Clyde, using a nickname he adulterated from Clyde Rerd's full name. "Sideward, you gonna fertilize the street when you're done mowin' it?"

"I might, and if I've got any left over you can spread it on those mushrooms growing under your bar stool. Although I can't imagine they're hungry with your nutrient-rich narrative sprinkling down on them all day."

Tom laughed and checked beneath his seat.

Clyde slapped his hand on the cool granite top of the massive oak bar. "Gentlemen, next one's on me. Grandpa's buyin' you a drink." Exuberant congratulations echoed off the tin ceiling tiles. "Yup, Edgar Allan Rerd Junior is now of this earth."

The room went silent except for Drew, who choked and coughed in the middle of taking a drink.

"That's, uh…" Wilbur faltered. "That's a name, all right."

Drew recovered from his coughing and sat up straight. "I'm happy for you Clyde, I really am. But you could have let me know."

"Easy there, Drew, I just left the hospital, and I came right over here to see you." Clyde's gaze remained on Eloy, who poured a round of beer.

"I have a cellular telephone now, you remember that, don't you?" Drew laboriously extracted it from his pocket and held up the incriminating evidence. He pointed it at Wilbur. "See, I have a cellular telephone now."

Eloy set their drinks on the bar.

Clyde lifted his glass. "To a healthy happy life for my grandson. Bottoms up 'til it's all down, boys."

"Hear, hear!" they replied.

A slurpy moment followed, then four empty mugs clonked onto the bar.

"A beer and a bump on me." Tom pulled out his wallet.

Drew's right eye twitched. "That's some rare generosity."

"Thank you kindly, Tom." Clyde started to reach for his hanky but settled for a couple of quick sniffs instead.

The shot glasses and the beer mugs were filled by Eloy.

Tom raised his glass. "Long life to you and yours."

"Hear, hear!"

They tossed down the whiskey and their shot glasses clacked onto the bar.

"Whew doggie." Clyde reached for his beer. "I'm already one over my limit. I believe I'll be sipping on this for a good while."

Drew watched him like a hawk for the next forty-five minutes. When Clyde finally drained his glass Drew immediately flapped his outstretched arms at Eloy to signal for another round.

Wilbur gazed out the big front windows as the driver of a minivan took a third approach at the space in front of Clyde's mower, wrestling with the lost art of parallel parking.

"That's a fine tractor you've got there." Wilbur took a sip of beer.

Clyde sighed. "Well, it's no Grass Thrasher, but it's got the Twin Twenty." He took a long drink.

Wilbur's eyes grew wide. "Twenty horsepower," he whispered.

"With full oil presshur..." Clyde belched quietly, "pressurization." He finished his beer.

Tom laughed at Wilbur. "You should be a big fan of that, being fairly lubricated yourself."

Ignoring Tom, Wilbur called out to Eloy. "Set 'em up again, on me." Eloy pulled another round and Wilbur raised his glass. "To the best tractor a grandkid could ever want." His voice croaked a little.

Clyde stared at his full glass of beer for a moment then

quickly gulped it down. He wiped the foam off his lip with the back of his hand. "Boys, let's go see the little Rerd." He spoke in a mostly outdoor voice.

Wilbur shook his head. "No, no, no. I just finished my route. I don't wanna go draggin' myself all the way over to the hospital."

"A journey of a thousand inches begins with a single step, but even so I would never tempt a postman to walk. Y'all can ride in my trailer."

Tom looked out the window and frowned. "That overgrown child's wagon? Do you intend to stack us like lumber?"

"Nah." Clyde shook his head. "Maybe if it was a side tipper. They're better suited for dumping bulk goods."

Tom slapped at the bar in feigned mirth. "Ah, railroad humor. Almost as funny as the flu."

Eloy took off his apron and stepped out from behind the bar. "Clyde, I would not let you drive a car right now, but I will go if you stay in low gear. Low gear is even slower than you walk anyway."

On their way out of the bar Eloy flipped the sign in the window around to read "Back in 5 Minutes."

Clyde threw a leg over the driver's seat and the men shuffled around the small trailer.

"Hold it, fellas. Wilbur and I can't fit on the same side." Tom put his hands on his hips. "We're too many axe handles wide."

Eloy and Wilbur switched places. Then all four men stood with their backs to the trailer, two on each side. When they sat down their legs hung up and over the low railings. The springs on the trailer creaked, groaned, and bottomed out. Sand and pebbles sprinkled onto the street around the squashed tires and a homemade sign hung with baling wire rattled against the tailgate. It read "Caution - Clyde Load."

"Hey, quit pushing on me, Tom." Drew leaned back against Tom, forcing him to bend forward.

"Can't breathe." Tom puffed his cheeks. "That's straining things that shouldn't be strained." He pushed against Drew.

Clyde looked back over his shoulder. "You kids settle down now. Don't make me come back there." He reached out his right hand for the ignition switch then stopped suddenly. "Where's the dern key?"

"Over there." Eloy pointed to Clyde's left hand. "You have been carrying it around since you came into the bar. I watched to make sure you did not set it down somewhere."

"Good man that you are, Eloy. You always know how to find stuff."

"My Comanche grandfather taught me how to be a tracker."

"Where were you last Thursday when I searched all over creation for the wallet that turned out to be in my front pocket?"

Clyde fired up the engine and shifted into gear. His foot slipped off the clutch pedal and the power of the Twin Twenty shot the front end of the tractor up into the air like a bucking bronco. Clyde held on tight to the steering wheel, battling to regain control. Back in the trailer Tom's and Drew's heads clacked together like coconuts and most of Eloy lay hidden beneath Wilbur.

Clyde laughed when the engine stalled and everything came to a lurching halt. "Whew! I sure am glad that part's over."

"I have changed my mind." Eloy's muffled voice floated out from under Wilbur.

"Aw, that was just a little crow hoppin', Eloy. I'm all freshened up now."

Eloy wormed his way out of the trailer and approached Clyde. "I must be crazy. You do not belong behind the wheel of anything." Eloy removed the key. "Either I will drive or you will walk."

"Fair enough." Clyde danced a little jig on his way back to the trailer.

Eloy sat down behind the wheel and restarted the engine. Driving in low gear they did crawl along at a very slow walking speed. The leisurely pace allowed the travelers to pass the time with townspeople they met along the way. Clyde shouted out his new grandparent status to almost everyone he saw.

Tom waved back to a group of people on the sidewalk. "We're a spontaneous one-vehicle parade, except we don't have any candy to throw."

Drew turned to look at Tom. "If we're a parade, what's the theme of our float?"

"Why, we're the harvest float, of course."

"Harvest float? How do you figure that?"

"Well, Eloy there is a fart farmer, you see, and he's got him a bumper crop of dusty old farts back here."

Drew scowled at him. "Call yourself that if you like, but don't go including me. I'm not a fart."

Wilbur giggled, and Tom made a loud fart noise.

Swinging wide for the one left turn on their route, Eloy came close to hitting Mavis Drew's Kettle Corn Cart. He leaned to the left and wrestled with the steering wheel. "This thing drives like a mule."

"Watch where you're going, Eloy!" Mavis followed after them, pushing her cart and wagging her finger.

Tom slapped at the side of the wagon. "Red alert. Road rage comin' up behind."

Clyde waved at her. "Sorry about what almost happened, Mavis. Please don't boil us in oil."

"Pshaw, oil's too expensive for that. Here you go, Drew." Mavis winked and tossed him a bag of popcorn.

Drew held up the bag and smiled. "Did you guys see what

she did? I got popcorn. Mavis threw me a bag of free popcorn."

Eloy pulled the tractor into a parking space at the hospital and shut off the engine. Clyde sprang out of the trailer, and Drew struggled to hoist himself up and over the railing. Wilbur's legs had gone to sleep and he needed a hand to get up. Tom's back got stuck in bent mode and he needed two hands. Once back on his feet, he exclaimed, "Oy, my hip."

Drew shook his head. "We all know there's nothing wrong with your hip."

Tom patted Eloy on the back. "You did an extremely adequate job hauling us over here."

The five men wandered into the hospital. Their festivities continued indoors with Clyde calling out over and over, "New grandpa comin' through!" The spectators were not as receptive indoors and the men were met with several shushes and disapproving glares.

Crowding around the window of the nursery, they had no trouble spotting the newest Rerd, Paxon Chute being a small town and Junior the only baby at the time.

"He's going to be a fine young man," Drew whispered loudly. "That blotchy swelling will go away, and his head will get rounded. It has to, because I've never seen an adult that looks like that."

The other men were mumbling their own creative sincerities when a loud voice rang through the hospital halls.

"Clyde!"

The voice belonged to Penelope Anne.

Instinctively the men drew closer together, darting glances all around trying to locate her. She and Richard lived in the neighboring town of Peyton and had been unknown in Paxon Chute before Beth and Edgar were married two years earlier.

"Clyyyyyde!" her voice grated out again.

"P. A." Tom hissed.

Eloy winced. "I yah! Is she on the intercom?"

"No, a real PA system is more intimate," Tom continued to scan the halls, "and has a more human quality about it."

"What's she doing here still?" Clyde muttered as Penelope Anne approached the nervous and fidgeting pack. "This is way beyond her parental attention span."

"Clyde! I just came back from the Peyton Plaza Mall. You're going to love this adorable little thing I bought."

She held up a black apron adorned with pink rhinestones that spelled out "Glamorous Grandmother."

"I had to bring it by for Elizabeth to see, but she barely woke up long enough to have a look before she fell right back asleep. And I came all the way over here to show her."

Clyde scrutinized the apron. "Do you cook much?"

"This will be great to wear if the grandkids ever want a glass of vegetable juice, or maybe a sugar-free Popsicle. Out on the porch, of course, because I've got white carpeting after all. But what am I saying? You know that, you've seen my white Berber carpeting."

Drew reached out to touch the rhinestones. "I'd be afraid one of those shiny stones would fall into my chili. Someone might crack a tooth on it."

"There's enough rocks in your chili already." Wilbur wagged his jaw around.

"One time!" Drew held a finger up in the air and shook it. "One time I missed a rock sorting my beans, and you never forget, do you?"

Tom grinned. "Oh, lighten up, Julia Child. It's not all the gravel anyway. You put in too many tomatoes."

Drew's face reddened and his lips compressed. "How many blue ribbons have you won, Tom? How many?"

"Nothing funnier than a bunch of gringos arguing about chili." Eloy chuckled.

"Grown men fussing about cooking, and you all seem to

have forgotten that I'm the one with a new apron." Penelope Anne abruptly stuffed her apron back into the bag. "Well, my interior decorator is bringing new wallpaper samples over this afternoon, so I'm off." She drew her face into a tight smile and quickly walked away.

Tom rubbed his chin. "Yeah, she's off all right."

"Off in a hurry." Clyde pushed back the cap on his head. "Wish I knew how we managed that."

Drew pointed down the opposite hallway. "There's Edgar, guys. Edgar! Hey Edgar!" Drew held his arms up and waved.

Edgar joined the group. "Thanks for stopping by. Whew! Smells like you've been busy. I hope you're driving them, Eloy."

"I am making sure they are okay." Eloy nodded slowly.

Edgar stepped close to Clyde and spoke quietly in his ear. "You're keeping track, right? You know how you forget. I don't want some crazy event of yours to deal with today."

Clyde laughed. "We'll be fine. Your very capable uncle will see to that, won't you, Drew?"

"Well yes, of course, yes I will." Drew bobbed his head in agreement. "I will, you can count on me, Edgar."

"Oh, and Dad, I need your help tomorrow in the park. Some knucklehead dismantled the boulder pile in the playground again. I swear I should put up a sign that says, 'Leave 'em alone, someone's already looked for treasure here.'"

"Tomorrow? What about Beth, and the baby?"

"I'm only doing it because Chief Turner called and said he didn't think it was safe, the way they're strewn about now."

Clyde's eyebrows scrunched up. "Why don't you let Garth take care of it?"

Edgar shook his head. "No, they're pretty tricky to get stacked right. If you help me with the front-end loader we can get them squared away pretty quick and I can get back to the hospital."

"Sure, I'll be there."

Edgar stared at his father. "I mean it, Dad. I really need your help."

"Got it. You can count on me."

"Let me see your pad, I'll write it down for you."

Clyde extracted a leather-bound notepad from his shirt pocket and handed it to his son.

Edgar removed the pen from its holder inside the cover and wrote a message on a blank sheet, then ripped it out and handed it to his father. "I put the time too. Is eight o'clock okay?"

Clyde took his cap off and stuck the note inside. Pulling the cap back down on his head, he smiled at Edgar. "See you then."

* * *

When Clyde, Wilbur, and Tom sat down in the trailer for the ride back to The Snorting Bull, Drew headed up front to the tractor instead. "I think I should drive us back, Eloy. After all, I'm the one keeping us safe."

Eloy shook his head. "That would clearly be less safe."

"Tell you what, two is better than one." Clyde pointed at the tractor. "Drew, you stand on the footboard there, and you can be our copilot. Everyone knows the copilot is the one who keeps things right side up."

Eloy continued to shake his head. "That is even more less safe."

Drew smiled and his shoulders snapped back into his posture of responsibility. "Oh no, I can definitely keep things in order better from up here." Drew's boot slipped on the footboard and he slid down the side of the tractor. "Don't worry everybody. I got it, I got it." Drew clambered into position.

Their parade resumed, and a number of townspeople walked alongside to give Clyde their congratulations.

"Not too close, stay back." Drew held up his hand to fend off the crowd.

Tom snorted. "Drew, they're all on the sidewalk."

"Yes, that's right, everyone stay on the sidewalk." Drew nodded vigorously.

Clyde leaned forward in the trailer so he could reach the aoogah horn mounted on the rear fender of the tractor. He squeezed it several times.

Mavis wove her Kettle Corn Cart among the crowd, offering a half-price special in honor of Clyde's news. Arriving at The Snorting Bull, she parked her cart behind the trailer.

A gaggle of customers sat outside the bar waiting to celebrate with Clyde. Many of them had taken the opportunity to close their shops and booths on the town square, leaving signs ranging from "Be Back Soon" to "Sorry, Found Somethin' Better to Do."

Clyde rubbed his eyes. "I do believe I'm going to call it a day and head back home."

Eloy put the key in his shirt pocket. "Clyde, you come inside and sober up before you go anywhere. I have a new menu item for you to try. Thai roast duck curry. You like curry."

"Yes, sir. Yes I do." Clyde smacked his lips.

* * *

Two hours later Eloy shook his finger at Clyde. "Your hot curry is now very cold, and you have forgotten to stop drinking."

"I gotta get outta here. It's not easy to sober up in a bar, 'specially one filled with so much hos-pi-tal-i-ty." He took his time with the big word.

"You still cannot drive. You will mow your foot or crash into something. Peter just got here, he can take you home."

"It would be my pleasure to see that the honorable new grandfather survives home safely."

Tom cleared his throat. "I think you mean 'arrives.'"

"Ah." Peter held up his index finger. "One can arrive but yet still not survive, you see."

Peter Martel taught history and drama classes at Paxon High School and had also founded the local community theater group, The Interpretarians. He turned slowly and projected his voice, "For our young Junior Rerd 'cannot find the peace of home, on grandfather's battered tomb.'" With a flourish he bent over and draped himself across the bar. After briefly holding this pose, he jumped back upright and held out his arms. "That's Yeats, you know."

Tom made a cricket chirping noise during the ensuing silence.

Drew frowned. "Well, that was dark."

"And misquoted." Eloy tossed a desalted pretzel into his mouth.

Clyde squinted at Peter. "And probally pur-pun-dic-ular to the point."

Peter smiled and shook his head. "I can't understand what you're trying to say. But, come, let us sojourney together." He led Clyde out of the bar amid a round of raucous final congratulations.

Unfortunately, even though sober, Peter did not drive in a straight line. A bad wheel bearing on his car made a high-pitched screeching sound, but Peter discovered the noise stopped when he made right turns. So instead of having it repaired he drove in a perpetual arc to the right until he ran out of road then jerked the car back to the left as quickly as he could amid the howling screech of the bearing. Once he resumed his lazy right turn the noise would stop again. Tom dubbed the car Twister because it traveled in a circular motion and had the potential for great destruction.

Clyde held onto the dash and closed his eyes as Peter zigzagged him back home. "Gently, Peter." Sweat broke out on Clyde's forehead. "I've drunk...to verge of...," he licked his lips, "biological...regret." He swallowed then exhaled through his mouth. "Riding Twister...not helping."

Peter came to a halt in front of Clyde's half-mowed lawn. "Aaaand here we are, safe and sound, eh?"

Clyde exited the car and took a deep breath of the cool evening air. "Thanks for gettin' me home." He clung to the door.

"Always a pleasure to provide the services of my shining armor at night." Peter giggled and patted the dash of his car. "Say, I want to talk with you about a new story I'm writing, and it concerns you very deeply. Would you be able to come by the school tomorrow morning?"

Clyde squinted, swaying with the door. "Seems like I've already got somethin' tomorrow."

"Here, let me see your pad. I'll write you a note." Peter's pen flurried across the notepad then he tore out the sheet and handed it to Clyde. "Now put that in your hat, right?" Peter pulled the door closed and honked as he drove off.

Clyde made his way up the steps of the front porch with careful deliberation and sat in a rocking chair to gaze at the stars.

After spending the better part of an hour on the porch, Clyde blundered his way into the darkened house and prepared his third pimento cheese sandwich of the day. Crunching loudly on a jumbo dill pickle, he took out his notepad and wrote at the top of the page in large squiggly letters "Things to do with Junior." Underneath he listed fishing trips, ball games, and construction projects.

Clyde pulled out his handkerchief and wiped his nose. He

wrote on the chalkboard next to the refrigerator "Congrats, Granny Rerd! Luv U 4 V R."

He finished his supper with a large slice of buttermilk pie. Pulling off his cap he immediately looked inside and extracted the notes from Edgar and Peter. Clyde squinted and lifted his glasses then shook his head and gave up trying to read Peter's flowery script. He rolled into bed still working on his last mouthful of pie. Smiling, he mumbled, "Life's better'n I deserve."

Clyde fell asleep immediately. When his left hand relaxed it released the crumpled notes, which fell onto the floor between the bed and the nightstand.

CHAPTER THREE

Clyde woke the next morning with traces of buttermilk pie in the corners of his mouth. He slowly rolled out of bed and shuffled into the bathroom, where he rinsed out his mouth then stared into the mirror, rubbing his temples.

Ruth looked him over when he walked into the kitchen. "I do believe someone got run over by a snorting bull."

"Shoot." Clyde smiled but his chuckle sounded forced. "Just sideswiped a little, the horns missed me."

"Hmm." Ruth shook her head. "You don't quite look mission capable, as you like to phrase it."

"Nah, my teeth barely even hurt when I smile."

Ruth set Clyde's breakfast on the table. Three strips of bacon happened to form a giant smiling mouth right below the yellow eyes of two fried eggs. Clyde bumped the plate as he fumbled into his seat. The bacon slid around and became a leering grin. The greasy yellow eyes wobbled and mocked him. He dabbed at the beads of sweat on his forehead with a napkin.

"Do you not feel like eating?"

Clyde held up his hand. "No, no. I'll feel better afterwards. Unless I feel worse." He shuddered.

The morning sun filled the breakfast nook with a golden glow. Ruth topped off their heavy white coffee mugs and steam danced up into the light.

"That Junior is something, isn't he?" Clyde blew on his coffee.

A small smile crept up the corners of Ruth's mouth. "Of course he is. He'll always be something special."

Clyde stared at the tablecloth. "You know, I've never claimed to be perfect."

Ruth laughed. "Good thing, that."

"I know I fall down like everyone else. But moments like this make me think I must have done at least a few things right, to have so much more than I'm due." He sat back, sipping coffee and rubbing his belly.

"None of us are due anything when you get right down to it." Ruth squeezed his hand. "By the way, I set your herd free when I got home last night. They were all penned up in the kennel."

"Whoops." Clyde's eyebrows shot up. "I had 'em back there so I could mow. Can't get anything done with that much help around."

Ruth set her napkin on the table. "What have you got going on today?"

"Nothing, my hat's empty." He glanced at the iron skillet clock on the wall. "I think I'll potter about with my tree for a while, then go to the hospital."

"What tree?"

"A tree of life." Clyde made a wide sweeping gesture.

Ruth folded her arms. "You know good and well that doesn't tell me anything."

"It's inspired by the tree of life in Revelation, which bore twelve manner of fruits, and yielded her fruit every month. I mean to graft eleven different fruits onto a peach tree so it's producing something all year round." He held the heels of his hands together and spread his fingers apart to emulate a tree.

"What do you know about grafting trees?"

"Well nothing, but now is as good a time as any to learn.

I'm going to start simple with pears, then plums. I hope I can eventually get coconuts, bananas, grapes, and maybe olives going, but I don't yet know what's possible."

Ruth gazed out the window at an unfinished totem pole planted in the lawn out by the road, listing noticeably to the east. "Sounds like a good project for the backyard. Way, way in the backyard."

Clyde stepped onto the porch and the doleful cry of several doves echoed through the quiet morning. He breathed in the dewy air heavy with the strong, sweet scent of fresh-cut grass. During the night someone had driven his tractor home for him, finished mowing the lawn, and parked the tractor in the barn. In the trailer were packages of diapers, baby formula, and a fifty pound sack of pinto beans.

"That's just dandy!"

The sound of Clyde's voice set Shimei to barking. The black Labrador retriever came tearing around the corner of the house, followed by two Scottish terriers, Donald and Mac. Then Luther fluttered up, a Canada goose whose honk sounded more like a bark. Thatcher the bulldog lumbered along behind, chuffing and snuffling loudly through her abbreviated snout.

Shimei ran onto the porch and rooted his wet nose into Clyde's hand, licked it, then barked some more.

"Why should this dog bark at his master?" When Clyde held his hands up in the air Shimei stopped barking and sat down, his tail wagging. Clyde took a moment to scratch each pair of dog ears and stroke Luther's smooth head.

The turbulent herd followed Clyde out to the barn. He sat down and quickly flipped through the pages of a thick book titled *Graft Craft: The Splice of Life*. Luther flapped up onto the workbench and pecked at the book. Clyde shooed him away and stared at one page for a few seconds.

"Sharp knife. Okeydokey." He jumped up and searched his

workbench. In a drawer he found a cordless phone that had been missing from the house for several days. "Ah, we meet again, you shameless wanderer." He almost dropped it when a shrill ringing reverberated through the barn.

Shimei barked, Luther honked in reply, and Thatcher, who had been staring up at the proceedings, sneezed on Clyde's leg.

Clyde tried to answer the newly discovered phone but only heard a dial tone. The ringing continued, and he tried to answer again. On the fourth ring he pulled the cell phone out of his pocket and answered that instead. "Clyde's arboretum, who's this?"

"Dad, where are you? You were supposed to meet me at the park at eight o'clock. I wrote it down."

Clyde took off his cap to double-check. "I'm sorry son, but I don't have it. What are you doing at the park? I thought you'd be at the hospital."

"I would be by now, if you had showed up on time to help. The boulders, don't you remember the boulders? I need help setting them back up."

"Well, I'll be there straight away." Clyde pocketed his cell phone, and then lost the cordless phone again when he dropped it back in the drawer. He stopped at the barn door and passed his hand slowly in front of the animals. They all stayed in the barn, watching Clyde as he left.

He got into his green surplus Forest Service truck and headed to town. Clyde drove past the meadows along the busy river. Summer vacation started in a few weeks and the early tourists were already showing up for a day in the chutes.

Clyde turned off the town square and into Nickel Rock Park, which ran for six miles along the banks of the upper Cobb River. The town park had been named after a large limestone outcrop in the river that formed the centerpiece of the chutes. The roundish rock nearly thirty feet across resembled a coin sitting at an incline atop a pedestal. The river split into fast-moving chutes on either side of the base. Water spilled onto the low upstream end of Nickel Rock where a bow wave formed as the rock cleaved the endlessly flowing river.

Clyde walked down the grassy bank over to one of the playgrounds in the park. There Edgar thrashed about with a chain, trying to flip a boulder up into the front-end loader. His reddened face glistened with sweat.

"I'm sorry to be late."

Edgar did not look up from his work.

Clyde tried again. "Seems like you've got a good start getting the base set up."

The chain slipped and the boulder tumbled away from the loader. Edgar danced out of the way to avoid getting his feet flattened. He kicked the boulder. "Stupid thing!"

"How can I help?"

"You could be here when you said you'd be here, that would be colossal on the scale of things that help."

"I honestly don't remember you asking me."

Edgar finally looked at his father. "You know, it's just not fair. Maybe you did forget, or maybe it's your ADD and you got distracted with something else, which happens on a regular basis. Or maybe you were too drunk when I asked you."

"You know I—"

Edgar held up his hand. "I'm not finished. It really doesn't matter why, because whatever the reason, I never know if you'll be around when I need you. I can't even count on you when I've got to get back to the hospital to see my wife and my day-old son. Your grandson!"

"Well, I'm here now."

"Hmph. I've been drafting a stern letter of disapproval." Edgar tapped two fingers on his temple.

"Yes, I believe I heard you dictating it to the rocks as I approached." Clyde's phone rang and he dug it out of his pocket. "Clyde's rock quarry."

"Oh my, I'm certain there's an interesting story behind that. This is Peter, whatever time are you coming to the school?"

Clyde's eyebrows scrunched up. "Doesn't sound familiar."

"I wrote you a note."

"I tell you what, I must have stuck my head up under the wrong hat last night. I'm right sorry, Peter, but it'll have to be some other time. I'll talk to you later."

Edgar shook his head and chuckled. "At least it's not just me."

A man with a metal detector approached them. He wore black fingerless gloves. His numerous leather equipment belts and straps creaked with every step. "Say, I was gridding this area a few days ago, although I'm sure it's a pounded site." His jaw worked relentlessly on a piece of gum. "I wanna sweep around the base of these rocks. They were all piled up earlier. Never know."

Clyde laughed. "If pounded site means someone has been here before you, then yes, this whole county was pounded to smithereens about a century ago."

The man put his hands on his hips and gum-smacked even louder. "So? I still wanna scan it."

"Nathan, someone's left an 'n' off your shirt." Clyde pointed at the red, white, and blue letters on the man's shirt that spelled N-A-T-H-A.

"My name isn't Nathan. That there's for North American Treasure Hunters Association."

Clyde held out his hand to shake. "It's a pleasure to meet you, Nathan with one 'n', from the North American Treasure Hunters of America."

The gum smacking stopped. "You're hilarious." He took Clyde's hand and gave it a quick shake. The brisk smacking resumed. "One of us will find big bucks here someday, make a name for ourselves." He stepped closer to the rocks.

Edgar stood up and put his park ranger cap back on, then turned to face the man. "Sir, this is a crime scene. If you know anything about the vandalism of this property I'll take you down to the station and get your statement. Otherwise, move along."

The man held his hands up in mock surrender. "Whoa there, easy now. I don't know anything about any vandalism. I'll just be on my way." He strolled up the riverbank, looking back occasionally.

Clyde clapped Edgar on the shoulder and chuckled. "Boy, you're in a mood today. Crime scene? Station?"

"I know, but if I thought he had anything to do with this I'd have Chief Turner come haul him in. But Nathan wouldn't need to search right now if he'd been the one who tore it down earlier."

"Why were you trying to roll that boulder over, instead of scooping it up where it lay?"

"Because, look." Edgar fished out a sheet of paper from his back pocket. He unfolded it and showed his father a photo of the neatly stacked rocks. "See, that boulder goes right here, pointy side up."

"Your first step should have been to throw away that picture. This is just a pile of rocks. You're not reconstructing London Bridge."

"Sure, go ahead, Dad. Show up late and then make fun of me." Edgar shoved the paper back into his pocket. "I happen to use the picture because it's hard to get the rocks to fit together so they don't fall over. Someone could really get hurt if that happened. It's less stressful this way, working with something to guide me."

"Fair enough, son, fair enough. Now that you've explained, it makes perfectly good sense to me."

Edgar threw his hands up in the air. "Whatever, Dad. I know you'd never do it this way. You'd lob them up there and it would all magically work out perfectly for you. But I have to fight and struggle for anything to ever work even halfway right."

The heavy chain dangling from the loader fell free, banging its way down Edgar's shin and onto his foot. "Dang it!" He hopped around on the other foot and rubbed his shin. "As if to illustrate my point." Edgar pulled the paper back out of his pocket and threw it on the ground. "You figure this out. I'm going to see my son." He limped up the bank in the direction of the town square.

Clyde started to call after his son, but the paper fluttered across the ground and he chased it down. He glanced back and forth from the picture to the pile of rocks, then hooked the chain onto the loader and wrapped it around the boulder Edgar had been working on. He drove the loader back, which rolled the boulder over, but it kept on going and slammed into the loader bucket wrong side up. Clyde dumped the boulder onto the ground then got out of the loader to work at it with a pry bar, trying to flip it right way up.

"That's what it did to me, too."

Clyde whirled around at the sound of Edgar's voice behind him. "Ah, you're back." He gestured towards the loader. "As you can see things don't always work out so magically for me, either."

"You just don't get all bent out of shape like I do." Edgar stared at the ground.

"It helps if you set your expectations with the understanding that rocks will tend to behave like rocks." Clyde handed the piece of paper back to Edgar. "A similar principle applies to people."

"I apologize for lashing out at you like that." Edgar picked up another pry bar. "Come on, we'll knock this out in no time between the two of us."

CHAPTER FOUR

Marlon Ezell approached Paxon Chute mid-morning on Farm to Market Road 2325 with Led Zeppelin blaring out of his black BMW. He drove aggressively through the many winding curves. Swerving past a tractor poking along the highway with the right wheels on the shoulder, Marlon gave a quick nod of his head. "That's right, Mr. Joe-Bob Farmer, you've been passed by a man of significance, driving an expensive European luxury sedan in a hurry to get somewhere important. Oops." As he passed a policeman on the side of the road he immediately glanced at the speedometer. "Only ten over." He kept his eyes on the rearview mirror but the police car remained parked. Marlon pumped his fist in celebration. "Yes!"

The billboards on the way into town were much the same as they had been for decades. Driving over to George's Goods, Marlon gazed at the south side of the town square where a constant flow of pedestrians spilled into the streets. They clotted up traffic, interfering with the chaotic affairs of the lumbering buses. Each bus had its own rattling trailer in tow for hauling tubes, rafts, and ice chests back up the river. Marlon watched several buses racing out of the town square and smiled.

Turning the steering wheel sharply he pulled into a parking space with tires squealing. Before the car came to a stop he opened the door right when Robert Plant sang about going to Chicago. Marlon rewound the song repeatedly on his way into town to get the timing right. He threw the gearshift into park, pulled the keys from the ignition, and exited the car in a brisk, smooth motion. Walking away he held the remote just above his ear and pointed it back towards the car. He clicked the button with a big snap of his wrist, cocking his head to hear the piercing chirp-chirp of the alarm.

In the middle of the north side of the town square, George's Goods looked out on the massive live oak in the open center of the square, and the view continued past the tree all the way down to Nickel Rock. The building started out as George and Molly Paxon's home in the 1860s. The couple invited their friends to visit and word began to spread about the chutes. More and more people frequented the area and swimming in the river made them powerfully hungry, so George kept ever-increasing amounts of food on hand to feed them all. Eventually other homes were built and the residents would often turn to George for provisions because they could always count on him to be well stocked. One day while inventorying a dozen barrels of flour in his storm cellar, George realized he had accidentally become the proprietor of a general store.

The ownership of George's Goods changed hands many times over the years. Ward Ezell, Marlon's father, worked there during his school days and eventually negotiated a deal to buy the business.

Walking up the steps of the store Marlon glanced at the old-fashioned red and white lettering on the windows. Much of the original structure remained and the building looked very similar to the rustic Western storefront George added onto his home in the 1870s.

The bell above the front door jingled when Marlon entered. He took two steps then paused to rock his weight onto his back foot where a soft spot in the floor made a froggy squeak.

The shelves inside were made with hewn pine branches and stocked with sunblock, clothing, novelty items, and snack foods. Cowhide rugs of various colors lay on the dark hardwood floor. Marlon looked down at the low stools bolted to the floor in front of the soda fountain bar, the very stools he struggled to climb as a toddler. Smells of cinnamon and other spices mixed in with a general background scent of wood and leather.

Customers browsed the aisles and a young family of four worked on their milk shakes at the soda bar. They all jumped a little when Ward stepped out from behind the counter, held his arms out, and proclaimed, "Well, well, well, the prodigal has returned!"

Marlon matched Ward's volume. "I think you must mean the profitable!" He pointed his thumb to his chest.

"That's what you keep saying in your emails." They shook hands and Ward pulled him in for a hug.

Marlon patted his father's back a few times then quickly pushed away, his nostrils flaring. "Aqua Velva," he mumbled.

"What's that?" Ward tilted his head.

"So you got my emails, eh? Seriously, Dad, it's too easy, like shooting fish in a barrel. I just know how to pick the winners. The Chicago Market never knew what hit them."

"I bet you hit them. Like a bug splatting the windshield. Ha ha ha!"

"Really? You're comparing me to a dead bug on a windshield? Anyway, they knew Marlon was there, that's for sure."

"I know when I've hit a bug, but it doesn't affect me much."

"Thanks, Dad. Supportive as always."

"Aw, now, you know I'm just giving you a hard time."

Ward turned on his toothy smile. "I'm sure you did great up there. You're my son, right?"

Though trimmer and taller than his slightly pear-shaped father, they had the same Roman nose and a rather hungry look about their dark eyes.

"Is Mom at home…" Marlon stopped. "Sorry, Dad, kind of a reflex, I guess."

"Unless she's dating a locksmith she's not in my house."

"What? She's…" Marlon looked around and lowered his voice, "dating?"

"I don't know what that woman is or is not doing, and I don't care. She left, she can stay gone."

Marlon waved his hand. "I don't even know what's going on with you two, and I don't want to talk about it."

"Aw, she claimed our bed was getting too crowded." Ward smiled and winked at a man and woman in the next aisle. "You know how sensitive women can get if they think they've got a little competition."

The couple stopped in their tracks. The woman's face turned bright red. The man coughed and jerked his head towards the door. They set the items they were holding onto the nearest shelf and quickly walked out of the store.

"Thanks for stopping by. Y'all come see us again!" Ward turned back to Marlon. "Listen, son, a man has needs. Your mother did what she could, I guess. I'm just too much for one woman."

"That's niiiice." Marlon held his hand on his stomach. "I think I'll go vomit."

The parents at the soda fountain bar stared wide-eyed at Ward. The woman held a dribbling spoonful of milkshake in front of her open mouth.

Marlon stepped closer to Ward and whispered, "Do you know how you sound?"

"Hey, I just call it like it is. Someday you'll understand, if you ever get married. Don't judge me until you've walked in my shoes."

"Whatever, Dad. I guess I'll stop by the house and drop off my bags."

"Hold on there. I'm expecting company later, and she's kind of shy. I think it would be better if you bunked somewhere else for a while, maybe at Emily's Place. Last I heard that's where your mother's staying."

"Fine. I'll figure something out." Marlon walked over to the door.

"What's that you're driving now?" Ward rubbed his tubby belly and eyed Marlon's car through the big storefront windows.

Marlon tilted his nose up slightly. "It's a BMW, Dad. 'The ultimate driving experience.'"

"I can see that, and it's 'driving machine,' not 'experience.' What year is it? Looks a little long in the tooth."

"Second generation 3 Series are ultra-rare collector's items. I had to search everywhere to find one."

Ward inhaled deeply, expanding his chest. "I tell you what, I can't imagine what anyone would pay for something like that, but I made a steal of a deal, on a real car. It's a six month old Cadillac I bought for way under wholesale. Plus I turned a profit when I sold my old one. Your old man is quite the horse trader, eh?"

"That's all right I guess, if you want an American—"

"It's more than all right. Six months old, she's practically brand new." He resumed his visual inspection of Marlon's car. "They sure do rust out up North, don't they?"

"Okay Dad. Great talking with you, as always." Marlon's shoulders slumped. He turned and walked away, muttering under his breath.

"What's that you say?" Ward sounded cordial enough, but focused a steady gaze on his son.

Marlon turned and flashed his own toothy smile. "I said I guess I'll catch you later."

He got back into his BMW and drove away in silence, searching through his music. He finally selected "I Won't Back Down," pressed play, and turned up the volume.

Marlon went by Emily Yates' bed and breakfast, located right off the town square, next door to a children's home called Emma's House. The similar names, Emily's Place and Emma's House, frequently led to people looking for the right thing in the wrong place.

His mother, Linda, happened to be outside the bed and breakfast unloading groceries from her minivan.

Marlon stopped and yelled out the window, "Hello there, woman!"

Linda turned from the van, both arms wrapped around grocery bags. "Marlon! Hello, sweetie. Wait, did you just call me 'woman'? That's a fine greeting for your poor old mother."

"Aw, Mom, think of it as a compliment, in reference to the fairer sex."

"Well get out of that car and give me a hug. Or at least help me with these groceries."

Marlon remained in his car. "I just rolled into town and here you are trying to put me to work."

"I'm so glad to see you. Where are you staying?"

"Oh, everyone is arguing over who gets me. But maybe I'll stay here so I can spend some quality time with you. I bet old Emily puts us up for free, am I right?"

"I'm sure she'd be willing to work something out with you in exchange for some help around here. That's what I've done. You could wash dishes, scrub toilets, or even carry groceries." Linda held the bags out for Marlon.

"Pay money and work as a maid? That's two strikes at once. What kind of friend is she?"

"The dearest kind of all, which maybe someday you'll learn

to appreciate. Emily's been a great help during a difficult time, but she's got a business to run. She can't give rooms away."

"Ah yes, difficult times. Well, Edgar's been bugging me to come see him so I'll probably stay at his place. I'll drop by for some face time after I get settled in."

Marlon drove away, using his knee to steer so he could look up an address on his phone. He turned onto a dead-end street lined with houses that were old, small, and well maintained. At the end of the street he stopped and got out of the car. Double-checking the address, he squinted as a thin cloud of smoke from the BMW's smoldering exhaust blew into his face. Immediately after the chirp-chirp of his alarm rang through the quiet neighborhood, a baby started crying. The crying became more intense when Marlon banged his fist on the door of the smallest house on the street. A note taped over the doorbell read "Please knock SOFTLY, baby sleeping."

Edgar opened the door. "Marlo! I should have guessed, but I didn't know you were in town already."

Marlon frowned. "No one calls me Marlo anymore."

"Come on in." Edgar stepped aside.

They shook hands and Marlon entered the house. Inside, the sounds of the crying baby were heightened by the bare wooden floors and minimal furnishings.

Marlon looked the place over. "So, how's life here at Rerd Manor? Everything going as planned?"

"Yeah, things are tight, but it's good. And you?"

"Couldn't be better, Gar, couldn't be better. I've been showing those guys up North how it's done."

"Yeah, I keep reading that in all your emails."

"Now, now." A smile slid up one side of Marlon's face and he held up his hand. "We'll have plenty of time later to catch up on all the thrills and chills of my latest triumphs. First things first. You're a proud new daddy, right? A baby..." He trailed off and raised his eyebrows.

"Boy, yes. He's a 'junior,' remember? That was Beth's idea, actually."

"Aaah, yes, I remember now." The smile disappeared. "Here's the deal, Gar. I really need a place to stay. And check out your humble little place here, all blinged up with antiques." The front room had a sofa, a coffee table, a small TV, and not much floor space left over. "This is a good, practical way to start out, until you can afford something more updated. So you're okay with me staying here for a while, right?"

"Um, I dunno. We've got the baby now, and things are pretty hectic. How long is a while?"

"Hard to tell, I'll be in town for some time and I've gotta steer clear of my parents right now. Oh, and there's that killer deal I need to get you up to speed on. We can hammer out the details into the wee hours."

"If I'm up late now, it's to change a diaper. We don't have a room for you though." Edgar shrugged his shoulders. "Or even a bed."

"Not a problem, I can sleep on the couch. Is it a foldout?"

"Sorry, it's not."

Marlon tried to fluff up one of the saggy cushions. It retained its sagginess. "That's all right, I can straighten my legs during the day."

"Hello, Marlon." Beth stood in the doorway of the nursery holding the protesting baby.

"Hey, Beth." Marlon quickly walked across the room and hugged her.

"Easy there, don't crush my baby." Beth smiled and took half a step back.

"Congratulations on the little one." Marlon barely glanced at Junior, then patted him on the head as if he were a bell on a hotel desk.

"Thank you, Marlon. It's good to see you." Beth's nostrils flared. "What's that smell?"

"Probably my Manitude cologne. I'm sure you've never come across it in old Paxon Chute." Marlon smiled. "I use their full regime of products. It's a robust, layered approach to a more fragrant life."

"Yeah, there's definitely the cologne, but also something that smells like burning oil."

The smile left Marlon's face. "No idea. Must be from your working man over there." He nodded towards Edgar. "It's really loud, that baby. How's motherhood treating you?"

"I love being a mom, but it is a lot of work, around the clock."

Marlon glanced at her rumpled hair and the teddy bear pajamas peeking out from under her pink robe. "Wow, you sure look different from the last time I saw you, at the wedding."

"Well that's to be expected, isn't it? Excuse me, Marlon. Edgar, would you come here please? I need your help with something."

"Sure. Have a seat, Marlon, I'll be right back."

Marlon sat down and pulled out his phone to check his email.

* * *

Beth entered the nursery and eased herself down into a rocking chair. She motioned for Edgar to close the door behind him. Junior quieted down as he started nursing.

"Did Marlon ask if he could stay here?" she whispered.

"Yeah, he says he needs a break from his parents."

"I can understand that, or at least with his dad. What a troll." Beth's eyes narrowed.

"I told him I didn't know, because of the baby, and we don't really have any room for him."

"No, he should stay with us."

"What? Are you sure?"

Beth took a breath and sighed quickly. "It's a sacrifice for us, no doubt. Anyone can see that. But he needs to be around good friends right now. Not his creeper dad."

"He's not creepy."

"You just don't see it because you've known him all your life."

"Hmm." Edgar paused. "Maybe you're right. If you look at something too long you kind of forget exactly what you're looking at."

"And to top it all off, Linda Ezell is the sweetest thing ever." Beth poked Edgar in the ribs. "Go tell him he can stay here as long as he needs to."

"I don't think I'll tell him that, exactly. I think it's better if we keep an exit sign on the horizon."

"Why do you say that?"

"Marlon's been a good friend my whole life. I used to tell people in college that he kinda has to grow on you. But he can grow into you, too."

* * *

Clyde drove into the parking lot of Paxon Chute High School and went around to the back. Tucked away behind the newer brick addition sat the much older limestone block building where Clyde had spent his school days. He opened the door and stepped onto the creaky hardwood floors, which were covered with scars from years of hard service.

The old gymnasium had been transformed into the Fine Arts Performance Hall. Clyde crossed the lobby to the set of inner doors. Inside the dark theater a girl stood alone delivering her lines on the brightly lit stage. Peter sat in the middle of the third row, surrounded by the rest of the students. Most of them were also members of The Interpretarians.

Clyde went to the back row and folded down one of the red bristly crushed-velvet seats and settled in to watch.

"All the world's a stage, and all the men and women merely players—"

"No, no, Jenny." Peter cut her off with a wave of his hand as he examined the script. "The line is 'All the world's a stage, and the men and women *are* players.' Listen up, cast, everyone should be off book by now. I know spring fever is going around and school is almost out, but we're performing this next week for heaven's sake."

"Sorry Mr. Martel." Jenny stared at her shoes. "I've heard it the other way my whole life and it's hard to remember all the changes you've made."

"I understand. But we have to update it, make it pop, you see, so it's more relatable to the audience of today."

"Yes, Mr. Martel."

"Also, the emphasis needs to be on the word 'players,' and spice it up a little. Make it more streetwise, say 'play-yuhs,' understood? Again, please."

Jenny swallowed and started again. "All the world's a stage, and all the men and women are play...uhs. They have their exits and their entrances; and one man in his time plays many suckers."

"That's what I'm talking about, but spice up 'suckers' the same way. Say it 'suck-ahs,' and show me some rap hands for emphasis."

Jenny frowned. "What are rap hands?"

"You know, the machinations a rap artist makes when he's performing. Thrust your arms out and point at me with the back of your hands, with some attitude. Goodness Jenny, this is what all you youngsters do these days. Must I explain your own culture to you?"

"Umm." Jenny bit her lip and her eyes fixed on her shoes again. "I'll try, Mr. Martel. But, uh, running through my lines last night with my mother, well, she said that in *As You Like It* the main characters left the city to live in a rural woodland, and it was kind of ironic that you were making everything more urban."

Peter blinked his eyes rapidly several times and the room grew silent. Then Peter's voice filled the theater again. "That's a very well thought out point, Jenny, and I applaud you for bringing it up. Let us just say that it's good the way Shakespeare wrote it, but there's always room for improvement. Understood?"

"But how is that an improvement over—"

The clanging school bell interrupted her.

"Very well, class." Peter waved them along with his hand. "We'll pick up there tomorrow."

As the students filed out Peter waved at Clyde. "Greetings and salutations, Mr. Rerd," Peter shouted. "Thank you for stopping by." He walked up the inclined floor to the back of the theater. A jingling sound with each step drew Clyde's gaze to a pair of low-cut Italian boots. The random musical accompaniment came from the dangling zippers on the sides.

"Greetings yourself, Peter. You've got some sharp students in that class."

"Ah, yes." Peter sat down in the seat next to Clyde. "Jenny is wonderful, but headstrong and a bit gawkward."

"So tell me about the new project you're working on."

"Oh, it's a charming little story I'm writing, focusing on the real-life events of our own dear Paxon Chute." Peter clasped his hands together.

"That's an admirable idea."

"Well thank you Clyde, I thought so. My idea is to show how our simple lives here burn brighter than most people could ever imagine. I'm calling it 'Chuting Stars,' as in c-h-u-t-i-n-g, get it?"

Clyde laughed. "'Chuting Stars'?"

"Yes, marvelous, is it not?"

"I wouldn't have thought of that in a million years."

"Well, we all have our talents." Peter's eyes twinkled.

"Yes, everyone needs to be good at something." Clyde nodded slowly. "All righty then. How can I be of assistance?"

"One of the fascinating stories I want to include is the time when you were struck by lightning. I'd like to run through the details with you, that is, if you approve my including it in the story."

"Uh," Clyde pulled at his shirt collar, "I think I'd be honored."

"I know it was a very life-changing event and it's very brave of you to share this with the whole world. Your courage is to be contemplated."

"I believe you're right, though most everyone in my world's already heard—"

Peter interrupted. "That may be, but they'll experience it in a new way, through your eyes, but really," Peter leaned well into Clyde's personal space, "through your very soul."

"You think so?"

"Absolutely." Peter sat back, opened a leather-bound notebook and uncapped his brown Waterman fountain pen. "Now, you shared the story with me before and I've written down what I remember. But I want every detail, so tell me all about that fateful stormy day so very, very long ago." Peter leaned in again.

"Well, not that long ago. Let's see, it happened right before Japheth's birth, and he just turned twenty-two." Clyde shifted his weight onto the armrest away from Peter.

Peter looked at the manuscript in his notebook and drew a line through the second "very."

Clyde shook his head. "Also, the skies were clear that day, not stormy, that's partly what made it so unusual."

"What?" Peter threw his hands up in the air. "Not stormy?

But you were struck by lightning. There must have been a storm."

"I could see a thunderstorm, miles away off to the southeast, but for me it had been sunny and calm all day."

"That's unheard of. The lightning strike must have affected your memory." Peter tilted his head slightly. "It must've been stormy, you just don't remember."

"It's not common, but it has been heard of. They call it a bolt from the blue, when lightning strikes on a sunny day."

"Okay, I'm with you, I'm with you." Peter wrote a note on the manuscript that read "memory definitely affected – have to fill in gaps."

Clyde glanced at Peter's notebook and then resumed his story. "So back then I still worked for the railway of course. And I had just moved the old speeder onto—"

"Oooh, speeder, I like that. It sounds very Luke Skywalker-ish."

"It's a small motorized car, back then we used them to inspect the tracks."

"Mmmm, small and very fast, I assume?"

"No, not really, maybe thirty miles an hour. Speeders were just faster than the human-powered cars they replaced. But we never went very fast in them, if you did you couldn't inspect the tracks. They'd be nothing but a blur."

Peter wrote down "gap" again on his manuscript and next to it wrote "blur." He held up his finger. "Okay, you were saying you had just moved the speeder. Where did you move it?"

"Right, I moved it onto the siding where we often kept it stored."

"Siding, that's a section off of the main line?"

Clyde nodded. "It's used to allow trains to pass each other on a single line like we've got running through Paxon Chute."

"Yes, yes, I see. And if that main line is not cleared then

disaster could strike at any moment, right?" Peter bumped his fists together to indicate a train collision.

"We don't have a main line, it's a branch line, and we never had much traffic on it. Back in those days we normally had a couple of freighters per week coming over from Job."

Peter wrote "gap" again, and added "Jobe."

Clyde pointed at the notebook. "It's spelled j-o-b, there's no 'e.'"

"There are so many towns around here I've not heard of yet." Peter scratched out the extra letter. "So the speeder is on the siding, what next?"

"I had to switch the tracks back so when the freighter came through later that week it wouldn't be diverted onto the siding."

"Aaah, yes." Peter's eyes opened wide. "That would be catastrophic, would it not?"

"Not really, it's a low speed section of track anyway. It'd just bump the speeder around."

"I see." Peter wrote "gap" again.

"As I walked up to the switch I noticed a metallic taste in my mouth, and all my hair stood on end."

"And that's when you saw the burning fireball headed right at you?" Peter pointed up in the air.

"Not exactly. I remember seeing kind of a blue-white light all around me. It didn't really have any shape, but everything kind of glowed real bright. Then I felt this tremendous pressure right here." Clyde ran his fingers across the left side of his chest.

"That must have been your heart deceasing." Peter made another note.

"Can't say one way or the other. My crew thought I had died when they found me. I do believe I could have, if I had so chosen."

"Oh, my. Wait, what? What do you mean?"

"I almost crossed over, to the other side." He paused, nodding his head slightly. "I found myself looking down on my own body lying next to the tracks, and I could see them working on me. Then I felt God Almighty calling my name, pulling me to eternity."

Peter's eyes widened and his face became flushed. "Okay. So what happened next? When did you come to?"

"Hold on, we're not there yet. I'm telling you, that had to be the most peaceful experience of my life. It's difficult to put into words, just so much beauty that I wanted nothing more than to give in to the calling of my name. But then there came the slightest tug back to earth, like a thread, and I could have broken it so easily if I wanted to. Do you know what it was that tugged on me?"

"I'm sure there were lots of confusing sensations. It's hard to account for all we imagine when we've been knocked about a bit." Peter wrote down "too heavy, leave out."

"Regret. That's what tugged on me. I regretted not being the father I should have been. The things I always wanted to do for my children that I somehow never got around to doing. I wasn't quite ready to walk away from this world. That little thread provided just enough resistance to keep me here. I promised God I'd be a different man when I came back." Clyde stared at the empty stage. "But I'm not so sure how well I've kept that promise over the years."

Sweat broke out on Peter's upper lip. "Good, good, you stayed here and we are all very grateful for that. What next?"

"The next thing I knew, I came to in the field beside the tracks with my ears ringing to Kingdom Come."

"Whew!" Peter exhaled. "And when you came to, you were naked, right?"

"What? No, not naked. Why would I be naked?"

"The lightning, of course. The lightning burned your clothing right off of you. I'm positive you told me that before."

"I can guarantee you I didn't, Peter. That's the craziest thing I've ever heard."

"But when they found you, they could see the scorch marks on your body from your head all the way down to the soles of your feet. How could they see all that if you still had your clothes on? I think this affected you more than you remember." Peter raised his eyebrows.

Clyde laughed. "I'm certain I would have remembered that, and besides, there were no scorch marks to see. I didn't have a single mark of any kind on me. But they did find some petrified lightning nearby."

Peter frowned. "I've never heard of such a thing. What is that?"

"Sometimes lightning melts the soil where it strikes the ground. They found some right behind the switch, so they think maybe the bolt hit me and then jumped to the ground. It's probably what kept me from being nuked into a cloud of smoke."

"Yes, I see." Peter tilted his head and looked at the ceiling, then quickly wrote down "nuclear."

"And that's about it."

"What about the lingering side effects?"

"There aren't any. Except my chest feels kinda weird sometimes when it rains. But I think that's just my imagination. So, no side effects."

"None? You're forgetting the ringing in your ears." Peter wrote down "gap."

"That went away after a few days."

"But it threw off your equilibrium, forcing you to retire."

"Equilibrium? No, I didn't retire for another twenty years."

Peter's pen flew across the page. "Okay, I can fix all that."

Clyde's lips pursed. "Yeah, that's what scares me."

"Yes, it can be scary, and wonderful, and fantastic, all at

the same time." Peter put the cap on his pen and smiled. "I'll
let you know when I get this all tidied up."

CHAPTER FIVE

Two days later Beth sat on the bathroom counter straightening her hair. "Would you check and see how many diapers are in the bag?"

"Mm-hmm." Edgar leaned around her to spit toothpaste into the sink. He wiped his face on a towel. "Dang it. This must be Marlon's, it's sopping wet. I swear he must dry off his water before he showers with it."

Junior sat in his bouncy chair on their bedroom floor making bubbly noises. Edgar bent down and squeezed his son's doughy foot as he walked by. "There's eleven diapers in the bag," he called out from the nursery.

"Hush!" she whisper-yelled back at him, "you'll wake up Marlon."

Edgar glanced into the living room at the inert, tangled mass of Marlon, quilt, and pillows on the couch. Marlon's dirty socks were on the coffee table, partially draped over a half-full casserole dish of baked spaghetti that he appeared to have been eating from and then left out all night.

"So what! You should see the selfish waste in here. I swear, what he doesn't eat he ruins. We'll have to make other plans for supper tonight." Edgar walked back into their bedroom to put on his shoes. "Anyway, he could get up and go to church with us."

"Badgering him is not going to help if he doesn't want to

go, you know that, don't you?" Beth unplugged her hair straightener. "Are you about ready? Did you put more diapers in the bag?"

"Yes. I am completely ready. No." Edgar pedantically answered Beth's series of questions in the order presented to him. "I told you there's eleven in the bag already. Church is only an hour long."

"Please put a few more in, just in case. And make sure there's enough spare changes of clothing, too."

"How many spare changes do you want in there? That dang diaper bag weighs more than I do."

"You're so silly. Anyway, it's still easier than carrying a baby around for nine months. You can put the bag down whenever you want."

"Yeah, I know, childbirth gives you the upper hand in every discussion we have from here on out." Edgar pinched her when he walked past the bathroom into the nursery.

He snickered and hid Junior's hooded winter coat in the bottom of the bag, and then crammed in ten more diapers. As he set the bag by the front door he looked at the spaghetti dish again. Edgar walked to the coffee table and smashed the socks down into the spaghetti, soaking them with the staining red sauce. He lifted them up and set them atop the spaghetti in their original positions.

Edgar crept away smiling, until he sniffed his fingers. He washed his hands at the kitchen sink. Twice.

A cookie sheet lay in the dish drainer. Edgar opened the drawer under the oven and dropped the cookie sheet into the drawer. Raucous metallic thunder reverberated through the house.

"Blunnnhh." Marlon moaned and rolled over.

"Get up and go to church with us, you slug." Edgar kicked the drawer shut.

"Sssh!" Beth whisper-yelled again, but Marlon remained

fast asleep. "Would you load the bag and the stroller into the car?"

"Why do we need the stroller?"

"You never know, I like to have it handy."

Beth ran her fingers through her hair one last time and swooped Junior out of his chair. He burped and spat up on her dress as she lifted him onto her shoulder. "You little stinker." She laughed and kissed his forehead. "Always, always, right when I'm ready to leave." She grabbed a washcloth from the nursery and laid it on her damp shoulder. "Let's go, Edgar, we're late."

Edgar stood at the front door twirling his keys. "Waitin' on you."

"Argh. I can't believe how long it takes to get ready to go anywhere now."

* * *

The service had already started by the time they crept into the back of the chapel. Edgar carried Junior's car seat in one hand and the diaper bag in the other. Beth patted their baby, sleeping on her shoulder.

The morning sun sparkled through the stained glass windows at the back of the church, creating a cascade of brilliant hues that lit up the white limestone walls inside. Exposed wooden beams held up the steeply pitched roof. Edgar and Beth went to their usual section in the middle of the right-hand side. Clyde and Ruth were there, along with Edgar's Uncle Drew.

Drew turned to Edgar and Beth, nodding to them with the beat of the music. He clapped his hands vigorously and with a great whacking sound, especially through a cappella sections, which he referred to as his clapping solos.

The music wound down and Pastor Kendall Brooks made

his way to the raised stage at the front of the chapel. He gave a short wave of his hand and greeted the Sunday morning crowd, "Hello, everybody. I know a lot of people, myself included, often find it difficult to just be where we are. Sometimes things are painful, and we want to escape, or maybe redo parts of our life in some way so that things could be different now.

"This week someone asked me about a Bible verse in Romans: 'And we know that God causes all things to work together for good to those who love God, to those who are called according to His purpose.' I was asked why so many bad things happen if God is supposed to make all things good. But it says 'God works for the good,' not that all things are good. We are living in a broken world, full of broken people who have free will, and bad things happen. I myself do them on a regular basis."

When Ken said the words "bad things happen," Edgar took out a pen. He jotted down some numbers representing their bank balance and several large bills either due or past due. The calculation resulted in a negative balance. He reworked the numbers and scribbled notes through most of Ken's talk. Edgar set down his pen for the conclusion.

"As I thought over what I would talk about this week, it struck me what a contrast the lottery is to the verse in Romans. I think the appeal of winning the lottery lies in the illusion of an instant life-fix."

A ripple of reaction went through the crowd, with some heads nodding yes and some shaking no. Beth elbowed Edgar.

Ken smiled and held up his hands. "To me it's not so much about whether the lottery is right or wrong, the bigger issue is where you place your hope. I've known people possessing fantastic sums of money, but all their wealth could not give them joy or peace. In general, the growing, healthy, healing things in life are a slow process, and most shortcuts don't work out. So I encourage you to be content with the journey you are on, and remember that even bad things can be used for ultimate good."

After the service, Edgar and Clyde stood outside the church in the shade of a large oak tree while Ruth and several other women helped Beth tend to Junior. People milled around, discussing the morning service and catching up on the latest town news.

Marlon called out as he approached from across the town square. "Hey man, what's up? I'm starving, what are we doing for lunch?"

"Well now Marlon," Clyde shook his head, "you just missed the main course. Ken served us up some food for the soul."

"I think we're getting boxes and hanging out on the square." Edgar motioned towards The Circle on the Square Café, which sold box lunches on Sunday afternoons.

Marlon clapped his hands together. "You know what, would you get me a couple of Brammies instead? I haven't had one of those in forever."

A sign in front of the butcher's shop on the town square told the origins of the Schwertner family and Schwertner's Meat Market. Thirty years ago Karl Schwertner married Felipa Garcia and they re-branded under the name Señora Schwertner's. Together the couple developed the award-winning bratwurst tamale they called the Bramale, also referred to as a Brammie.

Clyde pointed at the line in front of the butcher's shop. "You'd better get a move on. They usually sell out by noon, though you might still be able to get a Pollo Schnitzel Verde."

"Wait a minute." Edgar pointed at Marlon's feet. "Are those my workout socks? Beth gave me a pair like that for my birthday."

"Yeah, I knew you wouldn't mind. I found them in your

drawer. That is, as soon as I figured out which one was your drawer. If I'd been looking for a bra and panties I could've been here a lot sooner." Marlon thumped Edgar on the back and laughed. "You see, I had my last clean pair of socks laid out for today, but someone got spaghetti sauce on them. I'm not naming names, but I know how kids get into everything. Anyway, maybe Beth can get them clean when she catches up on our laundry."

"There's so many things wrong with that, I don't even know where to start."

Marlon laughed again. "Now don't look at me like that, Gar, I'm kidding."

Edgar turned to Clyde. "You know, Dad, I do want to win the lottery and I don't know why that's wrong."

"Well—" Clyde started, but Marlon interrupted him.

"I totally think I should win the lottery." Marlon put his thumb to his chest. "I could do so much good for so many with even a small percentage of my winnings. I would hang on to the rest, to manage it, so I can keep on giving for the rest of my life. You see, I believe God's more likely to make it happen for a generous guy like me." He winked at Edgar.

Clyde grinned at Marlon. "I'm sure God will smile a winning number down on you someday so you can do some of his heavy work through your lottery-funded philanthropy. But I will say you've got a good heart. I'll never forget you sticking up for Edgar that time all the Bruger boys had him cornered."

Marlon's face reddened and he looked down. "Aw, that was so long ago."

Edgar shook his head. "Yeah, long ago. So back to my point. I don't want to win so I can slack off all the time and life-binge on whatever. I still want to work, I'm just tired of being so stinkin' broke all the time. I know God could fix everything for me, but for whatever reason he hasn't, and I'm tired of asking."

"I'm sorry it's so hard for you right now, son. Is there something else you think you should be doing?"

"Even that question stresses me out because I have no idea. I just want to get on with it."

Marlon poked Edgar in the shoulder. "I think you've got to go for it, Gar, the way I did up in Chicago. Just be like a water drop."

"What?"

"You see, people always have to limit everything with a bunch of made-up rules and regulations. Water follows its own rules. It runs into and over everything. Does a river freak out about going over a thousand-foot waterfall? No, it pushes on and goes right over the edge. It crashes to the bottom and keeps going. Water can do anything, and nothing ever fazes it. Words to live by."

Clyde laughed. "Yes, water flows, but only because it falls under the unwavering jurisdiction of gravity and physics. So it has no choice. What if you, as Liquid Marlon, didn't want to go over the waterfall? And once you went over, where would you wind up? Maybe trapped in some underground aquifer. Or out to the ocean, caught in the Gulf Stream all the way up to the North Pole, where you might spend a few millennia frozen in a glacier. But I guess you'd have the happy memory of your fleeting cliff dive to keep you warm and content."

"You're forgetting—" Marlon started in.

Clyde kept rolling. "And I'd like to point out that water is utilized in many unpleasant processes. You might spend a few uncomfortable hours in a stained toilet bowl awaiting the next horrible event. Then there'd be the torturous journey through all nine levels of sewage hell before you could ever hope to find another waterfall to go rushing over."

Marlon spoke quickly when Clyde paused. "You're forgetting how dynamic water is. It can transform itself, evaporate into the air and become a cloud, travel the world, and then dive down, down, down as rain, all the way back to Earth."

Edgar frowned. "Well, this is all fascinating, but I'm not a water drop, and something's got to change."

"It will, once I get you hooked up with my new venture." Marlon smiled his toothy smile. "You know I'm right."

"Ah yes," Clyde raised an eyebrow, "when are we going to hear what this is all about?"

"The presentation pitch should be sent FedEx to me this week. The renderings have been in final review with my partners up in Chicago. You'll love it, it's epic."

The frown remained on Edgar's face. "We'll see. I guess. I may be sharp as a bowling ball when it comes to financial stuff, but I'm not getting sucked into some big risky idea."

"Trust me, buddy, I'm not putting lipstick on a pig here. This is the real deal."

"It's going to have to be, because I need real money to pay my real bills."

Clyde glanced at the gazebo in the middle of the town square. "Speaking of reality, there's the illustrious Mr. Martel, and he's got a manila folder tucked under his arm. Looks like we're in for another edition of Peter's Theater in the Square."

Edgar watched Peter walk up the steps of the gazebo. "Wonder what he'll share with us today?"

Clyde's face went blank. "I hope this isn't what I think it is."

From the folder Peter produced a set of papers and announced, "Listen up, people! Everyone gather 'round. I have some material to share from my latest project. It's titled 'Chuting Stars,' and it is about the good people of Paxon Chute."

"Oh dear." Clyde took out his handkerchief and wiped his forehead.

Beth and Ruth joined the men in front of the church. Ruth

held Junior on her shoulder, patting his back. She looked at the crowd gathering around the gazebo, sitting on benches or the grass. She giggled. "Oh, what a treat! Peter is going to perform. Let's get closer."

Clyde did not move. "I believe I'll hold back a little."

"Come on." Ruth nudged him with her shoulder. "What's the matter with you? You love this kind of thing."

Clyde slowly followed the group over to the gazebo but stopped behind Mavis's Kettle Corn Cart parked at the edge of the crowd.

"Ladies and gentlemen, children of all ages," Peter's booming voice carried across the town square as he walked in a slow circle around the platform. "For your enjoyification, from my original work 'Chuting Stars,'" he held the papers up in his right hand, "I present to you chapter four, titled, 'A Shocking Tale.'" He snorted and giggled, then flattened out his left hand and held it above his head, palm towards him, and drew it down in front of his face.

Calls for quiet sprinkled through the crowd and everyone settled in to listen.

Peter began reading. "The angry gray skies blew into Paxon Chute that day intent on unleashing their fury on anyone who got in their way." He shook his left fist in the air. "The wind had a strange oily feel about it that slammed Clyde's hair all about his head. Inside that head," he pointed at his own head, "was the thought that this was too dangerous a day to be outside, but he had a job to do, and if he didn't do it, people could certainly die." He nodded slowly.

The crowd let out a few gasps and at least one snicker. Clyde sat down and bowed his head.

"He had just finished performing a high-speed run aboard his speeder, checking to make sure the rails were still safe at top speeds. Railway testing was dangerous work even on a calm day, but on this day the wind had buffeted him terribly as the tracks blurred past, but the tracks were okay once again, this time, anyway." Peter paused his delivery but continued walking, slowly circling the inside of the gazebo.

"He had just moved the speeder off the main line and onto the siding, nuzzling it up to the coal train waiting there. Now the switch for the tracks had to be changed or the 12:24 p.m. passenger train from the nearby town of Job would plow into the coal train." He pantomimed extracting a pocket watch from a vest pocket and checking the time. "And not just coal. Among that long line of train cars filled with lumpy chunks of inky black gold there was also one lone, solitary white train car loaded with barrels and barrels of spent plutonium. Yes, if Clyde failed at his duties this day, not only would all of the people on the passenger train most certainly die, the entire region would have a nuclear disaster on their hands."

Mavis whispered to Clyde, "Goodness me, I don't remember any of this."

"You and me both," he mumbled.

Peter leaned into an imaginary wind. "Clyde struggled to maintain his footing as he desperately struggled with the switch amid the near hurricane-force winds." He made a violent wrenching motion with his left arm. "Then he saw something terrible and dreadful out of the corner of his eye. He spied up into the sky and saw his doom crashing down upon him in the form of a burning fireball that struck fear into the utterest depths of his soul." Peter clenched his fist and held it to his heart.

"He suddenly thought of what he had had for breakfast that day and that that was going to be his last meal and that he wished he had had something other than oatmeal for his last meal, but as it turned out it was indeed not his last meal, and he would actually enjoy many more meals again that he cooked himself. It was the last day for the clothes he wore that day though because the burning fireball that crashed down upon him in the form of lightning burned off all of the clothes he had been wearing and even burned off every hair of his body including the hair under his armpits and hair in other places too sensitive to mention except his ear hairs were not burned off which disappointed him because he wanted those gone." Peter frowned.

"The lightning knocked him unconscious for some time, and during that time he experienced some unpredictable experiences, probably hallucinations or daydreams. Who knows?" Peter shrugged. "But Clyde knew these were things best kept to himself and he never shared them with anyone ever." He pointed his finger and wagged it from side to side.

"When he regained consciousness he had no idea how long he had been out but knew he had to act fast or people would unquestionably certainly die.

"Singed and smoldering, completely naked and hairless, except for his bushy ears, Clyde shot like a cannon over to the switch trembling with fear and managed to switch the tracks as the passenger train safely sped by just in time." With great pantomime effort Peter moved the imaginary lever.

The crowd cheered.

"Clyde could see the people inside the train as it sped safely by, and he knew bitterly they were oblivious to the price he had paid to save them from extreme certainty of complete death. Except for the last car, where Clyde could see a little boy pointing at him and laughing. Next to the boy sat a beautiful woman in a red dress, and she began to laugh as well. At this, Clyde wept, and questioned whether anyone would ever care, and whether anything mattered, and he just wanted to die." Peter held the back of his hand to his forehead.

"Later that night though, he was proven wrong. Word began to spread about his heroic deed and his house was filled with many appreciating train passengers who somehow heard about what he had done, and learned his name, and where he lived, and collectively managed to make their way to his house to shower him as a conglomerated group with the well wishes he so deserved and songs of merriment also. Clyde hugged his wife and children and began to cry tears of real joy as they gathered around the piano in his house and sang 'What a Wonderful World.' There was a long-term price to pay though. His hearing became impaired in a certain complicated way that interfered with his equilibrium, which meant no more speeder runs, because doing them required exaggerated balance and reaction during such a dangerous task. Yes, for the rest of his career it was desk work from here on out for poor Clyde, no longer a high-flying railway car test pilot. Another chapter of another great life of sacrificing community service here in Paxon Chute."

Peter plunged into a deep bow for several seconds. The crowd clapped and cheered. Straightening up, Peter smiled and blew kisses with both hands. "Thank you, thank you!"

Tom Walker grabbed Clyde's shoulder, leaned in close, and shouted in his ear, "We all appreciate your gallant sacrifice!"

"You know I can hear, dang you, Tom."

"Well, I should help steady you though, what with your complicated hearing and all." Tom held onto Clyde's arm above the elbow.

Clyde looked at Edgar and shook his head. "Let this serve as a lesson to you on the importance of living in reality."

Ruth laughed. "Exactly, Clyde. You do tend to exaggerate."

CHAPTER SIX

Saturday at six o'clock in the morning Edgar got busy cleaning the pavilion in Nickel Rock Park. He started by emptying all the trash bins then scrubbed, bleached, and hosed them out. Ashes were meticulously scooped out of the barbeque grills. The park's big backpack blower thoroughly removed all sand from the pavilion floor and adjacent sidewalks. Edgar wiped down the benches and tabletops to get rid of the sweaty, gritty, suntan lotion smears and wayward blobs of ketchup.

Edgar glanced around the pavilion then checked his watch. He paced back and forth a few times, glancing at his watch again before running over to the maintenance building to drag a garden hose back out to the pavilion. He sprayed down everything except the barbeque grills, though he did stare at them several times. Running back to the maintenance building, he grabbed several towels to dry the tables and benches.

The sun had risen a quarter of the way up the sky when Edgar paused to wipe the sweat from his face and neck. He walked over to a wooden pedestrian bridge that spanned the Cobb River. Sunlight sparkled on the clear spring-fed water flowing past him.

Standing on the bridge Edgar kept glancing back at the pavilion where he'd posted a sign that read "Reserved for Rerd Baby Dedication." He grimaced at the scattered clouds and shook his head. Checking his watch, he kicked at the bridge railing and groaned, "Come on, Dad!"

Edgar turned and faced downstream where several kids were scurrying about on Nickel Rock, playing King of the Nickel. Edgar laughed when the king of the moment grappled with a challenger then hurled him off in a smooth arc into the river. The defeated challenger floated along in the current. A lifeguard stood on one of the small wooden ferry rafts attached to the ropes strung between Nickel Rock and the riverbank. The lifeguard pulled on the rope to draw the raft closer to the swimming boy, who declined assistance and splashed water on the lifeguard. The boy veered over to the bank and exited at the main turnout point for the river.

A flash of something white drew Edgar's attention back to the pavilion, where a group of pasty tourists shambled towards the unoccupied shady haven. The only adult in the group, a woman, shouted orders at indifferent ears as she lugged a wheeled ice chest behind her. Caked with fresh mud the wheels left a clotted trail along Edgar's otherwise spotless sidewalk. The most energetic child in the group lost the top half of his Popsicle to the pavilion floor then tossed the remainder on a bench seat so he could punch and kick one of the metal trash bins. Two more children dropped their popsicles to join the attack on the defenseless can, yelling and screaming at the object of their unaccountable wrath. Their cantankerous racket shattered the peaceful morning.

Edgar ran over to the pavilion. "Excuse me, ma'am." His voice faded amid the uproar.

The woman turned her head and eyed Edgar through narrow slits. "Quit it!" She yelled at the children, to no effect.

Edgar shouted, "I'm sorry, ma'am, the pavilion is reserved this morning."

A lull in the battle ensued as the children paused to listen. The smallest child, a toddler, had been collecting and sampling the dropped popsicles. He tottered over to Edgar and gave him a hug, wiping his sticky hands on Edgar's shorts.

The woman gawked at Edgar and said, "What." It came out as a statement rather than a question. She stared at Edgar blankly, breathing audibly through her open mouth.

"As per the notification," Edgar pointed at the sign, "the pavilion is reserved this morning. But there are lots of covered benches available along both sides of the river."

"Uh." The woman squinted and looked around. "Where's a good place to be at?" She spoke in a moist, wheezy voice.

"There are a lot of options, so that depends on what—"

"They wanna play in the river."

"Well, yes, of course they do." Edgar looked the children over. "I think I know the perfect place for their ages. I'd be happy to help with your gear and show you the way."

"Okay. Sure." She opened her eyes a little wider. "That'd be cool."

Edgar took hold of the handle on the ice chest and wheeled it straight off the sidewalk and onto the grass to keep the mud trail from spreading. He led them over the bridge to an empty bench beside one of the wading areas along the river.

The woman thumped her oldest child on the arm. "Look at the nice man pullin' our cooler for us. You boys should be that way for me more."

The kids, running full speed, plowed into the water.

Pointing at the river, Edgar yelled, "Watch out, there's a drop-off!"

The child in the lead went under.

Edgar laughed. "That happens all the time. The water is so clear it's hard to tell how deep it is." The child remained underwater for several seconds and Edgar turned to the woman. "He can swim, right?"

"Delbert!" She shouted at the oldest child. "Pluck him up outta there! You know he ain't a fish. He's gotta come up to breathe. Don't make me come out there, I'll snatch you baldheaded!"

The boy slowly obeyed.

Edgar hoisted the ice chest onto the table. "Ma'am, I hope you all make some great memories today in Nickel Rock Park. I've got a few thousand of them myself."

"Thank you, mister park ranger sweetie-pants." Her face broke into a gap-toothed grin.

Edgar smiled and tipped his cap.

Crossing back over the bridge he checked his watch again and frowned. He walked to the parking lot when Beth pulled in.

"Twenty till, and he's still not here. I can't believe it." Junior kicked his legs rapidly and waved his arms around as Edgar fastened the car seat carrier onto the stroller. "Well, I guess I can believe it." He pulled off his cap and wiped his forehead. "But still, I can't believe it."

Beth gave him a hug. "Who's not here?"

"Dad's way late. He was supposed to be here earlier so I could get changed. It's so frustrating. He worked for a railroad all his life. For his entire career he had to work around a timetable."

"Oh, well I'm here now. Why don't you go ahead and get changed?"

Kendall Brooks walked over to the park from the town square.

"I can't. There's Ken and I need to talk with him. Then everyone else will be here. It's too late now. All his big talk about being a grandfather, but where is he?"

"It's not just talk. He comes over all the time to see Junior, but you know how he is."

"Of course I know. I know because I've lived it over and over and over."

"I'm sorry you didn't have a chance to change, Edgar. But

you know, people wear their uniforms for all kinds of ceremonies, even weddings."

"That's completely different. Those are dress uniforms for formal occasions."

"You look fine."

"Really? It's barely even a uniform. A brown shirt, khaki swim trunks, and water shoes? And you're all prettied up in a nice dress. Think what the pictures will look like."

"But it's what you do. I think it's neat."

"I feel totally out of place. And to top it all off I was scrubbing the garbage cans earlier. I smell like sweat, and picnic trash...and popsicles."

"I can't smell anything. Don't worry about it, just go talk with Ken."

"See those buses?" Edgar pointed where they lined up along the river, ready to haul people back upstream. "A bunch of the drivers have gone off and left them idling again. They're not supposed to do that. It's going to stink us out over here. Hold on."

Edgar cupped his hands to his mouth and shouted at a man and a young boy in the parking lot. "Sir! No digging allowed in the park, so put the shovels back in the trunk."

The man threw the shovels into the trunk and slammed the lid while the boy stamped his feet, complaining to his father.

Edgar resumed his conversation with Beth. "And did you notice those clouds?" He pointed at the sky. "The forecast was for a thirty percent chance of rain. I'm telling you right now, those are packing at least a forty percent chance of rain."

"You can't control that, you goober." She pushed him gently in the direction of the pastor. "Go on, now."

Guests began showing up at the pavilion, "oohing" and "aahing" over the gurgling baby. Presents piled up on one table and various desserts crowded another.

Five minutes before ten o'clock, Clyde and Ruth showed up. Edgar caught them before they got to the pavilion. "Dad, where were you? You were supposed to be here over half an hour ago."

"Sorry, son. Something came up."

"What could possibly come up? You're retired." Edgar stopped, and held up his hands. "Okay, I know that's not fair. I was really counting on you to be here earlier so I could get cleaned up."

Ruth gave him a hug. "I tried to move him along, Edgar, but here we are now."

Several guests pointed towards the parking lot at Richard and Penelope Anne. Richard wore a white suit and yellow tie, but Penelope Anne drew all the attention with the massive yellow floral pattern on her dress and a wide-brimmed hat that extended beyond the width of her shoulders. As an added precaution against the sun Richard held a frilly parasol over her head.

Penelope Anne glanced around, her lip curling up slightly, and sashayed over to Beth. "Picnic tables? Under..." She looked up. "Under a shed? Aren't these events traditionally held in a church?"

"Mother, I already told you. We wanted a more natural setting down by the river."

"But it's June." Penelope Anne fanned herself. "And we're in Texas."

"Yes, Mother, I've been trained in the use of both calendars and maps."

"It gets so hot." She fanned more vigorously. "It's supposed to be ninety today."

"Yes, Mother, in seven hours. Isn't it perfect right now?"

Penelope Anne said nothing. She walked around slowly, glaring at the wooden picnic tables.

By ten minutes after ten o'clock a sizeable crowd turned

up, and Mavis had her Kettle Corn Cart in the parking lot. Ken motioned for Edgar and Beth to stand beside him and then called for attention. Beth extracted Junior from the group of women taking turns holding him.

"We're here today to celebrate a new life." Ken gestured towards Junior. "And how fitting it is to be out here along this river that gives so much life to our town. Edgar and Beth are the proud parents of Edgar Allan Rerd Junior, a fine name that he will be proud to bear."

Beth held Junior so everyone could see him, his head bobbling in jerky motions as he looked around.

Ken opened his Bible. "Chapter one of the first book of Samuel records the story of Hannah dedicating her son, Samuel, to the Lord: 'I prayed for this child, and the Lord has granted me what I asked of him. So now I give him to the Lord. For his whole life he will be given over to the Lord.'

"God has brought to earth another eternal soul who will make his mark. Edgar and Beth, as we thank God for Junior and commit him to the Lord, do you promise to set examples of Christian living in your home as you raise up your child in the ways of the Lord, teaching him to love, honor, and chase after God?"

"Yes," Beth and Edgar said in unison.

Ken spoke about the influence the community would have in the life of Edgar Junior and the joy of watching a new generation grow up and find its place.

"To everyone gathered here, upon hearing the commitment of this family, do you promise to join these parents in using your gifts to teach and nurture him, living as an example of God's love before him? If you agree would you please say amen?"

The attendees voiced their agreement, followed by the sound of Clyde blowing his nose.

"And now let's pray. God, thank you for this child—" Ken

was interrupted by a high-pitched squealing and scraping of automobile brakes.

The sound came from Marlon's BMW as it pulled into the parking lot by the pavilion. The door flew open before the car stopped and Marlon's entrance music drowned out the shrieking brake noise.

> ...It's me, whuup-whuup, it's me. Time to get the party on, with me...

Mavis Drew piped up, "What did you say, Pastor? I can't hear you."

"Heavenly Father," Ken spoke louder, "thank you for this child—"

> ...I got-ta gotta be free...

"What?" Mavis said again.

Ken fought through, nearly shouting his prayer. "Please guide him in all his ways, and..." He faltered as the music beat on.

> ...'cuz there ain't no we without me...

Marlon finished combing his hair and turned the music off.

After a pause Ken continued in a much quieter voice. "Lord, we ask your blessing—"

Wham! Marlon's car door slammed shut.

By that point most everyone in the pavilion had opened at least one eye to find out who was making all the racket.

Marlon marched their way, holding up his remote and pointing it back at the car. He snapped his wrist and clicked the remote, but nothing happened. He clicked it again, and again nothing happened. Marlon stopped and turned to face the car, clicking the remote repeatedly.

Ken's eyes remained closed. "We pray that you look down on this child and say—"

Marlon yelled at his remote. "Come on! Would you just work for once in your life?"

Mavis cleared her throat during the ensuing silence. "Well, I heard that plain enough."

The chirp-chirp of Marlon's alarm provided the last nail in the coffin of propriety. Ken quickly closed out his prayer and invited everyone to help themselves to the desserts.

Edgar pulled Marlon to the side. "I told you it started at ten."

"Sorry, Gar. Really, it couldn't be helped."

"Couldn't be helped? And why is that? Oh yeah," Edgar slapped his palm to his forehead, "it couldn't be helped because you always have to be so unpredictable, Mr. Spontaneous, blowing around like the wind."

"It really is embarrassing to be so late, especially with the whole godfather thing." Marlon chuckled and shrugged his shoulders.

"Godfather? I never said anything about a godfather. We don't really do that."

"Oh?" Marlon paused. "Really, why not? I thought you were going to surprise me."

"Ah, I think I get it now. The drama caused by the godfather being late, is that it? Concerned attendees asking," Edgar turned his body to the right, "'Is the godfather here yet?'" Turning to the left, "'No, but he is a very busy man.'" Turning back to the right and nodding his head, "'Yes, Junior is so very, very lucky.' Gimme a break, Marlon. It's not actually spontaneous if you plan it."

"I don't even know what you're talking about." Marlon glanced around quickly, his ears turning red.

"You know, it would not have been such a big deal if you had turned down the music and not shouted at the top of your lungs."

"Uh, music? Wha…what do you mean?"

"Yes, Marlon, good to hear from you again." Clyde's voice boomed through the pavilion. He smiled and shook hands with Marlon. "You always have such a cacophony of festive sounds accompanying you. But I say it's a good thing you got that alarm working. There's no telling how many ruffians have infiltrated our quiet little town, waiting for the right opportunity to purloin an antique BMW."

Ruth gave Marlon a hug. "Don't pay any attention to these two. It's always good to see you, and I'm glad you're here. It wouldn't have been the same without you."

"Thanks, Mrs. Rerd." Marlon's face flushed and he smiled at her.

Beth called out to Edgar. "Would you get some pictures of everyone? The camera is in the diaper bag."

Edgar rummaged through the cavernous baby-blue bag. He finally found the camera among the two dozen diapers, changing pad, spit-up cloths, four extra changes of clothing, and numerous blankets.

Edgar's Uncle Drew and Beth's father, Richard, stood a little off to themselves. Edgar walked over to them.

"I checked on that one you told me about, but I wasn't willing to pay that much for a garden hose." Drew shook his head.

Edgar took his first photo and looked at the camera's view screen. His uncle sported a slight scowl on his face and pointed his finger at Richard. Edgar smiled and aimed the camera at the men again.

Richard shrugged his shoulders. "How much should you pay for a garden hose?"

"I dunno, maybe half that, at the most."

"Why do you say that? If they all cost four times as much would you just not buy one?"

"But they don't cost that much." Drew's brow wrinkled.

"Yes, but how do you determine how much something is worth? It seems like however much something costs it's not worth that much to you. Does living with your decision afterwards ever factor in?"

"I can't live with spending that much. So I went to Buck Mart and found one for way less."

"And how is that working for you?"

"It kinda kinks up, and the connectors leak a little."

Richard nodded. "I spend a good bit of my time washing Penelope Anne's car. I don't know how many Buck Mart hoses I would have worn out by now, and hated every minute I used them. That's worth something to me."

"But the other ones cost too much."

"How much is your frustration worth?"

"But it costs too much."

Richard held up his hand. "Look, I'm not one to pass up a good deal, if it really is a good deal. But sometimes it's just not worth it. Like that LASIK commercial on the radio. I'd never trust my vision to someone who's having a sale where you 'buy one eye, get one free.'"

"Really?" Drew pushed his thick glasses back up his nose. "Who's offering that deal?"

The final shot Edgar clicked of the two men captured his uncle's excitement. Richard and Drew made their way back to the dessert table for another pass.

Penelope Anne's voice rang through the pavilion. "Richard, watch out for the Jell-O, it has carrots in it. You know they bother you."

Richard sighed and rolled his eyes.

Penelope Anne resumed her conversation with Mavis. "I keep telling Richard's doctors that he's allergic to carrots. None of them seem to understand, but I'm the one who sees how both his mind and body get completely out of sorts when we visit my mother and she puts carrots in everything. You've got to keep a sharp eye on these doctors. A sharp eye, I'm telling you."

Edgar took a picture of Penelope Anne and managed to get another scowling, finger-waving moment.

"I believe you're right, Penelope." Mavis wagged her head in agreement. "I went—"

Penelope Anne interrupted Mavis, her voice syrupy but firm. "It's Penelope Anne, dear."

"Oh, yes, of course. I was saying, I went to some poor doctor over in Peyton last year and I don't think he really knew what he was doing. He tried his best, I'm sure, but he didn't do a thing about my bunions until they were nearly the size of those grapes." She waved her hand over a bowl of red grapes.

"Oh my." Penelope Anne's voice fluttered and she looked around.

Clyde and his Snorting Bull companions, Tom, Wilbur, Eloy, and Peter, all stood together, staring right at her.

Tom pointed at the bowl. "Well, those are now doomed to never be eaten."

Edgar got a nice shot of all the barflies laughing.

"Won't eat them? Why not?" Mavis's hands went to her hips. "They're fresh off the vine."

Drew raised his arm up high. "I'll sure have some. Mavis grows the best fruit around these parts."

"Yup, and there's lots more in my backyard ready for the taking." Mavis sidled up next to Drew. "You should come over, Drew, and pluck some." She winked and nudged him gently with her elbow.

Edgar had Mavis lined up in the viewfinder and captured a picture of her winking at Drew.

Drew smiled and blushed. "I love a good, honest grape all by itself." He spoke rapidly, his voice a little higher pitched than normal. "I don't understand why people have to put them in so many dishes where they clearly do not belong. Like tuna salad. If something's got salt, pepper, and vegetables in it, then grapes are clearly out of place. It would be like Mavis here adding peaches to her garlic kettle corn." He laughed loudly.

Tom looked at Drew. "It has come to my attention that you often blather on about the most inane subjects whenever Mavis is around."

Drew puffed his cheeks. "I—I do no such thing!"

Edgar followed his mother over to the other side of the pavilion where Marlon's mother, Linda, chatted away with Emily.

Ruth sat down next to them. "How are you doing, Linda?"

"I'm fine. I keep praying for a good ending, that Ward will come to his senses."

"You'd take him back after all he's done to you?"

"Pshaw. He hasn't done nearly as much as he's thought about doing. I guess if truth be told I moved out because of what he was thinking."

"What are you saying Linda, that he's innocent?"

"No, if he was innocent I wouldn't have left."

Edgar caught another scowling composition, this time from Linda, but she did not wag her finger at anyone.

"I'm confused." Ruth shook her head.

"I don't blame you." Emily laid her hand on Ruth's arm. "She's been staying with me for a couple of weeks and I still don't understand."

Linda stood up. "Oh, let's don't spoil this moment. I'll tell you about it later. Look there at your beautiful daughter-in-law holding your grandson."

* * *

An hour later the crowd started to thin out. Edgar walked over to Beth and tickled Junior's bare foot. The sudden sound of rolling thunder made Junior startle, and rain began falling in heavy drops.

Edgar looked around at all the people, presents, and food. "Oh, great. That's perfect. Now what will we do?"

"Now, now, Edgar." Peter held his hands behind his back. "As Dickens said, 'Heaven knows we need never be ashamed of our tears, for they are rain upon the blinding dust of earth, overlying our hard hearts.'"

Clyde laughed. "Peter, it may have escaped your attention that everyone here appears to be *not* crying." He turned to Edgar. "Son, it's best to let it rain. Just let it rain. I happened to bring one of those newfangled umbrellas, and they do a marvelous job of keeping things dry."

Clyde popped open his umbrella, offered his arm to Beth, and walked her and Junior to the parking lot. Several other men followed suit and escorted the women out to their vehicles.

Marlon came trotting back from his car with a cardboard mailer tube. He pointed the raindrop-splattered tube at Edgar. "Okay, we've got an opportunity for some face time now, so let me paint the picture of your brightly lit future."

CHAPTER SEVEN

"Right here?" Edgar gestured to the pavilion.

"This is actually the perfect place, because it involves the river." Marlon set the cardboard tube on a picnic table.

"Hmm." Edgar grunted.

Marlon laughed. "You don't sound very excited."

"Just waitin' to see what this is all about."

"Look behind you," Marlon pointed towards town, "at the ceaseless, traffic-clogging, noise-polluting, pedestrian hazard that is our local busing nightmare. You can even smell their nasty fumes from here. Everyone around here hates those buses to death, am I right?"

"Well, I'm not so sure." Edgar watched several of the buses pull away and roar out of town.

Marlon smiled. "Of course you're sure."

"I do have some concerns about them, and most people are probably not too fond of them, but the river outfitters might argue the point with you."

"I don't think so, you see, because I've had meetings with them, with Bruger, and Hector over at Sloops, plus a few other outfitters. They hate the buses more than everyone else all put together. They're expensive to insure and operate, they break down all the time and leave people stranded, which infuriates their customers, I can guarantee that. It's an all-around headache that's bad for business."

"Maybe you're right. I will admit we've needed a better solution for a long time. It's not good when we let our visitors down."

Marlon picked up the mailer tube and removed one of the end caps. "I pitched this idea to some of my associates in Chicago during a late-night poker session. They jumped at the idea and all want a piece of the action."

He slid out a set of rolled-up papers from the tube and spread them on the picnic table. Reaching into his pocket he pulled out several shiny red casino plaques, which he used to hold down the corners of the papers.

"What are those?" Edgar started to reach for one of the plaques but pulled his hand back when Marlon laughed.

"Why, those are the chips used in high-stakes poker games, my boy. I kept these as a souvenir from that night, didn't even bother cashing them in. Their memory is worth more to me than their face value." He held a plaque up so Edgar could see the $500 denomination etched in gold. "Good times," he smiled and tilted his head, "good times."

Marlon pulled away the blank top sheet of paper, revealing a page emblazoned with the words "River in the Sky." Below the heading a sleek projectile resembling a space capsule zoomed across the page. Robust youths draped out the capsule windows, laughing and giving each other high fives.

"Oops, I almost forgot the theme music." Marlon tapped the screen of his cell phone. The distinctive guitar intro for "Spirit in the Sky" rang through the pavilion. "I haven't nailed down permission to use this in our advertising, but I will. I have to. It's so perfect. The whole 'in the sky' theme, you know? Plus it has a tie-in to our overall space imagery, because it's one of the songs the Apollo 13 crew played during their mission to the Moon."

"Yeah, I remember that from the movie. We must have watched that a dozen times when we were kids." Edgar rubbed his chin. "But I also remember they had an explosion and almost didn't make it back alive."

"Really?"

"Yup, they barely survived. I hope that's not fitting as well."

Marlon frowned. "I thought they landed on that asteroid and blew it up to save the Earth."

"Wow. I'm speechless."

"Maybe I should watch that movie again."

"Also, this song is about dying, and the afterlife. So what is this supposed to be," Edgar pointed at the drawing, "some kind of celestial shuttle?"

"Ha ha. Very funny. No, this is all about getting rid of those nasty old buses and moving this town into the future, into our fantastic future. Behold!" Marlon pulled back the sheet with the logo and waved it around like a matador's cape, revealing the next sheet.

The drawing depicted Nickel Rock and the chutes around it. A number of great shiny metallic towers jutted up out of the river and more of the space capsules were zooming around, suspended from cables strung between the towers. Smiling faces peered out the windows in the capsules going upstream. The empty units coming back downstream were headed for the turnaround point at a tower mounted directly onto Nickel Rock, where one of the capsules awaited its next load. Laughing people rushed up a sleek metal gangway, jostling to be the next lucky passengers. Bold red letters on a silver billboard attached to the gangway read "Step Up to the River in the Sky!"

"Well, what do you think?" Marlon's face broke into a smile that showed most of his teeth. "Huh, huh, huh?"

"That..." Edgar paused. "That's so completely wrong."

"Whoa there, Alligator Gar." Marlon startled backwards a little. "It's pure genius. What's not to like?"

"So many things in so many directions at once. I'm not sure where to start." Edgar stared at the drawing. "Probably the biggest thing for me is that it totally does not fit in with the river, or the town for that matter. There's nothing space-age about Paxon Chute."

"That's part of what's so perfect about it. It'll drag this dusty little relic ahead a few centuries. Face the facts Gar, this town has got to modernize and catch up with the rest of the world."

"Why? That's what people find so appealing. It's like stepping into the past."

"The past? The past is for dead people, not us. Besides, how nostalgic are those smelly old buses, anyway? But hey, how about we agree to disagree on that one for the moment. We can set that aside for now and come back to it later. What other concerns do you have?"

Edgar sat down and leaned over the table, studying the drawing. "Something like this would cost a fortune. Millions and millions. How are you going to come up with that kind of money?"

"Done." Marlon held out his hands. "I told you, I already secured the investors, that night at the poker game. You'll have to track things better than that if you're going to come on board, Egger."

"What do you mean come on board?" Edgar set both palms on the edge of the table and leaned back. "I'm not going to invest in this crazy idea."

"Who said anything about investing? Again, that's covered." Marlon snapped his fingers several times. "Stay with me here. We need someone who knows the park and the river like the back of his hand, someone who can oversee the whole project. I told the team I know the perfect man for the job, and I'm starin' at him right now."

Edgar looked up at Marlon and frowned. "I've already got

a job, and a new baby. I don't have time to fool around with this on the side."

"The side?" Marlon laughed. "Dude, I'm offering you a whole new job, doing something that will really make an impact."

"Um, wow." Edgar drummed his fingers on the table. "That's flattering, and a little nauseating at the same time. A job? Working for you? What could you even pay me?"

"Oh, I'm sure we can at least double your current salary, when you go full-time, that is. It will only be part-time for a while, until things really ramp up. But you'd also be in on the profit-sharing side. Think about how many thousands of paying customers will be partaking of this adventure every day."

Edgar smiled, just a little. "There's definitely some potential." The smile disappeared and he waved his hand at the drawing. "But that monstrosity doesn't even look feasible."

"You're thinking critically, that's good. I like that. And you're right, we have to get an engineering report on the riverbed, and Nickel Rock as well. We need to know what our options are from the very beginning in order to keep costs down."

"What kind of options?"

"There's a whole range of possible activities but it depends on what we find out with the initial report. We might find out we have to drive in some piers to evaluate the riverbed, maybe even get a core sample from Nickel Rock."

"Are you serious?" Edgar's eyes widened. "Everyone in town will freak out if you start doing that kind of stuff."

"They might, yes. That is a definite possibility, and that's why we need you, to iron out all those little wrinkles for us."

"They'll tar and feather me if I present this in a Town Council meeting, and I might be inclined to heat the tar for them."

Marlon slapped Edgar on the shoulder. "Nah, I've got all the confidence in the world in you."

"You clearly do not remember what happens in those meetings. The first one I ever went to there was a huge argument about people jumping off the new bridge."

* * *

Ten years earlier, the town built the pedestrian bridge and people discovered immediately that they enjoyed diving from the bridge into the clear water below. The Town Council tried to prohibit this due to concerns about collisions with the people floating down the river. Enforcing the ban proved difficult. Ward Ezell broached the subject at the first Council meeting after the completion of the bridge. Clyde took young Edgar along to the meeting as a way of introducing his son to the workings of the town's politics.

"I for one do not want to provide a breeding ground for that infectious scourge known as contingency lawsuits." Ward paused, frowning, and gazed around the room. "These people are out of control, and we need to…to…," Ward trailed off as a busty young woman in the audience bent over to pick up the pen she dropped, almost spilling out of her low-cut top. Ward stared in silence for a moment then suddenly looked up and stammered himself back to attention. "Ah, ah-hem. Uh, what was I saying? Oh yes, I can't tolerate all these people who don't have it in themselves to stop. So we'll have to do it for them. We need to arm the park rangers with the proper tools. I think it's high time they started carrying electroshock guns."

Reactions within the Council meeting ranged from indignation to laughter.

Clyde leaned over and spoke in a low voice to his son. "That's absurd, to shock people for jumping off a bridge. But Ward is a keen debater if you try to fight him head on.

Sometimes it's easier to kill something with sadistic agreement, especially if you slather it with copious amounts of courtesy. Watch this."

Clyde stood up and the mayor gave him the floor. "I think we may be onto something here, but we need to tweak it just a little, with all due respect of course for Mr. Ezell's original proposal. I don't believe that type of weapon would be effective if the intended target is in the river. So to amp it up a little we could mount a big diesel generator on the underside of the bridge. Then we get a bunch of extension cords and plug some toasters into the generator. If anyone jumps off the bridge you chuck a toaster their way. That should shock the daylights out of them. You don't even need a direct hit, just get it hand-grenade close, if you know what I mean."

Clyde sat down and a wide-eyed Edgar whispered to his father, "Would we really do that?"

"Of course not. It would be extremely dangerous, but that's not the point. I've just planted a seed. Let's see if it grows."

Clyde's idea did indeed spawn more sadistic agreement, moving on quickly to additional suggestions such as dynamite, boiling oil, and a gunship, leaving behind Ward's comparatively tame electroshock gun idea to die a quiet death.

Even the reasonable, legitimate policing measures discussed at the meeting were protested on the grounds that they went against the general spirit of the town. Finally Police Chief Turner came up with the idea of finding a safe way for people to jump. He proposed building a diving platform on the downstream side of the bridge and stationing a lifeguard there to monitor the activity. The upstream side of the bridge would have a floating barrier to keep the people coming down the river from drifting through the diving area.

Ward spoke out against the plan. "I'm telling you these people have to be controlled. One little platform will not accommodate all the people who jump off that bridge. Y'all are gonna spend all that money and there's going to be a huge line and everyone is still going to jump off wherever they please."

They voted on Chief Turner's idea and it passed.

Clyde whispered to Edgar, "See there, a few of Ward's comments actually have some merit but they've been cheerfully ignored because he's lost his credibility for the evening."

When the platform opened and the prohibition on jumping was removed, many participants discovered part of the thrill had gone and they left as well. So the bridge crowds thinned out and Ward proved to be a false prophet.

* * *

Marlon laughed at Edgar's retelling of the meeting. "That's why we're going to pay you the big bucks." He winked at Edgar, nudged him with his elbow, and made a click-click noise with his tongue.

A thumping sound drew their attention to the river, where a thin man walked along the far bank. He wore headphones and waved something around that resembled a metal detector. A stout woman walked beside him, striking the ground with the end of a large post as they slowly moved along.

Marlon stared at them. "What in the world are they doing?"

"Well, there's been tons of people out with metal detectors looking for Molly's treasure. That would be my first guess, except for the woman with the post. Maybe it's some kind of listening device?"

Marlon laughed. "Yeah, that's a giant microphone and he's listening for the rattling of gold doubloons when she whangs the ground. Idiots." He shook his head. "What's got them all stirred up again?"

"It's hard to say. You know how that story takes on a life

of its own. Someone heard something from someone about some map. No one has seen the map, and no one knows who the someone is, but word gets around and people start searching again."

"A map? That's ridiculous. You're the law around here, you should shut all that nonsense down." Marlon watched the man and woman make their way along the riverbank. "I said it once, and I'll say it again: Idiots. You make your own treasure with your own brain." He tapped his finger on his temple. "That's how I roll."

Edgar looked back down at the drawings. "This could give us a way to get rid of the buses. I'm no businessman, but I guess there might also be some money to be made…I dunno. But the townspeople…such an abomination…" He bit his lip. "I'm going to have to think this over."

CHAPTER EIGHT

Beth lay in bed that night staring up at the ceiling, rubbing the satin edging of the sheet between her fingers. "I don't know, sounds like it goes against so much that you value about the river, and what this town values."

"Maybe." Edgar pulled the chain on the ceiling fan then settled into bed next to Beth. "But if Marlon succeeds, this idea of his will get rid of the buses completely. And, it would be a huge attraction that would bring in more people to enjoy what we have to offer. Change isn't always bad, like the walking bridge they built when I was a kid. Some people were against it at first, but it's worked out great."

"At least that's a wooden bridge that blends in with everything else. What you're describing doesn't sound like it would fit in at all." Beth smoothed out the sheet. "But I want to know what *you* think about it."

"Maybe when you see the plans, it'll…" Edgar turned his head away from Beth, took a deep breath and frowned. "Maybe it'll make more sense to you. But don't forget what this could mean for us. Financially, you know?" He turned and looked her in the eyes. "It could solve so many problems."

"What problems?"

"Things are so tight, we're barely getting by, and now we've got the baby, and you're not working…" his voice trailed off.

"Tight, yes, but life is so good right now. We're all healthy, you love your job, and we're not missing any meals even with Marlon staying here." Beth paused. "Man that guy's got a huge appetite. And he can't do anything quietly. Every time he rifles through the pantry he wakes the baby. And—"

"See, I told you it wouldn't be long before you'd be ready for him to go."

"I admit it's been harder than I thought it would be." Beth sighed. "Anyway, I wish you had more peace about where we are, that you could just let it go and not worry so much."

"It seems like this opportunity would help me to do that, give us some margin so I don't feel so much pressure."

"Sounds like more stress to me, not less. Besides, the kind of margin you really want, you find it inside, not on the outside."

"I don't know what that means." Edgar rubbed his head.

Beth rolled over and placed her hand on his chest. "It means that peace lives inside of you, no matter where you are or what's going on. You don't go chasing after something to find peace."

"I don't think I'm chasing anything. It just fell into my lap."

"How would you even do this? Would you quit your job with the park?"

"No. Not in the beginning anyway. Marlon said it would be part-time until things got going."

"A part-time job? How many hours a week? You already work full-time. When would we ever get to see you?"

"Yes. I'm not sure yet. Ummm..." Edgar paused. "So maybe I haven't worked through all the details yet."

Beth poked Edgar in the ribs. "That's not like you."

"I've put in extra hours before, like when I was getting the nursery ready for the baby. Remember that?"

"That was short-term, for a specific goal, and it seemed more contained somehow. This is a whole different deal."

Edgar jerked the sheet up over his legs. "You know, this isn't fair. I supported your career decision to stay at home with the baby, but now you're not supporting me at all."

"Uh! That's—" Beth stopped short and rolled onto her back again. "Look, it's not that I don't support you. I do. I'm just asking questions. You're so defensive."

"You mean you'd go along with it, if I decided to do this?"

"Of course. I love you, and we're in this together."

"Well you sure don't sound very happy about it." Edgar sighed. "It seems like you want me to stay right where I am."

"No, but I do believe things are better than you realize. And I'm a little surprised you'd trust our future to Marlon. Just yesterday you wouldn't even ask him to load the dishwasher because you said he couldn't do it right."

"I admit there are risks anytime Marlon is involved but if his idea works it could fix everything for us."

Junior cried out in the nursery. Beth swung her legs to the floor and sat up.

"No." Edgar got out of bed. "You stay put. I'll go check on him."

He went into the nursery. Junior had worked himself into a corner of his crib.

"I know buddy, I know how you feel." Edgar picked him up and held him on his shoulder. "All wadded up and stuck in a corner."

* * *

The next week Edgar drove over to Peyton to get supplies for the restroom facilities in the park. At the supply warehouse he filled the backseat and trunk with gallon jugs of soap and cases of toilet paper, hand towels, and feminine hygiene products.

Edgar drove over to the Peyton Hills Country Club to see Daryl, a friend from college who worked at the club as a groundskeeper. Daryl had been working on a new fertilizer mix and wanted Edgar to try it out in the park.

Daryl struggled to cram the sack of fertilizer into the crowded trunk of Edgar's car. "Doesn't the park have a truck for you to use?"

"We drive utility vehicles on-site. To use one of the town's work trucks you have to get a request on the schedule, and check it in and out. Trust me, it's easier to drive mine."

"Well let me know how that fertilizer works, Edgar. I could use some good referrals."

Edgar eased into the driver's seat and grimaced as he inserted the key into the ignition. The starter on his old Crown Victoria made its usual harsh grinding noise then released a cloud of acrid smoke and went silent.

"Crap, crap, crap, crap, crap!" Edgar pounded his fist on the dash. He jumped out of the car and reared back to kick the fender but stopped when he turned and saw several of the country club crowd staring at the swirling cloud. At least they kept moving, unlike the members sitting down for lunch in the clubhouse, where a wall of windows provided a panoramic view of his plight.

Edgar held his foot in check and phoned Beth. "Our crappitty crap-crap car has crapped out on me."

"That's a fine hello for your wife."

"Well, I'm right here in the parking lot at the country club, and everyone can see me. The only one not staring at me is a woman in the clubhouse hiding behind a very large hat. I've got a feeling that's your mother."

"Oh, Edgar, I'm sorry it won't start. I bet you can get it fixed though."

"Yes, I'm sure we will, eventually, with enough time and money, wherever I'll come up with either of those." Edgar shook his head. "But that doesn't help me right now."

"Is there anything I can do?"

"I dunno. I guess I'll try to fix it this weekend, somehow. For now I need a ride home, and since we only have one car I'm completely stuck here in paradise."

"I'll ask Marlon to come pick you up. I was planning on taking Junior over to see my parents this afternoon anyway, so I'll ride over with Marlon. Dad can give me a ride back home later."

Edgar sighed. "I really don't like asking Marlon for anything. He tracks what's owed to him so diligently."

"He's staying in our home for nothing. He can certainly do us this one little favor."

"That's true enough. He should help us, even if he doesn't want to."

* * *

Marlon did not hesitate when Beth asked him. "Sure, I can treat you to a ride in the ol' Beemer."

A blast of hot air came out when Beth opened the passenger door of Marlon's car, carrying with it a strong odor of cologne and stale cigarette smoke. The men's fragrance emanated not only from what had seeped off Marlon, but also from the chrome air freshener hanging prominently below the rearview mirror. Beth smiled as she looked at the shiny three-dimensional representation of the male gender symbol. She squinted to make out the writing on the bottom of the air freshener. "Mag-ni-tude?"

"No, you say Manitude, because 'the g is silent, but they'll know you're coming.' That's their slogan. See how it's all uppercase letters, except for the 'g'?" Marlon tapped the air freshener with his finger, setting it to swinging back and forth. "Isn't that awesome?"

"How long have you been smoking, Marlon?" Beth wrangled Junior's car seat into the back of the aged two-door coupe.

"Huh? I don't smoke. Why would you even ask that?" Marlon's nostrils flared as he quietly sniffed, then frowned.

"Oh, nothing. I thought I smelled something, but maybe it was just the fog of virility."

"Yes, it is a very manly car, isn't it?" Marlon unfurled his smile up the right side of his face.

Junior fell back asleep as soon as Beth buckled him in. Marlon started the car.

"How about a little open air?" With a dramatic thrust of his arm Marlon punched the button to roll back the sunroof.

"Well, it's a little hot out today. Plus the wind might wake the baby."

The sunroof only went back a few inches and stopped. Marlon tried to close it but that only produced a steady clicking sound. Beth had to hold the button down while he pushed on the sunroof with both hands until it finally closed with a low moan.

"Ab-so-lutely, we can go modern instead." Marlon switched on the air-conditioning. The wheezy breeze coming from the vents smelled of old dusty plastic and had an even sharper scent of the previous owner's stale cigarette smoke.

They drove out of the neighborhood and Marlon hit play on the song he'd picked. The lyrics rang out.

...There's a ring still in a box inside his front pocket...

Beth glanced at Junior sleeping in the backseat and turned down the volume. "Wow Marlon, I never would have thought you'd be a fan of The Heartbroke Girls."

"Ah well, it's bittersweet. I had a chance for true love once, but, like the song says, the ring is still in my pocket." Marlon pursed his lips and nodded slightly.

Beth laughed. "You're so full of it, Marlon. We both know if you really wanted some girl you'd never stop pestering her."

Marlon's shoulders slumped. He pulled onto Farm to Market Road 2325 and flipped through the songs on his phone. With his attention diverted he failed to notice the pickup truck bearing down on him. The driver of the truck gave two short beeps on his horn to let Marlon know he was there.

"Dude, keep your pants on!" Marlon glared at the truck in his rearview mirror and gave the BMW full throttle. The car made a chuffing sound, sagged a little to the right, and ever so gently picked up speed. "How about giving me a little space to exist here?"

During this rant Marlon's carefully combed-back hair flopped down into his eyes. He laughed and casually preened his mane. "Sorry about that, I guess I'm used to a different caliber of driver. It's a bit of a throwback returning to old Paxon Chute."

Beth grinned. "Yes, I understand big-city drivers are demanding and relentlessly unforgiving. I'm sure you make a lasting impression everywhere you drive."

Marlon snapped his fingers and pointed at her. "You know that's right."

When they arrived at the Owens' home Penelope Anne came fluttering outside all in a dither. "Oh, it was so unfortunate, the whole thing. I just got back from having tea with my ladies' group. Edgar's car made such a scene right there in front of the clubhouse, but I think everything will be okay. No one knew who he was."

Beth's hands went to her hips. "Did he not want a ride from you, Mother?"

"Well I didn't ask him, of course. Richard was not there so I wasn't even in my own car and I couldn't impose on someone else, now could I?" Penelope Anne looked down her nose at Marlon's rusty BMW. She opened her mouth but Beth cut her off.

"Mother, would you help get Junior inside for me?"

"Of course, Elizabeth. Richard! Richard, come and get this car seat and carry our grandson."

Richard came scurrying out of their home and said hello to Beth and Marlon, then obediently carried Junior inside. Penelope Anne hovered around him every step of the way. "Watch the stairs, Richard. And don't brush the baby carrier up against my walls. Remember, they've just been painted."

Beth pulled the diaper bag out of Marlon's car. "So, Edgar's waiting for you at the country club. Thanks for going to help him, and for giving us a ride. It was interesting, as usual."

"My pleasure. Always willing to assist a lady in distress." He bowed and then got back into his car. "I must be off to my next quest. I'll see you soon, if not sooner." He drove off with a snappy wave of his hand.

* * *

Edgar paced in the parking lot, waiting for Marlon. He stopped and sat on the front of his car, watching the ducks swimming in the pond between the parking lot and the tennis courts. Leaning back onto the hood, he stared at the clouds until the unmistakable squeal of brakes announced Marlon's arrival. The noisy car drew many stares as it pulled into the parking lot.

Edgar winced. "Too bad that thing only smolders enough to draw more attention to itself. I could use a smoke screen right now."

Marlon ignored him. "Aaah, the plight of the poor American car." He whistled "Taps" as he unbuckled and got out. "That's why I drive a Beemer. You can't beat German engineering."

"At least mine doesn't belch smog and scream like a banshee."

"Of course it doesn't. It's silent as the grave, am I right?" Marlon paused and then laughed loudly.

"As much as I hate to do this in front of everyone," Edgar glanced around, "let's try to jump-start it and see if that will work."

"Certainly. Maybe my girl can breathe some life into your old thing."

They both popped open their hoods, then realized Marlon would have to move his car to the other side of Edgar's car. The other side of Edgar's car happened to be the exit lane of the parking lot. Several cars backed up behind the BMW as Edgar hooked up the jumper cables and tried to start his Crown Victoria again. Turning the key released more of the acrid odor but still the engine did not start.

"Aw, that's not gone well, has it?" Marlon waved to the people glaring at him from their cars, waiting to exit. Then he gave a thumbs-up to a silver-haired man in a brand new Mercedes sedan and shouted, "German engineering. Why can't more people be like us, eh?"

Edgar's face and neck turned crimson. "Please stop talking." He spoke through clenched teeth.

A number of people stared at them from the clubhouse, the tennis courts, and the driving range.

Edgar quickly unhooked the jumper cables and closed both hoods as quietly as possible, avoiding eye contact with the onlookers. "Marlon, move your car so these people can get out. Pull back in on the other side of me, where you were parked before."

"Ab-so-lutely. Cheerio, everybody!" Marlon waved, tapped his horn lightly, then drove around the parking lot. His brakes screeched again when he came to a halt.

Edgar winced and bowed his head. He opened the right rear door of his car and cut open one of the large boxes. "This won't all fit in your car, but I've got to bring at least some of these supplies back." He pulled out a few packages from the box and stepped back. Nodding at Marlon he said, "Would you open your trunk so I can—oof!"

The wind rushed out of Edgar as his shorts caught on the opened door, whipping him around to the ground. The packages flew out of his arms and several of them broke open, releasing dozens of tampons. They blossomed out in a fan-shaped formation, bouncing and rolling downhill, headed for the pond. A number of them made their way through the runoff path and into the water. There they bobbed along in the current, floating towards the clubhouse.

Marlon saluted them and shouted in a gravelly voice, "Anchors aweigh, me hearties!"

"Quit it," Edgar hissed, "it's not funny. Help me pick these up."

Edgar's left hand, elbow, and both of his knees were skinned and bleeding from the fall. He hurriedly stuffed tampons back into the boxes. Even though many were lost at sea, the ones he gathered would not all fit back into the boxes they came out of. Edgar's spasmodic efforts did not help them fit any better. Out of space and boxes, he took to gathering tampons in his shirt like an Easter egg hunter. Marlon wandered around the parking lot but never actually picked up anything.

A young boy watching the scene from the tennis courts asked his mother, "What are those things?"

"Hush your mouth." She pulled him along by the hand. "Don't worry about them, they're just two morons. Though I do believe one of them is married to Penelope Anne's daughter."

"Nice," Edgar muttered. His phone rang as he emptied the contents of his shirt into Marlon's trunk.

"Hello Edgar, this is Hazel over at the hospital. We got word back from your insurance, so we've been able to finalize your portion of the charges for your son's delivery."

Edgar's face went pale as Hazel read through the charges and then finally came to the balance due.

Hazel paused but Edgar didn't say anything. After a moment she continued. "I know it's a lot of money, sweetie, and I'm sure things are difficult, now that Junior's here, and Beth's not working. It must be even harder having that Ezell boy staying with you, I declare he eats like a hog. But we can set up a payment schedule. How much can you pay a month? Two hundred?"

Edgar wiped his sweaty hands on his shirt, almost dropping the phone in the process. He stared at a flock of ducks in the pond fighting noisily over what they evidently thought were bread sticks. His voice finally croaked out. "I'm going to have to get back with you on that, Hazel."

A man sprinted up to the pond with his tennis racket and frantically swatted at the water, trying to collect the troublesome bobbers.

Marlon snickered. "That's a little extreme, don't you think?"

The man cried out. "Help! The koi are trying to eat them. It'll kill them, our prized koi!"

"Well crap a thousand times over." Edgar walked across the parking lot and continued his mutterings as he waded into the pond to scare away the fish and hunt down tampons.

* * *

Half an hour later Marlon drove Edgar through Peyton. "I'm starving. How about some lunch?"

"I appreciate that, Marlon." Edgar rested his head on his hand. "I don't really feel like eating, but I haven't had anything since early this morning."

"You still smell like ducks, and fish." Marlon shot a spray of MAgNITUDE cologne at Edgar. "Are you sure your shorts are dry? That's leather upholstery, you know."

"Yeah, they're barely damp now. And I'm not going to put maxi pads underneath me, so don't ask again."

"Sorry, it's all we have. When in Rome, as they say."

Marlon drove to a restaurant in Peyton and ordered a rack of ribs with two extra sides. Edgar chose the grilled cheese.

Edgar picked at his sandwich and did not talk much during the meal. Their waitress checked on them when Marlon stopped eating. "You want a to-go box for all that?" She pointed at Marlon's substantial leftovers.

"Naw, none of this is much good reheated. Tell you what though, bring me a bourbon pecan pie to go, darlin'."

The waitress left their check on the table, which Marlon slid over to Edgar. "Here you go, old man."

"What?" Edgar sat up straight. "You said you were buying."

"You're confused. I said how about lunch, not that I was buying, which I would do in a heartbeat, without question, except I seem to have forgotten my wallet." Marlon patted his back pocket. "If I wasn't a better friend, I might mention that I just drove out of town to rescue you and your rogue tampons."

Edgar shook his head slowly. "If you were a better friend, you'd remember the free room and board I'm providing you."

"Now, now, let's not argue over these kinds of petty expenses. I'll pay next time, when I've got cash on me."

At the register, Edgar extracted a lone credit card from his wet wallet and handed it to the cashier. After swiping the card twice the cashier slowly pushed it across the counter back to Edgar. "The charge was declined," she said quietly.

Edgar emptied his wallet and found just enough limp, soggy cash to cover the bill. He held the bills up for the cashier, who grasped them by a corner and draped them delicately on top of the register. The change Edgar got back consisted entirely of coins.

"Sheesh, that makes for about a one-percent tip." He flagged down their waitress and handed her the coins. "The food and your service were great, but I'm a little short today, for the tip, I mean. I'll come by here next time I'm in town and make this right."

She lowered her eyes. "No problem, I understand."

"She wants to kill you." Marlon looked the waitress over and smiled at her. "I keep trying to give him a big fat job, but it's like he's allergic to money."

They drove up the on-ramp to the freeway and Edgar stared out his window at a sprawling automobile dealership. The monthly payments were painted in big yellow numbers on the windshields of the glittering cars.

Marlon laughed. "Ah yes, that looks like a place you really need to visit. If you're not trying to find a classic car, you know, like mine."

Distracted by the car lot, Marlon ran out of on-ramp with no room to get over. He tried to accelerate past a minivan just as the minivan accelerated to get out of Marlon's way. Marlon had to stand on the brakes and swerve wildly to avoid running into the guardrail.

"Come on!" Marlon grabbed the steering wheel with both hands and shook it. "You could've moved over, you psycho soccer mom."

At the very next on-ramp, Marlon held his position and didn't make room when another car tried to merge onto the freeway.

"Gotta pay attention, dude! It's your job to find a way in. Not mine."

Edgar checked his seat belt. "I see you still drive on one-way streets."

"Huh? What do you mean?"

"All streets you drive on are one way. Your way."

"Only because I'm right, that's all." Marlon nodded. "So what's the deal, where are we going? I've got big plans tonight."

"I already called my dad, he said I can borrow his truck. So just head to my parents' house."

They pulled up behind the old green truck at Clyde and Ruth's house and Marlon helped move everything out of the BMW.

"Let's get all this junk unloaded. I'm in a big hurry. You'll never guess what I'm doing tonight." Marlon grinned and rubbed his hands together.

"Hmmm." Edgar paused. "That's how you always looked when you had a date. I'd love to hear about how hot she is and all those sorts of details you like to share, but I don't want to make you any later. Thanks for the ride, Marlon." He got in the truck and quickly shut the door.

Edgar drove home and trudged into his house carrying several boxes of scuffed tampons. He bumped the front door closed with his hip. The door bounced right back open and the knob smacked him on the wrist bone.

"Ouch! Stupid thing." He shoved the door closed more firmly than necessary and wiggled the knob until it finally latched.

He sniffed his wrinkled shirt, which smelled of moss and MAgNITUDE, then turned and leaned against the door, staring into the kitchen.

Beth stood there smiling at him. "Hey there. Whatcha got?"

He dropped the boxes on the floor. "Long story, but the wrappers on these are dirty from rolling around in the street, so we can't use them in the park. Maybe I can donate them somewhere for art projects or something." Edgar sniffed again. "What is that nasty smell? I thought it was me, but it's not."

Beth scrunched up her nose. "Yeah, I noticed that earlier and I took out the garbage but it didn't get any better. Anyway, I've got some great news. I think I've got everything worked out."

"Really? How's that?"

"I was at my parents' house, and they obviously know we've got problems with the car. So, since I was there anyway, I asked them if they'd help us out."

"What? I don't want to take money from your parents." Edgar pushed himself back upright.

"It's okay, Edgar, it's okay. Father was very understanding and supportive."

"And your mother?"

"She wants things done in an orderly fashion, which I'm sure is no surprise. They have an attorney they use regularly, and they're going to have him draft up a simple contract—"

Edgar interrupted. "I am not signing a contract, and I am not borrowing money from your mother."

The smile left Beth's face. "We don't have to, of course. But it's an option, if we need it."

"That would stress me out even more."

"Oh. I'm sorry, I was just trying to help." Beth walked across the room and sat down on the couch. "Well, we can make things work out some other way. I'm sure we can use your dad's truck as long as we need it. They've got enough vehicles to spare."

Edgar joined Beth on the couch. "No, we need to get our car fixed, and we need to get another car so we've got a backup. A better one than we have now. One we can depend on. I don't want you and Junior stranded somewhere. I think we need to get a new car. Oh, and our credit card is maxed out, again. And the hospital called. They want two hundred dollars a month towards our balance, on top of all of our other past-due bills." He tugged at his shirt collar. "It's stressing me out so bad I feel all hot and dizzy."

"I feel kind of hot too." Beth fanned herself.

"Oh no. Not another blasted thing. Not today." Edgar walked over to the thermostat. "It's eighty degrees in the house!"

Beth turned her head. "But I can hear the air conditioner running."

Edgar held his hand up to the vent in the living room. "Hot air. The stupid air conditioner is blowing hot air."

He flopped back onto the couch, his head in his hands.

Beth ran her fingers through his hair.

"Sheesh, what a day." He lifted his head up and looked into Beth's eyes. "I admit Marlon's idea isn't perfect but right now I don't know what else to do."

"Well, I guess if it was a perfect plan they wouldn't need you."

"Exactly. Nothing worthwhile in life is easy. That job could make things so much better for us. I think I'm going to tell Marlon yes."

"You already know the concerns I have about that." Beth pulled on a tuft of his hair. "But if it's what you think is best, I trust you."

Edgar stared at his shoes. "Wow. I expected to have to convince you. Now I'm not so sure I'm convinced." He paused. "But it's really our only option, and it will make everything better. Right?"

Beth sat still for a moment. "Have you told your dad about any of this?"

Edgar winced. "No, not yet."

Cries from the nursery rang through the small house.

"Oh my gosh!" Beth jumped up. "The baby, Edgar. It's too hot for him." She walked quickly into the nursery. "We'll have to stay at your parents' tonight."

"Yeah, I guess you're right. I'll send Marlon a text and let him know where we'll be." He winced again. "I'm not ready to tell my dad about Marlon's idea. Not just yet."

CHAPTER NINE

The next morning Marlon sat on the large butcher-block island in the kitchen at Emily's bed and breakfast. His phone rang, interrupting a conversation with his mother. "Gar, what's up?"

"Just calling to see where you stayed last night. Sorry about the air conditioner."

"No problem, big guy. I wound up staying at your house." Marlon laughed. "I didn't get back 'til the cows came home and it wasn't too hot by then."

"Oh, good." Edgar paused. "Hey, I think I wanna join up with your deal. I mean sign on, or whatever."

"Outstanding!" Marlon let out a whoop. "Glad to have you aboard. You won't regret this, I guarantee. We need to get together and talk over our plan. So, I owe you lunch, don't I? Let's meet at Emily's."

"Okay, I'll walk on over right now." Edgar started to pocket his phone, then jerked it back up to his ear. "Wait, you are paying this time, right?"

"Relax, Edgar. The Marlon Express is gonna take care of you now." Marlon ended the call and smiled at his mother. "Hey, Mom, Edgar's coming over to talk some business. Would you whip us up a couple of sandwiches? Nothing special."

Linda straightened up from the farmhouse sink she had been scrubbing. A hint of a smile crept onto her face. "Of course, son." Her glasses perched on the end of her nose and she used her forearm to slide them back in place. "Did you hear what I was saying, before your phone rang?"

Marlon's brow wrinkled up. "I don't even remember what we were talking about."

"I was telling you why I moved out of the house."

"Oh, yeah. That." Marlon stared at his phone, tapping the screen.

Linda paused a moment. "I said he's not as bad as you're making him out."

"I'm not making him out to be anything." Marlon shook his head. "I was just telling you what he told me."

"I don't think he's cheated on me. Not yet, anyway."

"Uugghhh." Marlon slapped his phone against his thigh and looked up at the ceiling. "Do we have to talk about this? Besides, he told me I couldn't stay with him because he had some woman there at the house with him."

"A small town like this, word would get around if that kind of thing was going on."

"There's plenty of words going around about him."

"Words, yes. But," Linda held up a finger, "no names."

"So you're saying because there's no name, he's lying? Why would he tell a lie that makes him more horrible than he already is?"

"Marlon Ezell!" Linda stared at him over the top of her glasses. "He's behaving badly, but he's still your father." She pushed her glasses back up her nose again. "He probably told you that to try and get back at me for leaving."

Marlon lowered his eyes from her gaze. "If you think he's lying, why don't you just go back to him?"

"I love your father and want to be with him, but I will not," she shook her hand, flinging soap bubbles off the sponge in her clenched fist, "continue living with a shadow," more bubbles flew off, "of a man who can only give me a hint of a relationship." Foamy bubbles oozed out between her fingers. "I'm hoping this separation will wake him up so he can start learning how to step into reality, which is the preferred place for adults to live. The older I get the more I'm realizing how sparsely populated reality is."

"He'll never change."

Linda took a deep breath. "Let's not get ahead of ourselves. There's no point in worrying about tomorrow when today has enough excitement of its own." She bent back over the sink and resumed her scrubbing.

Marlon stared at the sink. "I guess, if you say so. Listen, I need somewhere to sit with Edgar and have a powwow, can we use one of the tables in the front room?"

Linda looked up over her shoulder at Marlon and smiled again ever so slightly. "I'm sure Emily wouldn't mind, but you should ask her."

"Will do. I've gotta grab something out of my car, then I'll be out front with Edgar. And don't forget about those sandwiches, okay?"

Linda chuckled. "Yes, sir."

Marlon went out the back door and retrieved his briefcase from the trunk of his car. He walked briskly around to the front entrance of the bed and breakfast instead of going through the kitchen.

"Hello there, Miss Emily." Marlon smiled and closed the door behind him.

"Well come on in, Marlon, and make yourself at home. I'll go tell Linda you're here."

"No, no, don't trouble yourself. I just talked with her so she's already expecting me. Listen, Edgar is coming by, is it okay if we sit in here?"

"Of course it is, sweetie, have I ever said no?"

Marlon glanced around the room at the tables with their yellow-and-white checkered tablecloths, each sporting a clear glass vase with fresh cut flowers. He pulled out a chair by one of the big front windows and sat down.

* * *

Edgar walked north on Downstream Drive, which ran along the western side of the town square, then he turned onto Short Chute. This appropriately named street ended after only one block, where it made a t-intersection with Ghyll Lane directly in front of Emily's Place.

Edgar breathed deeply the sweet smell of the honeysuckle growing over the white iron arbor at the front of the bed and breakfast property. Two ruby-throated hummingbirds whirred away as he walked under the arbor. An array of flowers, topiary shrubs, and ornate trees bore witness to Emily's love of gardening. The picturesque three-story B and B with its steeply pitched roof, big windows, and brightly painted siding stayed booked most of the year.

Edgar went up the front steps and onto the porch that wrapped around the entire first floor. He lightly pushed one of the many wooden rocking chairs on the porch, setting it to swaying gracefully. He stopped to sit down, until Marlon waved at him through the window. Edgar opened the front door.

"Gar! Come on in. Your life is about to get way better."

Edgar slowly closed the door behind him, leaving the beckoning rocker on the front porch.

"Pull up a seat." Marlon pointed at a chair. "I've taken the liberty of ordering for us, hope you don't mind."

Edgar hesitated as he was about to sit down. "What did you order, because I really like Emily's—"

Marlon interrupted. "Good, good, it's all good, then. Welcome aboard, again. This is gonna be so great." He pulled a legal pad from his portfolio and flipped through several pages.

"First things first, though. We need to have a meeting of the minds to get our plan of action down. Now, our investors are insisting on a feasibility study, which is the right thing to do, of course. They want to make sure the requisite towers can be built without major expense, and that all depends on the riverbed itself. If there's not enough solid rock we'd have to bore some big holes and build massive concrete piers. That could be a deal breaker. And we also need to check out the base of Nickel Rock because we want to shove a tower into that old thing as well. So we'll need you to get Town Council approval for an engineering study—hey, you all right Gar? You look a little funny."

Sweat broke out on Edgar's brow. "I think I need some water." His voice came out dry and raspy.

Marlon's mother came into the dining room bearing a tray with their lunch. "Here you are, two pecan and tuna-fish sandwiches. I know they're your favorite, Edgar."

"They sure are. Thank you, Mrs. Ezell."

Marlon stared at his notes and waved his hand absently. "Thanks."

Linda turned to Marlon, with no hint of a smile on her face. Before she could say anything several guests came downstairs into the dining room. She patted Edgar on the shoulder and said, "Well, I'll leave you to it, then."

Marlon leaned in closer to Edgar. "Relax, Edgar. Don't worry, we're going to start small. We'll do the dog-and-pony show, you know, let everyone see the plans and get approval to have an engineer evaluate the riverbed and the base of Nickel Rock. That's just preliminary, but it will help us ease into the more challenging phases, you know, the ones where all the little old ladies will cry and moan about how we're trying to destroy their beautiful park. We don't want to tell the Council everything at first and have them freak out."

Edgar sat up straight in his chair. "I'm not going to lie to people, Marlon."

"Of course we're not going to lie. That's never an effective long-term strategy. We just have to manage the communication process. Like they say, you can lead a horse to water but can't make it drink, so sometimes you gotta sneak up on him and splash some water in his face."

"Sounds like a good way to get kicked by a horse, and get him to *not* drink."

"They'll see, in the end. They'll see, and thank us both." Marlon smiled. "It's going to be great."

"Before we charge to the end," Edgar held his hand up, "let's back up a bit. You said this job would be part-time in the beginning. But it is a job, right?"

"Of course it's a job. I told you—"

"Yes, I remember what you told me. So do I need to fill out some kind of employment paperwork, or something? How do I track the hours I work? When do I get paid?"

"I don't really deal with those kinds of little details. I'll check with the investors and see how that's all set up. Don't sweat the small stuff, Egger."

"I'm not able to see anything small from where I am."

"Okay." Marlon slapped the table with the palms of his hands. "So the June Council meeting is tomorrow. I need you to get us on the agenda, but keep it pretty vague. Just call it 'Park Improvement Proposal,' with your name as the presenter. We don't want a bunch of crazy rumors spreading around town. That means we don't talk to anyone about this before the meeting. Not even your dad." Marlon leaned back in his chair. "My old man suspects I'm up to something and he's hopping mad because I won't tell him anything."

Edgar sighed. "I guess I'd rather take one public beating than a hundred private ones. I'll keep it to myself. Oh, except for Beth of course, no secrets from her, and she already knows anyway."

"She knows about the project, and that's all well and good. But as we go forward some things will have to be on a need-to-know basis."

Edgar's posture had relaxed, but he sat upright again. "Why? I don't like that."

Marlon shrugged. "Like I said, we have to manage the communication process. Plus, it's really for her own good. If people find out Beth has inside information, they'll pester her to no end trying to get it out of her. You know how everyone in this town likes to talk about every little thing that's going on."

"Maybe, but I still don't like keeping things from Beth. My dad is a different story. I'm not really looking forward to that conversation anyway."

* * *

Later that afternoon Edgar stopped by the Town Hall to see Orville Gardner, the principal of Creekside Junior High and part-time mayor of Paxon Chute. The Town Hall sat in the middle of the east side of the town square. The mayor's paneled office on the second floor had a view of Nickel Rock through the large windows directly behind his desk.

"Thanks for seeing me, Orville. I need to have an item added to the agenda for tomorrow." Edgar handed him a sheet of paper with one line of printing on it.

"Ah yes, 'Park Improvement Proposal.'" Orville winked at Edgar. "This must be the big new thing that Ezell boy has been bloviating about."

"Big new thing? What?"

"Oh, he's been working everyone's arm like a pump handle, shaking hands and telling them to be sure and come out for the next Council meeting. Says it's going to be big, real big."

"Did he now? That's interesting. I'll have to ask him what that's all about." Edgar drummed his fingers on Orville's desk. "Okay, so I'm all set on the agenda?"

"You sure enough are, though twenty-four hours' notice is cutting it close. I look forward to hearing what you have in mind, me and everyone else in town. It's gonna be a packed house."

* * *

When Edgar got home that evening Marlon was sitting on the couch, chomping on puffed cheese balls and watching an old episode of *The Bachelor*. Edgar grabbed the remote and turned off the TV.

"Whatever happened to us not talking to anyone about this before the Council meeting?" Edgar wiped cheese ball dust off the remote. "Orville said you've been yacking up a storm all over town about a big new park development."

"But I haven't revealed any details, or even a hint of what we have in mind." Marlon licked orange dust off his fingers. "I'm just giving everyone a heads-up to get a big turnout so the whole town is informed all at once. It's better that way. Plus it greases the skids a little, even if they don't know exactly what's coming."

"You could have let me know what you were doing, Marlon. I felt like an idiot when Orville already knew about it." Edgar sat down next to Marlon.

"Sorry Gar, didn't mean to leave you hanging. It won't happen again." He picked up the remote and turned the TV back on then shoved a couple of cheese balls into his mouth.

"You're not going to spring anything on me at the meeting tomorrow, are you?"

Marlon chewed and smiled. "Nah, just stick to those bullet points I gave you and everything will be fine. Trust me, buddy."

"I do trust you, Marlon. I trust you to be who you are."

"That's the spirit." Marlon slapped him on the back, leaving streaks of cheesy dust on Edgar's shirt.

CHAPTER TEN

The next evening Edgar left the park and walked to the Community Center on the square. A large crowd jostled to get into the Center for the Town Council meeting. Mavis had stopped her cart in the middle of the crowd and sales were brisk.

Edgar found Beth and Junior off to one side. Beth squeezed Edgar's hand but they said nothing to each other.

As they stood waiting to get in, Edgar glanced at the schedule posted on one of the front windows: Monday Texas Hold 'Em Tournament; Thursday Afternoon Bingo; Friday Night "Summer Squares" Square Dancing; Saturday Night Bunco.

Inside, noisy chatter reverberated off the exposed-brick walls. Additional folding chairs were set out in the large rectangular meeting room but many people were still left standing.

Edgar leaned over to Beth. "There's got to be two hundred people here." He looked around the room. "But I don't see Marlon anywhere. He better not be late."

They sat down on the left side of the first row where Clyde, Ruth, and Drew had saved two seats. The lectern for presenters loomed directly in front of them. Mavis came in and took a chair next to Drew right before the meeting started.

The Town Council members sat along a single row of

tables, facing the audience. Orville, being the town mayor, chaired the meetings. He settled down at the center table and called the meeting to order. As the agenda items were covered Orville repeatedly called for silence amid an increasing level of chatter, which mainly consisted of speculation about the last item on the agenda.

When Orville finally got down to the Park Improvement Proposal he stood up.

Someone in the crowd moaned. "Aw, man. Not Ollie's Follies."

Orville rapped his gavel. "Now before we move on, let's all get up and stretch a bit."

Tom already stood against the left-side wall near the front of the room, being one of many without a seat. "For those of us who've been standing up the whole time, can we take a sitting break instead?"

"Negatory, Tom, negatory." Clyde waved his arms. "There are no bar stools here, so we don't have a good donor match for you. Your highly refined fundament would reject anything so unfamiliar as these low, simple chairs."

Tom shook his head and laughed.

Orville held his hands up. "Come on now."

Shuffling and grumbling filled the room as everyone stood up.

"We don't have room to all touch our toes tonight, so let's reach straight up to the sky with both hands. Be careful, don't whack your neighbor. Good! Now wiggle your arms around in little circles, and walk in place."

The marching commenced. Several chairs slid across the floor, propelled by solid whacks from raised knees. The sound of stomping feet droned on for a while, then Orville had everyone raise and lower their hands, turn their heads left to right, and stretch from side to side.

"Excellent!" Orville smiled. "We all know that a little

cardiovascular activity works wonders on our dispositions. Keeps things from getting too ornery."

Orville let them cool down for a minute then had everyone take their seats again. Some were a little flushed, some panted, and many fanned themselves, but the level of chatter in the room definitely decreased.

Orville sat down. "Let's proceed. Next we have Edgar Rerd presenting a 'Park Improvement Proposal.' Mr. Rerd, you have the floor."

People whispered "shhhh" when Edgar walked to the lectern. Muffled, crunchy noises came through the speakers as he moved the microphone closer to his mouth. When he let go of the microphone, it sagged back down. He raised it up higher and it sagged down again, but not as low as before. He raised it up again even higher, and the crowd began to mutter. Edgar laid a manila file folder on the lectern and opened it. The meeting room became very quiet.

"Today," he spoke boldly into the microphone. Too boldly, as it turned out. His voice boomed through the room and made everyone jump. He took a step back and lowered his voice. "Sorry about that. Sorry. Is that better?"

Ward sat on the right end of the councilor tables, farthest away from the lectern. He leaned forward and cupped his hand to his ear. "Now I can barely make out what you're saying, and I'm certain those in the back can't hear you at all."

"Sorry." Edgar winced. "Okay, how's that now, okay? Is that okay now?"

Several people nodded, and Clyde gave him two thumbs up.

"Okay then, okay." Edgar struggled to take a deep breath and his eyes darted around the room. He wiped his sweaty hands on his pant legs.

"I've got something I'd like to present that I think will bring great, uh, great things to our community for years to come. Years. I've been presented with an idea, this idea for uh, um, a development project in the park." Edgar paused and used his shirtsleeve to blot at the perspiration beaded up on his forehead.

"What kind of development?" Even without a microphone Ward's commanding voice resonated through the room.

Clyde glanced at Ward. "He'll tell you, if you'd hush up, Ward."

Orville tapped his gavel gently. "Easy there people, easy."

Edgar reached out to adjust the microphone again then stopped himself. "It's an idea that will eliminate the shuttle buses, and make the whole process of riding the river much safer. What it is, is these kind of, uh, tram things that will carry people back up the river."

"A tram thing?" Ward shook his head and shrugged his shoulders. "What do you mean? This is all very vague, and does not inspire confidence."

Conversations broke out across the room. Most of what Edgar could make out came from Mavis and his Uncle Drew, who sat closest to the lectern where Edgar stood.

"I'll tell you what, Ward sure has his nasty side out tonight." Mavis pressed her lips together and sighed.

"He usually hates most any idea that's not his own." Drew's head oscillated up and down as he spoke. "But Ward will support his own son."

Mavis stared in Ward's direction, her lips still compressed in a thin line. "I don't know about that."

Orville stood up and rapped his gavel. Then he pointed the handle of the gavel at the crowd as he scanned the room, his left eye bulging and the right squinted up nearly closed. "I'd like to remind everyone that Mr. Rerd has the floor. We'll have time for discussion later." He shook the gavel vigorously. "If you all don't behave yourselves we'll double down on jumping jacks and sit-ups like last month." The crowd quieted immediately and Orville pointed the gavel at Edgar. "Please proceed."

"Uh." Edgar looked down at the bullet points provided by Marlon. He had already spoken to nearly all the items listed. "I guess that's most of what I've got here—"

Suddenly Marlon stood up in the back row. "With your permission, Mr. Mayor, I believe a picture is worth a thousand words, am I right? Wilbur, would you bring up the projector, please?" He buttoned his suit coat as he walked to the lectern.

Edgar's smile twitched a bit. "Yes, that's a great idea. Sorry everyone, sorry to surprise you." He glared at Marlon. "For no reason."

The room went completely dark except for the lamp over the audiovisual booth at the back where Wilbur scurried about. "Whoa there! Sorry, wrong switch." He flipped the house lights back on then tried another switch.

The lights above the screen hanging at the front of the room dimmed and the screen grew brighter as the projector powered up. After a few seconds the first page of Marlon's proposal came into view, and the words "River in the Sky" slowly came into focus. The giant, shiny, space-age capsule seemed to invade the room and the overjoyed youths spilling out of the windows were larger than life. Sweat flowed freely down Edgar's face.

Ward's voice rang out again. "Well, that surely is a pretty drawing, full of happy-happy people, but it doesn't really explain anything now, does it?"

Marlon stood beside Edgar at the lectern. "Let's back up here just a bit. Now we all know what a nuisance those shuttle buses are. Many a good idea has been brought forth over the years to try and resolve that bad situation. But so far nothing viable has materialized."

Ward snorted. "I've given plenty of viable options, like

increasing the speed limit and removing the seats. Everyone knows you can fit more people in with standing room only."

Orville banged his gavel repeatedly during Ward's grumblings. Ward finally quieted down and Orville nodded at Marlon to proceed.

"So the town has been burdened with running the buses, and all of us taxpayers have been stuck paying for them. They're expensive, unsightly, noisy, they smell awful, and clog up traffic. Face it, they're littering up our streets of paradise. And talk about an accident waiting to happen? Oh my goodness, just yesterday I myself watched helplessly as one of them drove up onto the curb and caught Mavis between her cart and a hard place, am I right, Mavis?"

Mavis sat bolt upright. "Ooh, yes. It was a near miss."

Edgar leaned over and spoke quietly into Marlon's ear. "Wow, you're doing great. I shouldn't even be up here."

Marlon shook his head and winked at Edgar. "Nonsense, it's a team effort."

A metallic clicking sound shot through the room and startled a number of those seated near the front. People looked around to see where the noise came from. The piercing "click-clack" sounded again. Marlon held the clicker up above his head and he clicked-clacked again, then turned to Wilbur. "What part of the clicker do you not understand?" He hit the button several more times. "Would you please advance the slide when I hit the clicker?"

"Jeepers, Marlon, you could have told me that before." Wilbur tapped the mouse button to bring up the next slide. "How do you expect me to know what that horrible sound is supposed to mean?"

The screen faded to black momentarily then the next slide appeared. Ruth gasped and someone muttered "oh my" at the sight of the giant towers jutting out of the river and the sleek capsules suspended from cables.

Ward slowly read aloud the words on the screen. "Step-up-to-the-River-in-the-Sky. Hmmph."

Marlon continued. "What Edgar was trying to say, is that this is a state-of-the-art aerial lift. Feast your eyes on that. Unlike the buses, there's nothing to detract from the natural beauty of our community. It's quiet and extremely efficient, and not just with energy consumption, although we all want to be carbon neutral, go green, and save the planet. But this is also highly efficient at moving people. With carriers capable of handling six passengers as shown, it is rated to transport over two thousand people per hour."

"What?" Ward frowned. "Are you sure about that?"

Marlon turned to his father. "Totally sure. And the time spent breezing back upstream would be a beautifully scenic twenty-two minute glide through the air, not scraping along for a hot, smelly, jolting, sticky ride on a crowded, rickety old bus." Marlon walked over and stood beside the screen. "I think we can all agree," he gestured towards the screen, "this is a beautiful proposition."

Ward took out a pocket calculator and punched the buttons on it rapidly. His eyes grew wide as he worked.

"So, let's go ahead and open it up for discussion now, Mr. Mayor." Marlon bowed slightly in Orville's direction.

"All right, we'll have informal discussion at this point." Orville set down his gavel. "As long as you all remain civil and take your turn, the floor is available for open discussion to present your point of view."

Ward spoke immediately as he raised his hand. "There may be some merit in this 'River Skies,' or whatever you call it—"

"It's 'River in the Sky,' Dad. See the huge red letters?" Marlon pointed at the image on the screen.

Ward continued. "There may be some potential here, and I emphasize 'some,' mind you. Although I'd like to see the numbers you're basing that capacity on." He waved his calculator in the air. "Two thousand an hour is nearly triple what we can accommodate with the buses we have now. But there are huge obstacles in your way, and you two greenhorns have started out all wrong. This should've been properly managed, developed, and promoted. If I had been consulted beforehand, well, I think everyone here is aware that I've been making things like this a success my whole life."

Edgar spoke up. "Mr. Ezell, we didn't tell anyone about this. I didn't even tell my own father. I wanted everyone to hear it at once so no one felt like things were happening behind their back."

Uncle Drew nodded emphatically. "Yes, that is very important. Good point. You certainly don't want any of that going on."

Ward looked at Edgar. "What is your involvement in all this anyway, Edgar?"

"Uh, well, Marlon asked me to, uh, he thought—"

Ward cut off him off. "Is this an official Nickel Rock Park project? Are you here to represent the park before the Town Council?"

"No no no, it, uh, it just seemed like something that might help us out—"

"Help us out, or help *you* out?" Ward pointed at Edgar. "What's in this for you?"

Marlon stepped in front of the lectern. "Edgar is helping us in an advisory capacity. We wanted to have someone who knows the park and is also committed to its preservation. He understands the park way better than I do, and I know he would never allow it to be compromised. That's important to me, and I think it's important to all of us."

Drew turned to face the crowd. "Well I certainly trust Edgar, and not because he's my nephew. He loves that park like his own child. He'd never steer us wrong."

"That's a fact." Mavis smiled.

Ward kept his gaze on Edgar. "Indeed. He'd never put his interests ahead of the community, would he?"

Edgar swallowed, his eyes fixed on the lectern.

Eloy stood up. "Have you researched the liability for this kind of operation? Amusement park insurance is expensive."

Marlon smiled for a moment. "Excellent question, Mr. Chibitty. And yes, of course, we've got a comprehensive plan covering all operational costs going forward on an ongoing basis, including liability insurance."

"Ah, yes." Ward pounced again. "Liability! Thank you, Mr. Chibitty, for bringing this up. That's a key concern for us all, in these litigious times. People are so irresponsible regarding their own behavior and then all too eager to blame everyone else for their own actions. Even in your own illustrations," he thrust his finger at the screen, "the passengers look ready to fall out. It would be impossible to control them without some type of substantial restraints in these…things."

Peter jumped to his feet, his face flush with excitement. "These conveyances are fabulous! This is not just transport, it is progress, depicted in functional sculpture, extracting us away from our little log cabin frontier town all the way into postmodern artistry."

Tom laughed. "You say that as if it's what anyone here wants, or needs."

Peter sat down and the room was silent for a while.

Clyde slowly stood up. "I am rather curious as to exactly what material those bright shiny capsules are to be made of."

Marlon smiled some more. "I don't have the exact details of the construction specifications, but I imagine it would be chromed steel. I think we can all agree it's a classic look."

"Classic, possibly." Clyde frowned a little. "But I do believe they'd get scorching hot in the summer, and be prone to rusting."

"Listen." Marlon held up his hands. "I'm not so much on the engineering side, but I can assure you—"

Clyde continued his train of thought. "Aluminum wouldn't rust, but it would transfer heat even more effectively to anyone who had the misfortune of touching them."

"Details, details." Peter waved his hand. "This is a fantastically beautiful design, such elegance. They are modern chariots in the sky!"

"More like Easy-Bake Ovens in the sky." Tom snickered.

Orville glared at him. "Behave yourself, Mr. Walker."

Drew stood and stretched his hand way up in the air. "Say, I'm curious about something. You've got that giant oil-derrick-looking thing bolted onto Nickel Rock, and in the picture that's the end of the line, everything just stops there. How are people gonna make their way to the capsules? Anyone on the bank who wanted to ride upstream would have to swim out to Nickel Rock, or pull across on a ferry."

"Good thought there, Drew." Clyde reached over and patted him on the arm.

Drew's face broke into a huge grin as he sat down.

"Well." Marlon paused. "Let me lay my cards on the table. That's an excellent point, Mr. Rerd, and to be perfectly honest, I brought this up with our illustrator. I said, 'Help me understand why it stops there?' Now, I'm not trying to throw him under the bus, but the fact is he dropped the ball. He made a mistake, and he's working overtime to correct it, to be sure, but this is what we have today. So, we would, of course, continue the lift on downstream to the riverbank, so people could get on there as well. The Nickel Rock boarding station was only supposed to be a focal point in the drawing."

Eloy stood up again. "I have another question. Where are the funds going to come from to pay for this development?"

Many heads nodded and someone piped in, "Yeah, where?"

"From a small group of investors." Marlon scanned the room. "Anyone else?"

Eloy remained standing. "So a private business is going to commercially develop the town park?"

"Yes." Marlon looked around the room again.

Many heads shook in disagreement.

Eloy continued his questioning. "Who will own the infrastructure that is to be constructed on town property?"

"Well, the investors, of course. They're the ones taking the risk."

"And these are local investors?"

"No."

"Where are they from?"

"Chicago, mostly."

"Chicago?" Tom stepped away from the wall. "Some group of people in Chicago want to build down here, tell us what to do and how to do it? They wouldn't care about what we want."

Grumbling began in earnest, and Orville rapped his gavel.

Clyde stood up to speak, "Now, now, let's not get all wrapped around the axle. But I must say, with all due respect to Mr. Ezell and the good Mr. Rerd, I think there may be some room for improvement here."

Edgar leaned over and whispered to Marlon. "Uh-oh, I think he's gonna use sadistic agreement to kill it. He'll agree, then add something on that's so ridiculous we'll get laughed right out of here."

For the first time that evening, Marlon started to sweat.

"I was thinking we could..." Clyde glanced around the room, then his gaze fell on Edgar and he stopped mid-sentence. Father and son stared at each other in silence. Clyde cleared his throat and continued. "As I was saying, with all due respect, that is, respecting everyone's concerns, I think we need to hear these gentlemen out. I'll admit that on first impression this may not be my cup of tea, but I'm all in favor of exploring our options for getting rid of those buses."

Several people in the crowd voiced their approval.

Marlon wiped his forehead. "Thank you, Mr. Rerd, thank you. Yes, we're just wanting to explore this as an option."

Eloy stood up again. "Then what is it that you want to do at this point?"

"Excellent question, Mr. Chibitty." Marlon smiled at the short bartender and clasped his hands together. "I'm not asking you all to sign on the dotted line, or even to agree tonight that this is what everyone wants to do. All I'm proposing is to have an engineer check out the river and write up a report. The first step is to see if the riverbed is even capable of supporting this type of system. If it's not, then the whole deal is off because the investors are only interested in developing this kind of unique vision." He waved his hand at the screen. "So, if we find that it's viable, then we can work through all the details being brought up tonight."

Orville peered at Marlon over the top of his glasses. "An engineering report, and what would that process look like?"

"It would barely look like anything at all, it would be so unobtrusive. We'd have an engineering diver evaluate the riverbed and Nickel Rock. People scuba dive in the river all the time, it'd be no big deal. And it won't cost the town anything because the investors are paying for it."

"So just the one diver, rootin' around as he sees fit for a while. Nothing else, right? No surveyors, no bulldozers, no excavating?" Orville's left eye bulged again and fixed on Marlon.

"Ha ha ha ha ha." Marlon laughed loudly. "No, none of that, Mr. Orville. We'll barely even disturb the waters. Edgar here will see to that, won't you, Edgar?"

"Uh, yeah. Yes. Definitely."

"All righty then. I guess we can vote on that, if there's no more discussion." Orville pointed his gavel handle around the room.

Ward stared at his notepad as he spoke. "I have a number of reservations, as I'm sure many of us do, based on the comments here tonight. But let's not get the cart before the horse and waste a bunch of time debating this before we know anything about anything." He glanced at his fellow Council members up and down the tables and nodded subtly. Several of them met his gaze and nodded in return.

Orville rapped his gavel. "Let's vote."

CHAPTER ELEVEN

Edgar's cell phone rang a week and a half later on a busy Saturday afternoon in the park.

"Gar! Marlonator here. Listen, everything is set, it's time for our surveyor to go splashy."

Children screamed and squealed in the river behind Edgar. He pressed the phone against his ear and stuck a finger in his other ear. "What did you say?"

"Our egghead is ready to goggle up."

"I've got a lot going on today, Marlon. What are you talking about?"

"The diver. Our engineer who's going to dive and check out the riverbed. I've got him with me and he's ready to get after it."

"Right now? You were supposed to coordinate that with me, Marlon."

"But I did."

"You did? You asked me if the diver could come on a Saturday, the busiest day of the week for me and the park, the day when it would cause the most disruption for everyone, and I said yes? You're telling me that happened and I've somehow forgotten it?"

"I said he'd be here any day, and you said to just let you know. And this is me letting you know. Right?"

"Marlon, the town is trusting me to not allow any

disruptions. Orville was clear about that. If this turns into a problem, I'll be responsible. You can't do things like this."

"Ah, well. Must have been a communication breakdown. You'll need to work on that, Gar, so you don't have these issues rearing their ugly head up on you. Every little detail can't always be ironed out to the nth degree, so you have to be able to roll with the punches a little."

"Why is it that I always feel like you're the one throwing them?"

"Oh, Gar, you crack me up. So we're good, right? 'Cause we're pulling into the park right now. Just meet us over by Nickel Rock." Marlon ended the call.

Edgar ran downstream. Two hundred yards away Marlon made his way towards the river. Beside Marlon walked a large man in a bright orange wetsuit. A number of people in the park stared at them. Edgar ran faster.

"Marlon." Edgar wheezed, trying to catch his breath. "He was supposed...to start...upstream...and float down."

"Diving here we can check out this portion of the riverbed and Nickel Rock as well. That's our best starting point and then we'll evaluate the rest of the river as we move forward."

"That's not the point." Edgar's breathing slowed as he recovered. "Divers always start out upstream. It looks weird, especially with a companion like you, in a suit and tie. You're making a scene. Everyone's staring at you guys." He took in one big breath and sighed.

"Everyone? Come on, relax, Egger. There's only a few bored onlookers. It'll be fine."

A young girl standing in the crowd nearby walked up to Marlon. "Hey, did somebody drown? Are you a cop? I bet somebody drowned and that guy's gonna go try to find a dead body."

"Ah, no no no, of course not." Edgar rushed over to the girl and waved her away. "They're here to, uh, enjoy the river."

Several more people joined the crowd.

The man in the wetsuit stood a few yards away, checking over his gear. He picked up a buoyancy-control vest with its attached scuba tank and slipped the vest on.

Marlon grabbed Edgar's arm and pulled him over to the diver. "Fritz Yunger, I want you to meet Edgar Rerd, the very man I told you about."

"I'm Fritz, the engineer." He held out his thick, meaty hand.

"Ah, I'm Edgar, the, uh, head park ranger." Edgar flinched when his hand disappeared in Fritz's crushing grasp. "Well, Fritz the engineer, it looks like you do a lot of this sort of thing."

Fritz's freckled skin had a coppery tint and the sun had bleached out his hair. Even the giant walrus mustache that enshrined his chapped lips appeared weather-beaten. "Not fond of sittin' at a desk." Fritz's attention returned to the buckling of his vest.

"I hear you. Being a park ranger I don't spend much time indoors. I've always wanted to get certified to dive but never got around to it." Edgar watched as Fritz checked the pressure gauge. "Where do you usually work?"

Fritz did not look up. "Gulf."

"Really? Lots of engineering jobs in the Gulf?"

"I'd say so. Oil rigs and hurricanes make plenty of work."

"Aah, yes." Edgar cleared his throat. "Of course."

A boy with curly black hair crept up by them and stood watching Fritz's preparations.

Marlon clapped Edgar on the back. "So, Gar, I've already briefed Fritz. He's going to explore around here and see what he can see."

"But he's going upstream to start out, right?"

Fritz glared at Nickel Rock. "The rock is right there."

"Whatcha doin', mister?" The boy's voice squeaked out.

Fritz did not look up. "Fixin' to get wet."

Edgar lowered his voice and smiled. "Trust me, it would cause way less fuss if you started upstream where everyone else—"

Fritz interrupted. "That's my focus." He pointed his thumb at Nickel Rock. "So I'm puttin' in here."

Marlon draped his arm across Edgar's shoulder. "Navigating around the chutes will be dicey and Fritz is the type who wants to tackle the most difficult part of the job first. Besides that, we have to know ASAP if we can sink a pier into Nickel Rock, because if we can't that changes our plans. Just relax, it'll be fine. He'll check out the rest of the river later and no one will think anything about it. Except you."

Edgar shrugged off Marlon's arm. He looked in the direction of the Town Hall where Orville happened to be walking briskly across the square towards the river. The barflies ambled out of The Snorting Bull, Uncle Drew waving at Edgar with both his arms up in the air.

"Really, Marlon?" Edgar wiped his sweaty brow. "I see lots of people noticing already."

Fritz pulled a pair of swim fins out of his dive bag and sat down with his feet hanging off the riverbank. The boy with curly hair followed him. Fritz pressed the purge button on the primary regulator and sniffed the air coming out. The boy reached over and pressed the button on the secondary regulator clipped to the buoyancy-control vest. Fritz jerked his shoulder away, glaring at him. "Hands off."

The boy's lower lip trembled and he scooted away.

Fritz put both fins on, pulled his mask down, inserted the regulator in his mouth, and slipped off the bank into the water.

Edgar watched the orange wetsuit moving closer to Nickel Rock. "He's not the friendliest guy, is he?"

"Yeah, he's got a few barnacles on him, and appears to have around a twenty-dollar-a-day donut habit. But Fritz is top shelf, best I could find. Trust me, this whole project is riding on what he can find out right now." Marlon called out to a group of people floating in the river and bearing down on Fritz. "All hands on deck! Diver down, diver down!"

The people frowned at Marlon and then at Fritz as their group split apart, trying to avoid a collision.

"Well, gentlemen, I trust this little shindig of yours will not disrupt our substantial number of Saturday visitors?"

Edgar spun around. "Orville! Sorry, I didn't notice you there."

"Seems everyone's noticed you boys, though. There's talk that someone's drowned?"

"Nothing of the sort." Edgar shook his head and smiled broadly, his face reddening.

Drew came tottering up. "Hi, Edgar. I hope nothing bad happened."

"It's just the engineer checking out the river, Uncle Drew. This is what the councilors approved at the last meeting."

"Pshaw." Orville shook his head. "More like what Ward approved. Everyone was against it except him and his cronies. I do believe Ward's got his eye on a piece of your pie." Orville's hands went to his hips. "You know, it would have been a lot less obtrusive if you boys had done this on a Wednesday."

Marlon smiled. "I hear you, Orville, I hear you. But we wanted the best man for the job, and it's hard to get on his calendar. So we had to be flexible. No worries though, Edgar here's got it all under control, don't you, Edgar?"

A woman floating in a tube bumped into Fritz and squealed. She kicked her legs to get away from him. "Hey! Watch out, freak."

"Um, yeah, doing everything I can." Edgar walked to the riverbank and waved at a cluster of people in tubes coming down the river. He pointed at Fritz. "Diver in the water!"

Fritz labored on and swam closer to Nickel Rock where the current grew more intense. The big fins churned up foamy water as he tried to maintain his position in the river. The force of the water proved too strong so Fritz reached out and grabbed onto Nickel Rock. A bow wave formed directly in front of his head. After a few seconds he lost his grip and the current immediately took him down through the chutes. Marlon held up a camera and took several pictures.

Just past Nickel Rock, Fritz circled around in the eddy and swam upstream along the riverbank near where he put in. Then he made his way over to Nickel Rock again. This time he went along the bottom of the riverbed.

Marlon and Edgar lost sight of him in the turbulent water near Nickel Rock. It did not take long for Fritz to reappear in the downstream eddy at the end of the chutes. Marlon took more pictures.

The third time around an inflatable raft plowed over Fritz. The impact knocked his mask sideways onto his ear and sent him tumbling through the chutes. A number of onlookers cheered and clapped.

Marlon put the camera back in his portfolio. "Don't need any more pictures of that."

Fritz tried the far side of Nickel Rock and the current quickly shot him through the other chute. Marlon and Edgar tracked his location by the bubbles breaking the surface as Fritz explored the calmer waters on the downstream end of Nickel Rock. After a while he swam back to where Edgar and Marlon stood on the riverbank. Edgar bent over and held out his hand to help Fritz up. Fritz ignored the gesture and hoisted himself out of the river.

Edgar laughed. "My apologies, Mr. Yunger. That was quite a wild ride to introduce you to our Paxon Chute Park."

"Hmmph." Fritz pulled off his fins. "If I wanted a wild ride I'd punch another cop." He cleared his throat and spat on the ground, then looked at Marlon. "No go on that upstream end. I can't hold my position."

"That's not the answer I'm looking for." Marlon frowned. "What if we dropped an anchor, or had some kind of rigging to keep you in place?"

Fritz shook his head. "Even with something to hold onto there's so much turbulence I can't see anything. And it's worse at the bottom. I couldn't find a parade of flaming elephants down there."

"Crap!" Marlon stomped his foot, staring at the river. "Well, what could you tell about the riverbed, I mean, away from the rock?"

"Not enough to make any decisions."

Marlon took a deep breath and smoothed back his hair. "It is what it is. Been there, done that. No point hanging around here all day. Come on, Fritz." He turned to Edgar. "We'll have to move on to Plan B."

"Plan B?" Orville stepped closer to Marlon. "You only have approval for Plan A."

"Understood, loud and clear, Orville."

Edgar raised his eyebrows. "I guess you'll tell all of us what Plan B is at some point?"

"Yes, exactly." Drew's head wobbled in affirmation. "We all need to hear what that is."

Marlon smiled. "Ab-so-lutely. It'll all be in the engineering report and we'll present our findings at the next Town Council meeting."

"But you're going to have Fritz check out the rest of the riverbed, right?" Edgar pointed upstream. "That still needs to be done too."

"May as well hold off now that we know a visual inspection of Nickel Rock won't tell us what we need to know. Remember," Marlon snapped his fingers, "if our concept won't work as we've drawn it up that's a game changer for the whole project. It could push our design out of the riverbed and onto the bank, and that's not the vision our investors have in mind. No vision," Marlon rubbed his thumb back and forth across his fingertips, "no 'vestment. Come on, Fritz, let's bail."

* * *

That evening, Marlon's phone rang when he and Edgar were discussing Plan B. Marlon glanced at the display then held the phone up to his ear. "Hey old man, what's up?"

"Old man?" Ward's voice came through loudly. "I guess I could still give you a run for your money."

Marlon laughed, then turned to Edgar and rolled his eyes.

"Well, son, did you find what you were looking for today?"

"We got exactly what we needed to make our next decision, but I swear half the town thought we were trying to find a body."

"Not surprising." Ward made a sucking noise between his teeth. "This town's always forgetting which end is up no matter how clear you make it to them. That's why they need people like you and me to keep 'em on track."

"You know that's right. We Ezells keep things moving, don't we, Dad?"

"Speaking of moving, I hate that you're not staying here with me. How long you been a guest over there at Edgar's?"

"Going on three weeks, I suppose."

"Now listen here, I kicked that little gal out. You're more important to me than her. Why don't you grab your gear and come on home? Your room is here waiting for you."

Marlon looked down at the short, lumpy couch he had been sleeping on in Edgar's living room. "That's music to my ears, Dad. I'm right in the middle of something but I'll head over there later." He dropped the phone onto the cushion beside him. "Well, Gar, the old man is still pining away for some father-son time and he's all begging me to come stay with him again. I've put him off long enough. I do appreciate you letting me stay here, but I need to get out of your hair anyway."

Beth shoved a heaping basket of Marlon's dirty laundry into the living room. "If you're sure you want to stay with your dad, maybe that would be good. For the two of you, I mean."

Edgar drew in a deep breath and smiled as he exhaled. "Yeah, some father-son time sounds like a great idea."

"Okay." Marlon clapped once. "Back to Plan B. So, Fritz was not able to see what he needed to see. That's unfortunate, but that's also why we make contingency plans. You can't have one little hiccup spoil everything. What we're going to have to do is get Council approval to extract some core samples from Nickel Rock."

"Oh man oh man oh man." Edgar grabbed two handfuls of his hair, his head hanging down. "That sounds awful."

"Now, Edgar. You know how you tend to spiral down into that negative mindset. I already told you we might have to do this, and it's not that bad. They'll be itty-bitty little holes. It won't take any time at all to drill them, and when we're done no one will ever even know it happened."

"Oh man oh man." Edgar shook his head.

"It's just another step in our journey. We'll get approval at the next Council meeting and then we'll move forward."

Beth hollered out from the nursery. "We'll all be there with you at the meeting, Edgar, just like last time."

Edgar released his grip and looked up, staring off into a corner of the room. His hair stuck straight up in two big clumps where he'd been holding onto it. "Oh man."

CHAPTER TWELVE

It was nearly dark the next Wednesday when Edgar got home after a long day in the park. "Well, Fourth of July week is crazy as ever." He kicked his shoes off and pushed the front door closed. It bounced back open and got stuck on one of his shoes, requiring Edgar to bend over and wrench it free before closing the door.

Junior lay on a blanket in the living room blowing spit bubbles onto his hands. He lifted his head and turned towards the sound of his father's voice, then watched as Edgar walked across the room and sat down on the couch. Junior smiled and started rocking his weight off his belly and onto his right arm.

"Look at you, big boy." Edgar leaned over and picked up Junior, who let out a belly laugh. "He almost rolled over, Beth, and he's still pushing off with his left arm. You're gonna be Daddy's little lefty, aren't you? Uh-oh." Edgar pulled on the back of Junior's diaper and sniffed. "There's that smell, and it's definitely not his diaper. What in the world could it be?"

Beth stood in the arched doorway that led into the kitchen. She stared out the living room window and didn't say anything.

Edgar looked at her. "Hey, what's the matter?"

"Aunt Fooze died."

"Who?"

"My great-aunt Fooze."

"I've never even heard of her. Fooze? Sounds like someone from your father's side of the family."

"No, my mom's actually, from Louisiana. We hardly ever talked about her. She wouldn't come to any family gatherings, then she quit responding to letters and wouldn't answer her phone or call back even when her own children left messages. Eventually everyone gave up and she just kind of disappeared from our lives."

"That's sad."

Beth smoothed out her apron then stared out the window again and sighed. "It is sad, almost like she died a long time ago. She was very…eccentric."

"I'd say so, based on her name alone. Fooze?"

"That's pretty tame compared to some of them from that Louisiana side. No one knew her real name but Mother thought maybe it was Fuchsia. She'd lived alone as a widow for years, and now she's died alone."

Edgar got off the couch and walked over to Beth, putting his arm around her shoulder. Junior, held in his father's other arm, turned his head back and forth to look at his parents.

Beth dabbed her eyes with a tissue. "I'm not even sure why I'm crying. I guess because she lived such an isolated life and was all by herself in the end. But she did something really sweet for us in her will. She's giving everyone in the family an equal share of her estate. The executor said we'll get a check in a couple of weeks. It won't be a huge amount of money but we'll be able to pay off some of our smaller bills, which will free up our budget to work on the big ones. We have a way out now."

"That's great." Edgar bent over and set Junior back down on his blanket. "Sure helps us out."

"I know, right? This changes everything. Now you don't have to do Marlon's funny little project, if you don't want to."

"Wait, what?" Edgar stood up and frowned. "What do you mean?"

"Well, you were only doing that because things were so tight, and now they're not, so there's less pressure."

"Don't get me wrong, I'm certainly grateful for the inheritance from your aunt. It makes some things better for today, but not forever. That hospital bill is a whopper. And what about the next time the car breaks, or something with the house, or whatever?"

"There you go," Beth yanked her apron string to untie it, "worrying about the rest of our lives when just today a whole bunch of our troubles were taken care of without any help from us." She turned away quickly and hung her apron on a hook.

Edgar shook his head. "I think it's irresponsible to just wait around for things to magically fix themselves for us."

"But we're not just waiting around, Edgar. You have a job you love, you're working, I'm working taking care of the baby. We're both doing the next right things for our family, the things that we agreed were important to us."

"The opportunity with Marlon's got potential. I really think we should ride that out and see what happens."

"So you're going to present to the Town Council, about drilling on Nickel Rock?"

Edgar stared at the floor. "Yes, of course."

"Did you talk to Orville and get on the agenda?"

Edgar scrunched his lips together. "Not yet."

"Interesting. You seem to be avoiding that."

"Just because I'm half terrified doesn't mean it's not a good opportunity."

* * *

The next day Marlon crept up behind Edgar in the park.

"Boo!" Marlon laughed when Edgar jumped and turned around quickly.

"Seriously, Marlon?" Edgar wiped his sweaty face on his shirtsleeve. "Fourth of July is already our busiest day of the year, but two of our park rangers are out and we're also short a driver." He pointed at a bus filling up with people. "As soon as that fills up, I've got to drive it upstream. I don't have time for whatever you're doing."

"Exactly. I knew you'd be busy and a break would do you some good."

Edgar frowned. "All right, let's get it over with. What do you want?"

"Nothing, nothing at all. But as long as I'm here, did you get us on the agenda yet?"

"No, but I'm working on it."

"Working on it?" Marlon shrugged his shoulders and held up his hands. "It's a simple action item, not a global project. You just do it. I hope you remember that the next meeting is less than two weeks away."

"Yes, Mother, I remember, and I'll get it done. You don't need to pin a note to my shirt. Speaking of action items, when are you going to show me the presentation for Plan B?"

"I'm waiting for the slide show. I can't control when they send me that, unlike your little task."

Edgar gestured to the crowds of people around the park. "I've told you I'm completely swamped right now."

Marlon stared at Edgar. "You're not thinking of bailing out on me, are you? Just because Beth came into that tiny little inheritance?"

"I wouldn't call it tiny. It'll take a lot of the pressure off."

"Gar, Gar, Gar. You're thinking too small, too short-term. That inheritance is like putting a Band-Aid on Godzilla."

"I have no idea what that's supposed to mean."

"Your current financial situation is like a giant radioactive monster." Marlon held his hands up like claws and roared. "You're barely scraping by now, you don't have a plan, and now you've got to think about your bambino's future as well because," Marlon's eyes opened wide and he pointed off into the distance, "here comes Godzilla!"

"Oh come on, he's only eleven weeks old."

"Look, I don't have to tell you how expensive it is to raise a kid in today's world. Food, clothing, toys, never-ending visits to the doctor. How is your medical insurance anyway? And speaking of insurance, wait 'til your wild little munchkin starts driving. And what's he going to drive? You can barely keep one old beater rolling for yourself. And it won't be long before you outgrow your tiny house even with just a family of three, let alone if you spawn more offspring. And don't even get me started on how expensive it is to get a kid through college."

Edgar's mouth hung open while Marlon spoke. He snapped it shut and took a deep breath. "You've certainly put a lot of thought into my life, probably more than you've put into your own. Want me to return the favor?"

"I only say these things because I'm your friend and I want to help. And, because I have the means to help."

"Speaking of that, when exactly will I start getting paid?"

"Setting up out-of-state payroll is not something you do overnight, but point well taken. I'll call our accountant in Chicago next week and see what the holdup is."

"What's wrong with this week?"

"Really, Gar?" A smile slid up one side of Marlon's face. "The whole office is shut down for the rest of the week. It's Fourth of July, don't you know? That's the good thing about the white-collar world, you get to spend your holidays on a holiday instead of working in an insane asylum."

The radio on Edgar's belt emitted a series of loud beeps and a tinny voice came through. "River Rat calling Eggman."

Marlon smiled. "River Rat, is that Garth?"

Edgar nodded then pressed a button on his radio. "Eggman here."

"Tubers clotting up river, big line to put in. Chief Turner says thin 'em out. When you coming upstream?"

"Leaving now. Eggman out." Edgar looked around the river in silence, then at Marlon. "I actually enjoy the park and the people who come here to appreciate what we have. As for insanity, I tend to encounter that in other walks of life."

* * *

Edgar walked across the town square the evening of the July Town Council meeting. He stopped beside a black BMW sprawled diagonally across two spaces. "Nice parking job there, Marlo."

Marlon rummaged around in the trunk of his car. "You like that, huh? I get less door dings this way." He pulled several sheets of paper from a gray metal file box. "I think I've got everything we'll need. Just let the road warrior shut down his mobile office." He closed the trunk lid and the loud "chirp-chirp" of the alarm made Edgar jump. "Let's rock 'n' roll, bro."

Marlon stuck all but one of the papers into his portfolio. He waved the lone sheet at Edgar as they walked to the Community Center. "You're sure we're on the agenda? 'Cause I don't see us anywhere."

Edgar stopped. "Yes, I told you a thousand times we're on it. I just didn't talk to Orville in time to get it on the printout."

"Easy there, big boy." Marlon circled Edgar, bobbing, weaving, and shadowboxing, his coat and tie flapping around. "Let's not come to fisticuffs. I was only double-checking."

"You've still never shown me what we're presenting tonight."

"Sorry about that, I only got the final presentation today and you were working. Don't worry, I'll drive during the meeting."

The two men approached a long line of people outside the Community Center.

Marlon whistled. "Agenda or no, looks like the word is out. There's even more people here than at the last meeting."

Inside, the muggy air smelled of various perfumes, colognes, and perspiration. Orville sat red-faced and sweaty at the councilor's table. Like most of the attendees, he fanned himself with a piece of paper. "Mr. Rerd, you are technically the last item this evening, but let's start with you anyway. Our air conditioner is struggling to cool the room with this many people packed in and I bet some of these good folks will leave after your moment in the sun." Orville chuckled. "Or on it. So, Mr. Rerd, please proceed."

"Oh, already? Uh, okay."

"Good call, Mr. Mayor." Marlon strode up to the podium, gesturing for Edgar to follow. "Let's get this party started! Am I right?"

No one said anything.

"So, if you'll bring the lights down and queue up our slides, Wilbur." Marlon snapped his wrist and the piercing clicker came to life.

"Yes, your majesty." Wilbur flipped some switches and the screen at the front began to light up.

A photo appeared of Fritz the engineer in his bright orange wetsuit tumbling down the chutes.

Marlon pointed to the screen. "As you can see, our engineering diver encountered some difficulties during his survey of the river."

Laughter rippled around the room.

Clyde tipped his cap back on his head. "Clearly you did not engage the correct resource. Oompa Loompas are only accustomed to working in chocolate rivers."

The laughter increased.

Marlon smiled and forced out a laugh of his own. "Good

one, Mr. Rerd. But seriously, anyone who's met Fritz Yunger knows he's no Oompa Loompa. We definitely underestimated the limited visibility, which prevented our diver from performing the requisite reconnaissance to provide a geotechnical recommendation regarding the viability of the river supporting our proposed tramway tower structures."

The crowd stared at Marlon in complete silence.

"Ah, I can tell I'm throwing around too much engineering jargon. Sorry about that everyone, I've been living and breathing so much technical stuff lately that I feel like an engineer myself. What I mean is that what Fritz went out there to find out about Nickel Rock, well, he couldn't find that out." Marlon spoke slower than usual and enunciated his words with great precision. "And the reason he couldn't is because that dern current is so tricky through the chutes that even with our experienced boss-hog diver, well he just couldn't see." He pointed to his squinting eyes. "So he was not able to tell whether or not we can put up the tramway towers." He shrugged his shoulders and held out his hands.

The crowd remained silent until Ward finally spoke up. "I'm no ignoramus. I understood you the first time when you used all those five-dollar words."

Marlon's face reddened but he continued smiling. "Excellent, Dad. Excellent. So everyone's with me? Good good good. If you remember, our number one priority at this point is to answer the question about the structural integrity of the riverbed and Nickel Rock. Since there's no way to do that with an engineering diver we'll have to move on to Plan B."

Ward folded his arms across his chest. "I believe you mean, we'll have to consider Plan B. We're not moving anywhere yet."

"Yes, of course." Marlon bowed slightly. "Just a figure of speech, if you know what I mean. Let's not get hung up on semantics. So here we have," Marlon pressed the clicker, "Plan B."

Gasps and exclamations came from the crowd when the next slide appeared. A photograph of Nickel Rock had been modified to include a tall drilling rig sitting atop the iconic river formation. Men in hard hats smiled as they went about their work on the rig.

"This," Marlon aimed a laser pointer at the drilling rig, "will give us all the answers we need."

Clyde chuckled. "Marlon, I don't believe we need that bright light to direct our attention. I'm sure everyone is staring at that gigantic tower."

"You know that's right, Mr. Rerd. Now look, I know this image is highly impactful. But honestly, it's really not a game changer and, obviously, it would only be temporary. The tower would be set up quickly, and once it's up the sampling wouldn't take long at all. We'd be doing AQ drilling, which makes the smallest diameter hole, and it's the fastest. So the drilling should only take one day. Then the tower goes bye-bye at that point and we've got our answers and we're done and we move on down the road."

Mavis bit her lip and frowned. "What is the purpose of that machine?"

"Very good question, Mavis. Yes, the drilling rig is there so we can extract some core samples from the riverbed and from Nickel Rock."

Drew's jaw went slack. "Oh my."

"Yes, yes." Marlon held up his arms. "Again, I know that sounds impressive, but the holes would be less than two inches in diameter, and then we'd patch them up good as new using the original rock we're extracting. You couldn't find where we drilled in a million years, unless maybe if you used a microscope."

"I don't believe a microscope would be the proper

instrument for that type of activity. A bloodhound might be able to find them," Clyde tapped his nose, "if you could train him to know what a hole smells like."

"Exactly." Marlon pointed at Clyde. "So, you see, it's really no big deal."

Eloy stood up. "It is a much bigger deal than a diver swimming around. But an even bigger deal is the permanent towers you want to put up. I am only one person but I do not like the way they look and I do not want it to happen."

Cheers and applause broke out, and from the back of the room someone yelled, "Well said, Eloy!"

Ward stood up and spoke over the noise of the crowd. "Mr. Mayor, with your permission, I have an agenda item coming up later, but it is pertinent to this discussion."

Orville took a deep breath and leaned back in his chair. "Proceed, Mr. Ezell."

Ward picked up a thick stack of yellow papers and held them above his head. "I'll go into the details later in the meeting but here in my hand I have some very troubling news. Last week the annual certification inspection was completed for our buses and there are a number of maintenance and safety issues to be addressed that will require a significant amount of repairs. I am afraid it's very grim indeed. The lower end of the estimate for everything required is two hundred and fifty thousand dollars."

The room turned quiet again.

Ward dropped the stack of papers onto the table. "That's a quarter of a million dollars, minimum, to keep us shackled to something we all hate. I think it's fair to say that we need to explore any other options we might have, especially with a proposal like Marlon's that comes with investors."

Drew raised his hand. "That sounds like an awful lot of money to fix the buses. Are you sure all that stuff has to be done?"

Again from the back of the room, "Yeah, Ward, what are you trying to pull now?" More grumblings followed.

Ward glanced around and waited for the comments to slow down. He picked up the stack of papers again and ran his thumb across the edge. "Look, I don't make this stuff up. The bottom line is we've got a lot of buses, they're older than dirt, and repairs are very expensive. We can keep throwing money at them, or we can have an open mind instead." Ward sat down.

Mavis shook her head. "Maybe you're right, Ward. But if that," she pointed at the screen, "is what comes next, I don't know. Maybe the holes would be small, but that thing looks like it would tear up our poor old Nickel Rock."

"No no no no no, of course not. It's just sitting there atop the rock. There's absolutely no damage to be done that way. However, I'm glad you brought up that point because there is one small matter that is somewhat related to your comment. I want to have full disclosure here, you know. Open kimono, no surprises." Marlon turned to Edgar. "What's that, did you have something to add, Edgar?"

Edgar's face reddened and he shook his head. "No, sorry. Just clearing my throat."

Marlon turned back to the crowd and smiled. He held his arms out wide. "We're all working from the same playbook, and trust is our number one player. So," he hit the clicker again, "there is this one little thing."

A document appeared onscreen. Printed in an Old English font, the title read "Release of Liability and Indemnification."

"Now let me say, with no offense to lawyers, of course, some of my best friends are lawyers, but this is just some legal mumbo-jumbo formality our corporate attorneys have mandated that we bind the town to contractually. Nothing, of course, would ever go wrong. This drilling technology has been around forever. But, just in case something did go wrong, we would need to spell out who is responsible for what. The main concern is that some unrelated misfortune might happen to damage Nickel Rock purely by coincidence during the time we're drilling. This contract clarifies that kind of what-if scenario. However, to be honest, I think it mostly pads the attorney's pockets. Ha ha ha."

"What is that section that cuts off at the bottom?" Eloy's eyes narrowed as he read aloud from the slide. "'The Town of Paxon Chute wholly and irrevocably removes all liability from River in the Sky, LLC, for any damage of any nature before, during, or after any exploration activities conducted on the rock formation known as Nickel Rock, including but not limited to crumbling rock, shifting (either locally to the drilling points or globally to the entire structure), fracturing, shearing, or fissures resulting in the partial or complete defacing, destabilizing, or destruction of the rock.'"

Clyde laughed. "So this eliminates any liability for your company for everything from a hangnail to a nuclear bomb, from the dawn of time until the universe collapses."

"Now, now, let's not exaggerate. We all know how attorneys are: Can't live with them, and it's illegal to shoot 'em. But seriously, the investors just want to cover all the bases because things happen naturally in nature all the time. They have to protect their interests in the unlikely event that some random event happens to happen while we're working there. That's all."

Orville's left eye opened wide and fixed on Marlon. "But your organization would still be responsible for any damage they might inflict?"

"Well, I'm no attorney, so I would recommend the town have someone review this, of course."

"I agree. Because I think it is not good for you," Eloy pointed at Marlon, "to have that rig on our rock with no responsibility."

Marlon swallowed. "Again, this is all standard—"

Mavis stood up and interrupted Marlon. "I guess I don't care so much who is liable. What difference would it make who's liable if you destroy Nickel Rock? It can't be replaced, and our little town wouldn't even be here if it weren't for Nickel Rock."

Boisterous agreement from the crowd drowned out Orville's gavel for some time. Orville finally stood up and shook the handle of the gavel as he looked around the room, his fierce left eye cutting a swath of silence in its wake. "Settle down now, you hear? Air-conditioning is a privilege, and I'll turn it off if you all don't get ahold of yourselves."

He sat back down and turned to Marlon. "If I might interject here, Marlon. There is some interest and some merit in exploring what you might have to offer. But if I could sum up the sentiment of what I am perceiving, the good people here are simply not ready for this." He stared at the screen. "Even if there were enough votes on the Council to approve it," he turned and frowned at Ward, "it would create bad blood in our town. I don't want that."

"Wel-l-l-l." Marlon hesitated. "One of our junior associates did throw out an idea during a brainstorming session."

Edgar grabbed a clump of his hair. "Another idea? There's a Plan C, and I'm just now seeing what Plan B looks like? Where's that open playbook, Marlon?"

Marlon leaned over and whispered, "Not a good time, we'll talk about this later."

"I doubt it since you never tell me anything."

Marlon addressed the crowd again. "Not everything in the playbook has been fully fleshed out, and some of the plays in there are a bit unconventional, if you will. There are some complications, and I don't know that it's the way we want to proceed."

Clyde raised his eyebrows. "Complications? Is it more

complicated than Nickel Rock washing downstream in the form of gravel?"

Spirited discussions again broke out across the room.

Edgar spoke into Marlon's ear. "You're losing them."

"All right, all right." Marlon held his hands up. "If you insist." He pulled a flash drive from his portfolio and walked to the booth at the back where Wilbur sat. "I think I've got a draft slide presentation on Plan C. We didn't put much effort into it, just capturing the idea, really."

Marlon and Wilbur huddled together at the computer pointing and clicking and mumbling, then another slide presentation came into view. A generic-looking plain white slide with blocky blue lettering read "Plan C (?) – Cofferdam."

Tom frowned. "What's a coffee dam?"

"It's coffer. Cofferdam, Mr. Walker, and I'll get to that in a moment. Please forgive the rough edges of this presentation and bear in mind that this concept has not been fleshed out yet, or even approved for that matter. I'll probably get flayed alive for even sharing it tonight. But hey, let's roll with it and see what we think."

Marlon pressed the clicker.

"So this is one type of cofferdam. There are several ways to do them, but the one shown on this photograph is from the 1911 salvage operations of the USS Maine in Havana Harbor."

In the black-and-white photo of the harbor, several dozen large, circular, interconnected islands of dirt about fifty feet in diameter surrounded the sunken ship. Interlocking steel pilings made up the perimeter of the islands, keeping the dirt inside. Within the wall of islands no water was visible and the twisted wreckage of the ship lay on the exposed floor of the harbor.

Marlon aimed his laser at one of the circular structures in the photo. "As you can see, they drove these interlocking pilings into the harbor floor to create a sort of container, which they then filled in with sand. Once this temporary wall was sealed all the way around the ship, the water within the wall could then be pumped out. You can see how this created complete open-air access so they could work on the wreckage."

"Are you proposing we allow you to proceed with constructing this type of massive earthwork around Nickel Rock?" Ward looked at Marlon over the top of his glasses.

Tom jumped in before Marlon could respond. "You've got to be joking, that's gigantic. Building that kind of thing would take a long time, and all of that kerfuffle would do way more damage than drilling core samples."

"Precisely, you've hit the nail on the head there, and I completely agree. What you see here, for us, would be like boiling the ocean, or the river, as it were. Ha ha ha. This photo is just to illustrate what type of work you can accomplish within a cofferdam. The technology has come a long way since 1911. There's new ideas, new ways of thinking, new paradigms, if that makes sense."

Marlon pressed the clicker and an aerial photo of a river appeared. A long blue tube formed a line from the riverbank and out into the water, about halfway across the river. There the tube turned and went downstream, then it turned back towards the bank and all the way to dry land again. The segmented blue line resembled a large letter "C" jutting out into the river. The area inside the tube formation had no water in it and the muddy riverbed lay exposed.

"This little setup is so sweet. It's about as complicated and risky as filling up water balloons. And this system works particularly well in rivers. All they have to do is anchor one end of the tube to the riverbank and then pump it full of water. Then the next tube goes on top of the first tube, and so on, until there's enough height, and bam! You're done. What you see in this picture was deployed in less than a day."

Abbie, the redheaded waitress from The Circle on the Square Café, folded her arms across her chest. "Talk about your lesser of two evils. Why didn't you just show us this in the first place?"

"Well, the cofferdam has a lower perception of risk, although I don't think the other one is risky myself. But perception is reality. Honestly, this is fast and easy and less expensive, but not as conclusive. At the end of the day all you have is a visual inspection. That's worth a lot, but not as much as a core sample. But, hey, I recognize that this is a team effort, and we need to work together. It's all good."

"You started talking about drilling," Ward jabbed his finger at the table, "and now," he jabbed his finger again, "you've moved on," then he started jabbing his finger, harder and harder, with each word, "to some damn coffee contraption." He slapped both hands onto the table. "It sounds like you're flying by the seat of your pants. Team effort? A project like this needs strong leadership, and stability, and direction."

Orville shook his gavel handle at Ward. "I do believe there are enough cooks in the kitchen at the moment, and I happen to appreciate the fact that your son is not trying to shove this down our throat." Orville turned towards Marlon. "But I will say, Mr. Ezell, that this is a mighty profound change of direction." He looked around the room. "What do you all think?"

No one said anything for several moments. Then Mavis stood up. "As long as it's clear that we're not agreeing to the entire project, just taking a look around, then the coffee dam seems way less scary to me."

Eloy stood up. "I still do not like the whole thing, but as I said before, I am only one person. So if the town wants to have more information before making a decision then I am in favor of getting that information without drilling."

"You realize," Edgar tilted his head and stared at Marlon, "that if we put this thing around Nickel Rock, the biggest attraction of our community will be shut down completely. When would you do this, and how long would it have to be in place?"

"Well, we wouldn't do it during the busiest time of the year, that's for sure. But, that's why we have you on board, Edgar, to coordinate these kinds of things. We'll minimize the impact, I can assure you."

The room quieted down again.

Orville drummed his fingers on his chin. "So what you are asking for is permission to erect a temporary cofferdam around Nickel Rock in order to determine whether a permanent tower can be attached, is that correct?"

Marlon nodded. "Yes sir, Mr. Mayor, that's correct."

Ward repeatedly ran his thumb across the stack of yellow papers as he glanced up and down the councilor tables.

Orville held out his hands. "Council, are you ready to vote, or do you need more information?"

The councilors indicated they were ready, and the item passed.

Orville pulled a handkerchief from his shirt pocket and wiped the sweat from his forehead. "Before we move on to the next item we're going to have us a snow cone recess." Orville rapped his gavel. "Meeting will resume when my snow cone's empty."

CHAPTER THIRTEEN

Edgar got home from work the following Wednesday just before five o'clock. He bumped the door shut and leaned his shoulder into it, wiggling the doorknob until it finally latched.

Beth called to him from their bedroom. "Finally, you're here." She stood in the doorway and sighed. "Wait, let me start over. I'm glad you're not working late for a change. Did you have a good day? Are you looking forward to dinner with our parents tonight?"

"Uh-huh. I think." Edgar stopped at the coffee table in the living room. He picked up a stack of mail and flipped through it.

"It'll be nice." Beth ran a brush through her hair. "Now don't stress out going through the bills. I had to write a big check for the pediatrician, so that set us back. We're over thirty days with the air conditioner repairman and the garage but I called them both and they said we could make payments."

"That's awesome." He dropped the mail. "It'll be great to have some more bills to pay on our old junky stuff, and every single month, too." Edgar unclipped his radio then unbuckled his utility belt and dropped them both onto the counter between the kitchen and the living room. He reached inside his shirt to catch the magnets that fell down as he pulled off his name badge. Edgar reattached the magnets and dropped the badge on top of the belt.

Beth walked over beside Edgar and collected all his gear.

"Here, I'll put these away for you, again, if you'll go get Junior. I can hear he's up from his nap." She went back into their bedroom.

Junior lay on his stomach, kicking his legs and slapping his hand on the stuffed elephant lying in front of him in the crib. He raised up and looked at Edgar coming into the nursery, then squealed and kicked his legs even harder.

Edgar laughed. "Hey, he just woke up? I thought we were laying him on his back to sleep."

"I did. I always do." Beth poked her head into the nursery. "Oh my gosh, he rolled over!" She walked quickly over to the crib. "Edgar, he rolled over onto his stomach all by himself."

"That's so cool!" Edgar picked Junior up out of the crib. "Too bad we missed it."

"Don't worry, he'll do it again." Beth tickled Junior's belly. "Yes he will. Oh!" She slapped Edgar on the arm. "Guess what? I'm so excited. I found out what that horrible smell was in the front room. Come here, I'll show you."

Edgar opened his mouth as if he were gagging. "Thank goodness. What in the world was it?"

Beth led the way to the front room, pointing at the couch. "A really old burrito, shoved way down between the cushions."

"Seriously? How did we lose a burrito in the couch?"

"Well, it still had the wrapper around one end. It was an Anita's Atomic Afterburner."

"Marlon." Edgar frowned. "I should have known."

"We can't say that for sure."

"I can. The whole time he was here if he wasn't stuffing his face with cheese balls he was gnawing on a 'Burner."

"I have to admit I was ready for him to leave," Beth rubbed her temples, "but I'm sure the 'Burner was an accident."

"Fah!" Edgar shuddered. "That odor's been haunting me for two weeks now. How long are we going to suffer through these enchanting reminders of Marlon's stay with us? That Gag-nuh-tude cologne of his must have a half-life of like a thousand years."

"It's Manitude." Beth struck a bodybuilder pose.

"Well, between that and the rotting burrito, I've taken to sniffing the diaper pail to clear my head."

She hugged him and laughed. "You exaggerate so much."

"I do not. In fact, his cologne just got stronger as we're standing here talking."

Beth sniffed the air. "You know, I smell it too."

Junior, Edgar, and Beth all startled when the front door rattled around under the assault of heavy knocking.

"Ugh." Beth slapped her hands on her thighs. "That sounds like Marlon, again. He's taking up all your time with that project."

Edgar leaned on the door and wiggled the knob until it opened. "Marlon. I thought it might be you."

Marlon smiled and pointed at his head and then at Edgar's head, then back and forth several times. "Great minds, eh? Think alike, am I right?"

"Well I guess they do, if you were thinking that you were at my house." Edgar bumped the door repeatedly with his hip to get it closed. Junior, held in the crook of Edgar's arm, giggled with each bump.

"Hi, Marlon." Beth checked her watch. "Edgar doesn't have time for an impromptu titans-of-commerce meeting right now because we're going to his parents for dinner." She paused and took a breath. "Why don't you come along with us?"

Edgar turned away from Marlon slightly and mouthed the word "no" at Beth.

"Thanks all the same, Beth, but I can't tonight. I just dropped by to share the good news." Marlon reached out and patted Junior on the head.

The baby scowled and looked around, his head moving in jerky motions.

Marlon dropped his full weight onto the sofa. He bottomed out the cushion and the sofa jettisoned a small cloud of dust into the sunbeams that lit up the room.

"Hold on there." Edgar held out his arm. "I have to ask. You don't have a burrito in your pocket, do you?"

"Edgar, hush." Beth stifled a laugh. "Ignore him, Marlon, he thinks he's being funny."

Marlon shrugged and looked at Edgar. "I heard back from Bag Barriers, they're a cofferdam outfit Fritz Yunger hooked me up with. They said they can support the schedule we discussed, so they'll be here to set up the Wednesday after Labor Day. Isn't that awesome? The earliest date we penciled in, and they're good to go."

Edgar sat down on the floor with Junior across his lap. "You already scheduled them to be here?"

"Yuppers, done and done." Marlon gave a thumbs-up.

"Okay then." Edgar pulled his phone out of his shirt pocket and opened up the calendar. "That gives us six weeks. Might be a little tight, but now we have a date so I can submit the permit request to TAGO."

"Yeah, that's gotta be done." Marlon waved his hand. "I know you'll get us all squared away. What's TAGO?"

"T-A-G-O, the Texas Agency for the Great Outdoors, they're kind of like our state version of the EPA."

"Hmmm, that sounds very complicated and very boring. I'm sure you'll earn your keep jumping through all their hoops."

Edgar folded his arms across his chest. "Speaking of earning, when do I get paid?"

"Yes! I almost forgot my other big news. I've got your paycheck." Marlon opened up his portfolio, flipped through some file folders, and extracted an envelope. "I know we haven't really tracked your hours so far, but I think this is fair compensation for the initial work you've done these past few weeks. It'll be more substantial each month as we ramp up."

Edgar tore the envelope open. He unfolded a perforated sheet of paper with blue printing. "Let's see, 'River in the Sky, LLC, a subsidiary of Sorrentino and Sons Investments, Inc.' Interesting. 'Payable to Edgar Rerd, five hundred dollars.' Wow. I'd say that's fair." Edgar read the memo line on the check, "'For…consulting services'?"

Marlon nodded. "Absolutely. That's the way to do these things until we're all systems go and you're on board full-time."

"That's exciting, isn't it?" Beth put her hand on Edgar's shoulder. "Five hundred dollars will sure come in handy right about now."

"Yeah, it's great." Edgar looked at Marlon. "Thanks, man. You sure you won't join us for dinner? You know Mom always makes plenty of food."

"Nah, the old man is bringing home some Schwertner's brisket tonight."

"Aw, that's so nice." Beth tilted her head and smiled. "Are you having a good visit with him? Just…" she paused. "Just the two of you?"

"Yup, just the two of us. He's going crazy trying to butt in on our little venture." Marlon laughed. "I walked in on him the other day, poking around my room. I'm sure he was trying to get more info."

Edgar laid Junior down in front of him on the floor. "He's snooping around your room? That's kinda weird, isn't it?"

"He knows a good thing when he sees it. I wasn't even surprised, really."

The distinct ripping sounds of a disposable diaper being unfastened echoed in the room, then Edgar slowly peeled open Junior's fully loaded diaper. "Atta boy, fired both barrels again."

"Wheew-eee! That's some dirty business there, Gar. You should warn me before you unleash a world of hurt like that." Marlon's eyes watered and he pinched his nose. "I'b godd a berry keen thense off sthmell."

Edgar paused his work and stared at Marlon. "How ironic."

Marlon let go of his nose when he reached the door but kept his hand over his mouth. "Hmm? Well, anyway, I gotta get out of here. Catch you all later. Oh, and you better jump on that permit process ASAP, eh?"

"Yes, Mommy. I will, Mommy. Junior, wave buh-bye to Mommy Marlon." Edgar cupped his hand and flapped his fingers up and down in a childlike wave.

"You're sooo funny, Egger."

"Goodbye, Marlon." Beth shoved the door closed and turned to Edgar. "We've got to get going or we'll be late." She went into the nursery and stuffed diapers and extra clothes into Junior's distended diaper bag.

Edgar changed out of his work clothes. "Are you nervous, about having dinner with all of them together?"

"Maybe a little." Beth bit her lip. "I really want to get there before my parents do."

* * *

When they pulled in Clyde and Ruth's driveway, Shimei was running around the yard, barking and wagging his long black tail. Luther the goose had Penelope Anne backed up to a rocking chair on the porch, his head held low as he maintained a nasally, hissing growl. Penelope Anne's eyes were wide and she did not move a muscle.

"Oh dear." Beth's face went pale. "This is one of the reasons I wanted to get here earlier. Go! Go help her."

Edgar jumped out of the car just as Luther snaked his neck

forward and poked his head well up under Penelope Anne's bright turquoise dress. When he cut loose with a series of great honking barks aimed at her nether regions, she shrieked and fell back into the rocking chair.

"Don't just stand there, Richard, help me!" She swatted at the squawking lump wriggling around in her dress.

Richard held a casserole dish, his hands encased in oven mitts, and an umbrella tucked beneath his arm. He tried to set the dish on the porch railing but it kept sliding around. Donald and Mac, the Scottish terriers, scampered around his feet. Their eyes never left the dish.

Edgar ran up onto the porch and thumped Luther's tail feathers. Luther flapped his wings and reeled his head out from under Penelope Anne's dress, but continued to direct his odd honking barks at her.

Thatcher the bulldog made her way onto the porch with her stiff-legged run. She looked up at the guests, wagging her entire stubby body, and sneezed on Penelope Anne's leg. Thatcher then licked Penelope Anne's shoe and passed gas noisily.

"I declare!" Penelope Anne scrunched up her face and turned away from the dog. "What a horrible zoo."

Clyde came out the front door. "Luther! No one wants to listen to any of your preaching just now. Away with you all, you domestic plague. Barn!"

The crowd of animals waddled, tottered, and scampered into the barn where they turned, sat down, and stared at the house. Clyde raised his hands and Shimei finally stopped barking.

Ruth hurried out of the house and over to Penelope Anne. "I do apologize for all that ruckus." She helped her out of the rocking chair.

Clyde put his hands on his hips. "I don't know what's got into them. They usually stay when I tell them to stay, though Luther can be mighty protective on occasion."

"Why." Penelope Anne let the word hang in the air as she adjusted her dress and patted her hair. "Is that dreadful huge bird here?"

"Sshhh." Clyde held his finger up to his lips. He looked around then whispered, "He thinks he's a dog."

"What a marvelous promotion in the animal kingdom for him." Penelope Anne took a tissue from her purse and laboriously wiped Thatcher's sneeze off her leg.

Beth quickly stepped up onto the porch with Junior cradled in her arms. "Hello, Mother. Look, here's your grandson." She tried to hand Junior over.

Penelope Anne held her hands up in the air like a doctor entering an operating room. She pinched a corner of the glistening tissue between two fingers. "No!" She paused and then applied a smile to her face. "I mean, I need to freshen up a bit first."

"Of course, of course. Come on in, dear." Ruth led the way inside.

Clyde held the door open for Richard, and Edgar followed with Junior's bulky diaper bag.

Inside, Beth settled Junior on a blanket she had spread in the corner of the dining room. "He's about to fall asleep."

"Ah, he needs his napping partner." Clyde went to the back door and called Shimei. The dog's chunky paws thundered across the porch and he came skidding into the house. "Nap!" Clyde pointed at the blanket.

Shimei nosed around in a basket by the door and came up with a stuffed doll in his mouth. He trotted across the room and dropped the doll on the blanket then licked the baby's foot.

"Good heavens." Penelope Anne shuddered. "Do you really think that's sanitary?"

Clyde scratched Shimei on the head. "He'll be fine, dogs have really strong immune systems." The dog curled up beside the baby.

"The point I'm telling you is," Penelope Anne tilted her head and stared at Beth, "dogs get into everything. Do you really want your baby sleeping with that barnyard animal?"

Junior smiled and gurgled sleepily. He stuck his thumb in his mouth and took one of the dog's ears in his other hand, rubbing it between his small fingers.

"See, it's fine, Mother. They're like best friends." Beth took a seat at the long farmhouse table in the dining room.

At each end of the table sat large gravy boats shaped like swans. Spread in between were two large bowls of tossed salad and many steaming dishes, including mashed potatoes and a platter piled high with chicken-fried steaks. The whole house smelled of fresh baked biscuits.

Everyone settled in at the table except Penelope Anne, who was still running water behind the closed bathroom door. She stuck her head out several minutes later, misting herself with perfume. "I'm just reapplying, I'll be there momentarily."

When Penelope Anne finally joined them at the table Clyde bowed his head and prayed. "Lord, I thank you for the excellent family members here with us today. And thank you for this great food." Thatcher barked at them from the back door. "And thank you also for our pets." Luther answered with a honking bark. "And for the grace you give us to not slaughter and eat some of those pets on occasions like today. I offer this prayer in the name of Jesus, amen."

Richard's shoulders shook under his repressed laughter.

"Oh my." Penelope Anne mumbled. "Slaughter?" She raised her head up and looked around. "That was, certainly, an unusual blessing."

Clyde scooped a large helping of steaming mashed potatoes onto his plate. "I believe prayer is merely another conversation, a chat with the Almighty. I'm just sharing with him what comes to mind."

Penelope Anne sat up a little straighter in her chair. "I

believe the Lord does not need to know everything that comes into our minds."

"Ah, but he already knows anyway, whether we're judging our fellow man or a fool of a pet. Comin' your way, Richard." Clyde dropped a heaping spoonful of potatoes onto Richard's plate. "Say when."

Penelope Anne leaned across Richard's plate and held her hand out to block the second spoonful that Clyde offered. "Oh, Ruth, those aren't instant potatoes, are they?"

Ruth smiled. "No. I've heard of such a thing but never had a mind to try them. These are russet, fresh from the market this morning."

"Oh, good, but that is enough already, Clyde. We're watching Richard's waistline." She withdrew her hand only after Clyde withdrew the spoon. "I only ask because those instant ones don't sit well with Richard's stomach, so we've had to give up potatoes altogether." She held a pair of serving tongs over the platter stacked with chicken-fried steaks. "These aren't the frozen patties, are they? They're so loaded with fat and nitrates."

"No, these are fresh cube steaks, I breaded and fried them myself."

The tongs continued to hover. "Fried, in lard?"

"Goodness gracious, no." Ruth chuckled. "Canola oil, it's good for your heart."

Penelope Anne poked around the patties and finally picked one out, set it on her plate, and cut it in half. "These are so big, Richard, we can split one. You know how fried foods aggravate your system."

Richard's gaze lingered on the platter.

"Aw, that's all right, Penelope." Clyde flipped the largest golden-battered steak onto Richard's plate. "There's plenty here to feed us all for several meals to come."

"That's not..." Penelope Anne struggled to speak, then looked at Clyde. "It's Penelope Anne, please."

"Whoops, my mistake." Clyde winked at Richard.

Beth passed a dish of green beans to her mother.

Penelope Anne stared at the dish. "Are these—"

Clyde interrupted her. "Yes they are, fresh from Granny Rerd's garden." Clyde held a serving spoon above the dish Beth's parents had brought. "Belladonna toadstool casserole, anyone?"

Ruth stared at him. "Clyde, you nut, she already told us that's spinach and portobello."

Clyde smiled at Penelope Anne. "It sounds so much more adventurous the other way."

Penelope Anne ignored him. "Everyone, now listen up. I've brought a special treat for you all called Saucy Spinach, it's from Mrs. Thins. Low in fat, cholesterol, and sodium, you see. It comes in a microwave bag. Like they say, 'So easy to make, just add your own appetite.'"

Clyde passed the basket of biscuits to Richard. "So tell me, how's everything back at the salt mine?"

Richard's eyes darted up from his plate. "Work? Well, about the same as always, I suppose."

"Oh, Richard." Penelope Anne held her hand up to her chest. "You must have forgotten, though I can't see how, about the big government investigation that's going on. You're the central figure in all that."

"Investigation?" Richard slowly wiped a red-and-white checkered napkin across his mouth. "Oh, you mean the audit? Yes, the state is conducting an audit of the city's auditing processes. I'm overseeing our staffing resources for the audit, which is challenging due to preexisting commitments that place limitations on our available resources, because that precludes our own auditors from undertaking a number of key objectives." Richard's smooth, even voice swirled around the room. "Currently we're trying to overcome these limitations by attempting to circumvent—"

Penelope Anne laid a hand on her husband's arm. "Yes, Richard. I'm sure we all understand," she turned her head slowly and glanced at everyone around the table, "that with an official government investigation at this high of a level, you can't share all of the behind the scenes goings-on. I have a suspicion," she raised her eyebrows, "that Richard has let slip a few details that even I should technically not be privy to. I would love to tell you even a fraction of what I've heard. Fascinating, just fascinating. And to know that Richard is holding the reins, representing our beloved city of Peyton so very competently, and with honor and integrity. We're all so proud of him. And now our young Edgar is an up-and-coming commercial developer." She tilted her head in Edgar's direction. "I knew there were bigger things in your future, young man."

"Bigger?" Clyde chewed on a mouthful of steak. "Bigger than what?"

"Bigger than, well, what he's been doing."

"Um, thanks?" Edgar flinched upon receiving a kick under the table from his wife. He glanced at her and shrugged his shoulders.

Clyde looked at Edgar. "For something that's so big I've heard very little about it."

"Uh, yeah." Edgar shifted in his seat. He stared at the potatoes, his cheeks turning red. "You know how secretive Marlon likes to be about everything."

"Indeed." Clyde sliced open a biscuit and spread some honey on it. "Marlon paints a colorful picture. It'll be entertaining to see what develops. But how do you see things panning out, son?"

"Well, it's hard to say at this point. It's all just getting started."

"I'm afraid we'll never see you when it really gets going." Beth's expression went blank. "We barely see you now as it is."

Edgar frowned. "You know the summer is always my busiest time of year. I hate being away. It's just how things are."

"I know that's how it is at the park. It's the Marlon stuff I'm talking about."

Clyde stopped chewing. "What in the world would be taking up so much time at this stage?"

"Well, you know Marlon. Wheels within wheels." Edgar tried to smile.

"Yes, wheels," Clyde rubbed his chin, "his seem to be eccentric, rather than concentric. Can you describe one of these wheels for me?"

"Oh, there's not much to talk about yet, really."

Beth shook her head at Ruth. "He rarely gets home before Junior is asleep. And when he is home, Marlon pops in all the time to keep the ball rolling so they're giving one hundred and ten percent to grease the skids and think outside the box so they can be on their 'A' game and make it a win-win situation." Beth exhaled, blowing a few strands of hair away from her face.

"Really, Elizabeth." Penelope Anne wagged her index finger.

Beth's lower lip stuck out in a pout. "You don't understand. Edgar spent his only day off this week with Marlon."

Edgar turned to Beth. He frowned but kept his voice low. "You know we had to scout out potential anchor points for the cofferdam bags."

Ruth patted Beth's hand. "That does sound pretty stressful, for all of you."

"I did get my first paycheck today, from the investors in Chicago." Edgar turned back towards Clyde. "It's a good start, and Marlon said it's only the beginning."

Beth looked over her shoulder to check on Junior. She pushed her chair back and reached out to pull a corner of the blanket up over him.

"Son, have you got with TAGO yet?" Clyde helped himself to more mashed potatoes and plopped another serving onto Richard's plate.

"Oh yeah, I've contacted them. Someone's supposed to be out here by next week to let us know what approvals we're going to have to get."

"Oooh." Clyde winced. "That'll be an ever-expanding universe. Never ask a barber if he thinks you need a haircut."

Penelope Anne leaned close to Richard and whispered, "What is TAGO?"

"Oh, that's all right, Penelope Anne." Clyde's voice took on a thicker sound coming through his mouthful of potatoes. "None of us knows everything. It's the Texas Agency for the Great Outdoors."

Penelope Anne frowned, opened her mouth to speak, then closed it again.

"Between the railroad and serving on the Town Council I've been through many a feisty exchange with TAGO." Clyde gently shook a forkful of mashed potatoes at Edgar. "They're just as happy over there as if they had good sense."

"But of course you know, Edgar, that Richard would be more than happy to share his real-world regulatory acumen with you. He's a tremendous wealth of information, right here in the family." Penelope Anne inclined her head towards Richard. "A tremendous wealth."

"Oh, yes." Richard's brow wrinkled slightly. "If you ever need any of your policies, processes, or procedures audited, I would be glad to assist. It all starts with the standards, and even though you are venturing into private enterprise, I would nevertheless recommend following the generally accepted government auditing standards. Yes, dear, what is it?"

Penelope Anne stopped poking him in the arm. "I'm so sorry to interrupt, but would you pass me the honey?"

The bottle of honey sat approximately six inches away from Penelope Anne's plate, next to Richard's glass of tea.

She turned to Edgar. "It's so nice to see you finally doing something with your career, making your way in the professional arena. I know you'll be happier there."

Edgar wiped the condensation off his tea glass, slowly turning the glass and wiping, turning and wiping.

Ruth stood up. "Beth, would you be a dear and come help me with dessert?" She stopped at Edgar's chair and laid her hand on his shoulder. "And would you come and scoop the ice cream for me?"

The three of them went into the kitchen.

Ruth set a pan of peach cobbler on the counter by Beth. "If you'll start serving that up for me, Beth, I'll be right back. I've got to get some ice cream from the other freezer."

Edgar stood close to Beth. "What was that all about? You kick me for barely saying anything when your mother talks about me like I'm dumb as a post, and then you go on and on and on, right there in front of everyone, about a bunch of stuff you've never even told me before?"

"I didn't plan on doing that, it just all came out. You're hardly ever home, and when you are, I never want to ruin what little time we have together." Beth pulled a tissue from the box on the counter and wiped her eyes. "This is exactly what I was afraid of, and I told you that when we first talked about it."

"You said you'd support me in this. The whole thing is barely getting started, and already you're digging into me with 'I told you so'?"

"This isn't about me being right. It's about what's important to you."

Edgar leaned over and gripped the counter with both hands. "Really? Isn't it obvious how important you are to me? And Junior? Can't you see I'm doing all of this for us?"

"I'm taking time off from my career so I can be with our

baby. That's what we agreed we both wanted for our family. But when you're never around, we don't even feel like a family."

CHAPTER FOURTEEN

Early Friday morning Clyde and Peter walked along the west side of the town square. Their reflections shifted as they passed each pane of glass that made up the rounded front of The Circle on the Square Café. They turned and went into the café.

Abbie stood behind the counter rolling silverware in paper napkins. Her pink t-shirt had "To Serve and Protect" printed on it in big white letters, with the café logo on the sleeve. Peering over the top of her glasses she called out to the two men. "I was beginning to think you weren't coming in today." She pointed at the clock on the wall. "It's after seven, and I've been here since four thirty."

Clyde tipped his cap. "You can't rush brilliance like mine early in the morning."

"Sit anywhere you like." Abbie pulled two coffee mugs from under the counter.

"We'll just roost on our usual perch here." Clyde took off his cap and the two men sat down at a booth by the window.

Abbie walked over to their table and set the mugs down. "And what will you two creatures of habit be having today? Your usual? Or do I need to bring you a menu? Our special this morning is the Four Squares with Pears."

"I'm not really in the mood for waffles, Abbie. I'll have the Full Circle breakfast," Clyde drew a circle in the air with his finger, "but instead of just one choice of meat I'd like bacon, sausage, and ham, with eggs over easy, hash browns, and can I substitute a bowl of grits for the toast?"

She stared at Clyde. "I guess I can make that happen. For you." The pen scratched across the ticket.

"You're awesome, Abbie." Clyde winked at her.

"Don't expect it every time you come in." She blinked slowly as she turned towards Peter. "And you, sir, what can I get for you today?"

"Yes, Miss Abigail, yes, you know, I was thinking that what Clyde ordered sounds wonderfully indulgious. Could I trouble you for the same arrangement?"

"No." Her pen scratched some more. "Only one per table." She walked towards the counter. "I'll be right back with a pot of fresh coffee."

Peter's eyes followed her. "So, she'll be bringing me what you ordered, right? Because she said no, but I didn't order anything else."

Clyde laughed. "You act as though you've never spoken with Abbie before."

"It can be difficult to know when she jests." Peter's forehead wrinkled and he looked over at her again.

"Sit back and relax, Peter. You'll soon have more food than's good for you."

"Yes, of course. I've never tried the Full Circle even with just one meat. It's convexing to me how you can eat so much."

"I don't make a habit of it, but I'll not be having anything else until late this evening. I'm meeting with a bunch of guys from my old crew. Retirement has bored them out of their skulls and they're pining for a new hobby."

"You certainly never seem bored. Perhaps they should simply follow you around."

Clyde removed his glasses and held them up to the light, then wiped them with his handkerchief. "Not everyone is interested in where life leads me. They declined to join me at yoga class, at least one of them is too claustrophobic for spelunking, and none of them can even spell accordion."

Peter's mouth hung open. "You are an accordionist?" He slapped Clyde on the arm. "Please explain to me why I've never heard you perform."

"I only play by request, so that keeps the old one-man band silent most days of the year."

Abbie stopped by their table with the coffee. "That's because you only know the one song. Learn something besides 'Camptown Races' and then maybe people will show more interest." She filled their mugs with steaming coffee and walked away.

"I for one am eager to hear you play." Peter poured a steady stream of sugar into his coffee. "So, what group hobby is it that you all are going to pursue?"

"Apparently they all miss their jobs because they want to jump back into railroading. Did I ever tell you about speeders?"

"Aaah, yes, indeed. There's one in my book, remember? Where I relay the details of the time you were struck by lightning."

Clyde gazed out the window for a moment. "Yup, I do believe I'll always remember your book. You were able to elaborate on so many details, it's almost as though you pulled things out of me that I didn't even know had happened."

"You are too kind, Mr. Rerd."

"Not at all. It's the mark of a great storyteller. And you make stories like no one else I know."

Peter sighed. "I am so pleased that you enjoyed it."

"So, the guys wanna go over to the Rail Equipment Depot for some parts to get their speeders running." Clyde took a sip of coffee. "Most of us got ahold of one when the railroads quit using them, but no one ever did much with them."

"What in the world is there to do with them?"

"Oh, they have clubs with meetings, and they'll take them out on short runs. Sometimes they go on longer trips."

"That sounds delightful. And are you interested in this as well?"

"I've always enjoyed puttering along in those things. It's the best view of the country you can imagine. Still, I might try and talk them into something a bit more interesting."

Abbie walked by again, barely slowing down as she slid a ticket across their table.

Clyde called out to her. "Why, Abbie, you've remembered the bill but forgotten our food."

Abbie glared at Clyde, then tilted her head slightly and opened her eyes wider as she stared at the piece of paper.

Clyde picked up the ticket. Abbie had written on it:

> **BE QUIET! Your nemesis just came in, at your four o'clock (that means he's behind you at the counter).**

He checked over his right shoulder where a wiry man wearing a fedora sat on one of the round stools at the counter. Clyde quickly turned back to Peter. "Samuel. I might have guessed he'd be the one they'd send."

"Who is Samuel?" Peter reached for Abbie's note. "Nemesis? Oh, I must hear about this." Peter opened up his leather notebook.

"No, I'm sorry, Peter." Clyde held up his hand. "This has to be off the record. It can't go in your book."

"But why?" Peter took the cap off his fountain pen.

"Because he can be a mite touchy. I wouldn't want anything to get him all worked up into a self-important lather. I mean it, put the pen away or I'll not tell you a thing."

"All right." Peter capped the pen, his lower lip puffing out.

"That there," Clyde jerked his head towards the man, "is Strickland Samuel. He's from TAGO, and I've had many a tangle with him over the years. I'm sure he's here to nose around about the cofferdam."

Abbie brought their meals to the table. "You had the Full Circle with grits and every available manner of meat." She set a plate in front of Clyde.

"Thanks for the recon, Abbie, you're the best." Clyde saluted her with his coffee mug.

"Of course I am. They don't let just anyone be a waitress, you know." Abbie slid the other plate over to Peter. "And you, sir, I believe you had the same as Mr. Clyde. Enjoy." She walked off.

Peter spun his plate around slowly, trying to find an easy way in. "So much food, I have no idea where to start."

Clyde took one bite and set his fork down. "Excuse me, Peter, but I gotta let him know I'm here." He looked over at the man again. "Strickland Samuel." His voice resonated through the restaurant.

Strickland slowly put down his coffee mug then swiveled on his stool. "Mr. Rerd. We meet again."

"You know as well as I do that we would meet again with you coming in here on a Friday morning." Clyde nodded his head a little for emphasis.

"Best breakfast in town. Plus, I know Abbie misses me."

"How can she miss you when you keep coming back?"

"Leave me out of this, you two." Abbie topped off Strickland's coffee.

"Thanks for the warning, Abbie." Strickland smiled at her and tapped his finger on the ticket in front of him.

"Why, Abigail, you double agent." Clyde pointed at her and laughed. "Leave me out of it, she says."

She shrugged her shoulders. "I'm like Switzerland, I try to keep the peace for the benefit of the other patrons. Things go just a little smoother when neither of you is surprised by the other one."

Strickland swiveled again. "I saw your brother Andy. He shed some light on a number of things for me."

"Clyde has a brother named Andy?" Peter's eyes went back and forth between Clyde and Strickland.

"You probably know him as Drew Rerd." Strickland wagged his jaw around as he slowly struggled to say the name. "I call him Andy to save a lot of undue wear and tear on my mouth."

"At least he manages to keep his names in their proper order. You've got yours backwards," Clyde tapped his finger to his forehead, "just like your thinking."

"I have to think backwards when I'm here so I don't get run over by you."

"Okay, that's pretty funny." Clyde chuckled. "What is it that brings you to town?"

"Don't ask questions you already know the answers to. It wastes both our time. When the agency got the permit request for a cofferdam here, they assigned their best field agent to come out for the site inspection."

"Oh, thank goodness." Clyde wiped his hand across his brow. "I'm so relieved to hear that. When will she be here?"

Strickland folded his arms across his chest. "You ought to be more civil to me. There was a chance that the cofferdam could have been worked out without too much trouble. But now we've had a recent development and everything, and I mean everything, might be fixin' to change around these parts."

Abbie set a tall stack of pancakes in front of Strickland. "Change? What do you mean?"

Strickland kept his attention on Clyde. "You probably don't know anything about the Barton Springs salamander. Most people don't."

"Well," Clyde shifted in his seat to face Strickland more directly, "I'm not most people, as you'd do well to remember.

They're an endangered species and their only known habitat is Barton Springs in Austin."

"That's right, or it was right, until last week. One of your zealous treasure hunters claims to have found one in the Cobb River, about two miles upstream from here."

Peter paused with a forkful of ham in front of his mouth. "Say, that is something, is it not, Clyde?"

Clyde's eyes darted in Peter's direction. He raised his eyebrows and nodded. "What are you playing at, Strickland? You're not going to use this to scuttle my son's project, are you?"

"Me?" Strickland held his hand to his chest. "I'm from the government, and I'm here to help you. But we have in our possession a Barton Springs salamander that was found in your river. If my investigation confirms you've got an endangered species here, the cofferdam will be the last thing on your minds. Your access to the entire river for recreational use might be blocked by the Feds. I imagine that would not do your economy any good, though I suppose people could still come stare at the river and enjoy your charm, Clyde."

"Oh my," Peter said quietly. "No more swimming in the river? That's a plague on both your houses."

Clyde leaned close to Peter and lowered his voice. "No, this plague would only be on Paxon Chute. Shutting us down won't bother the government at all. I'll have to see if I can determine what Strickland's up to. He might try to roll out a red kerfuffle carpet for us, if he can." Clyde drummed his fingers on the table, then went back to work on his food.

After finishing off two of his three breakfast meats Clyde called out to Strickland. "So you said this was a treasure hunter who found the salamander? I can imagine that, we've got so many of them this year, they're worse than the mosquitoes."

"Yes, he was working alongside the river."

"Interesting. Was he a local, or a visitor?"

"I'm not going to share that kind of information with you. It's on a need-to-know basis until we get to the bottom of this."

Clyde held up his hands. "Fair enough, I understand." He paused. "They can be an annoying lot, those treasure hunters."

"Yeah, this one 'bout drove me crazy smacking his gum."

"Hmmm. A gum smacker, eh. They set me on edge as well. Leave a lasting impression though, don't they?"

Clyde focused his attention on drizzling honey over his grits. He ate them in silence, frowning a little. He stuck the last spoonful in his mouth then dropped his spoon in the bowl. "Aha!" He looked around and lowered his voice. "Oops. That was loud. But I remember now."

Peter inclined his head. "Remember what?"

"I'll tell you later, when I know for sure." Clyde took out his notepad and wrote down "Search for Nathan with one 'n', the gum-smacking treasure hunter." He stuck the note in his hat then picked up their ticket. "It's my turn this week." Clyde went over to the cash register and paid the bill.

Peter laid his hand on Abbie's arm as she walked past. "Miss Abigail, thank you for the wonderful meal. I may want to order that again sometime. Who could blame me?"

"You can have it again, but only if you remember what it is that you ordered. I can't do everything for you." Abbie chuckled. "See you next time."

Clyde paused at the door and abruptly hollered at Strickland, "Ruth will have supper ready at six, are you going to be there or not?"

"I guess I might, if you're inviting me."

"Well I guess I am." Clyde pushed the door open.

"Fine. I'll see you then."

"Fine." Clyde walked out.

"Did I just hear you ask him over to your house?" Peter pointed back towards the café.

"Yes you did."

"I'm not at all convinced that you two like each other."

"And I can understand why you'd think that."

"Then why ever did you invite him?"

"I expect Ruth will want to visit with him. They're cousins."

CHAPTER FIFTEEN

The deep blue sky, uninterrupted by clouds, offered no relief from the broiling August sun. The air even smelled hot. A substantial crowd of people at the park were cooling off in the chilly spring water of the Cobb River. Laughter and shouting punctuated the steady background noise of the river flowing through the chutes at Nickel Rock.

The pavilion in the park offered shade but actually intensified the heat. A low wall around the perimeter kept the air from moving freely, and the brown paint soaked up the sunshine, radiating it back out in withering waves.

Marlon slouched at a picnic table under the pavilion. His white dress shirt clung to his sweaty skin. After several attempts his slippery fingers managed to unfasten the top two shirt buttons. "Explain to me what is so important that we're meeting here, now, at the absolute worst possible time of day?"

Edgar walked back and forth in the pavilion. "Because it's hard for me to get away from work on Saturdays and I've already got something going on with Beth in a little while. And TAGO is supposed to come by the park later."

"Couldn't we meet afterwards, when it's cooler?"

"I called you last night when it was cooler but you didn't answer." Edgar tossed his park ranger cap onto the table. "And it was cooler this morning when you didn't answer again." He grabbed a clump of hair and tugged on it. "If you'd listened to my messages you'd know why it can't wait."

Marlon fanned himself with a manila file folder. "I sort of listened but didn't catch all the details. You sounded like your hair was on fire, although now that I see you, it only looks like a cat's been sucking on it."

"That stupid cofferdam, that's what's up. Or not up, or up the creek, or whatever, but it's a mess, or it's gonna be a mess. No, it's a mess already."

"Slow down there, take a breath and complete a sentence for me. And have a seat. Watching you pace around makes it hotter in here."

Edgar stopped beside the table but remained standing. "The cofferdam will disrupt the flow of the river, which requires a permit, so I submitted the request to TAGO for that."

Marlon gave him a thumbs-up. "Yes, and good for you. I don't know what you're so worried about. It'll be fine."

Edgar resumed walking. "Thanks for sharing that with me. And how do you know it will be fine? Have you ever been to a TAGO Waterway Impact hearing?"

"Gar, you act like the government is out to punish you. Listen, they're only going to justify their existence for a little while and then they'll crawl back into their little hole and we'll march right on along."

"Oh, but wait. It gets better. The cofferdam's only a minor point now. Someone supposedly found a Barton Springs salamander in the Cobb River, just upstream from Nickel Rock."

"You say that like it's a bad thing." Marlon fanned himself more vigorously. "What's that got to do with anything?"

"They're endangered, Marlon, and only known to live in Barton Springs. Until now."

"But now there's more of them. With them being found in

the Cobb River, they must not be so rare. See, problem solved already."

"Wrong. They're just as endangered as they were before. The federal government could come in here and shut everything down."

"Hmm. Well, that's certainly not optimal. Could definitely delay us. But—"

Edgar slapped his hand on the picnic table. "You don't get it! This is not about our project anymore. They could restrict the entire river, no more swimming, no more tubing, nothing. It's all a ginormous wad of worry now."

Marlon stopped fanning. "That is different."

"Aha!" Edgar pointed at Marlon. "See, that's what I've been saying. We'll be older'n dirt before TAGO gets done with us."

"Whatever." Marlon stood up. "Look, even a pig poops out a nickel once in a while."

"What?"

"I mean it'll all work its way through and something good will come out in the end."

Edgar blinked several times. "And you'd want that nickel, would you? This metaphor is not making me feel any better."

The smile slid up Marlon's face. "I'll make it happen, I always do. So, who do we know at TAGO?"

"Actually, Strickland, the agent they sent, he's my first cousin once removed on my mother's side."

"Sweet. Why didn't you tell me that before? That'll grease the skids nicely."

"It's not like that. At all. He and my dad don't get along very well, I don't think. Dad always put up a fuss when dealing with him over TAGO business, and most other times as well."

"But the Marlonator is not your dad. I'll just work my magic with Mr. Strickland."

"No! Don't ever call him that, he'll go nuts. Strickland is his first name. His last name is Samuel."

"Oy vey. Your family and their names. What's up with that?"

Edgar's face, flush from the summer heat, turned a shade redder. "Said Mr. Ezell."

"How can I get in touch with Strickland? You got some contact info for him?" Marlon sat down and resumed his fanning.

"I don't think that's a good idea. Last night my dad told me he's already working on Strickland. He also said he's checking on something that might shed more light on the whole salamander situation."

Edgar's phone beeped and he fished it out of his pocket. "Dang it. Strickland just emailed me and said he's coming over right now."

"Awesome." Marlon smiled. "I can meet and greet and start workin' him over to our side."

"Yes, and this also messes up my thing with Beth, so it's doubly awesome." Edgar pulled up Beth's contact info on his phone and pressed send, then held it up to his ear. "Hey, sweetie, it's me. I'm really sorry, but I'm going to have to cancel today. Strickland went and changed our meeting time to right now."

"This is my surprised voice." Beth spoke slowly and quietly.

Edgar made a fist and lightly thumped it against his head. "Don't do this to me, Beth."

"I'm not doing anything to you, Edgar. You're doing this to yourself."

He closed his eyes. "It's not me, it's TAGO, for crying out loud. They show up when they want to, and I've got to meet with them. I don't have any choice."

"Uh-huh. Just like the two other times I rescheduled because you couldn't make it."

"It's only a haircut. They'll give you an appointment all day long most every day. Just, please, reschedule it again, and I promise I'll be there next time."

"No. You promised before. This is your son's first haircut."

"His hair's not really even that long yet, is it?"

"Long enough that people over in Peyton have asked me what her name is. This is a big event that's important to me and you've blown it off three times in a row now. I've got the appointment set up. Again. My parents and your parents are going. Either come on and be there for this special moment with your son, or his life will roll on along without you. Your choice."

"But it's TAGO, the whole project, even the whole river, it won't—"

"I love you, Edgar. But I have to go now so I won't be late." Beth hung up.

Edgar shook his phone in the air. "Dang it. What am I supposed to do? It's the blasted, inflexible, all-doing, unknowing TAGO."

"Mr. Rerd?"

Edgar turned around.

A man with sharp features spoke again. "Mr. Samuel, from TAGO."

Edgar swallowed. "Yes, uh, yes, Mr. Samuel, we've met before, if you'll recall. Thanksgiving dinners, family reunions, my wedding."

"All that goes away in this context. This is strictly business and by the book, which I do happen to know, by the way." Strickland folded his arms across his chest.

Marlon swooshed up beside Strickland and held out his hand. "Mr. Samuel, Marlon Ezell, I'm the director of operations and also the on-site investor liaison for this project. I'm so glad to have a chance to meet you."

Strickland ignored Marlon's hand. "I don't know that

you're going to have a project to manage." He turned to Edgar. "I came up yesterday and did a preliminary inspection. Let's go upstream and have a closer look."

* * *

Ruth hollered at Clyde from down the hall. "You know we're going to Junior's first haircut. We have to leave in a minute."

"Today?" He took off his cap. "I don't have anything on that."

"With or without a note, it's still today, and I aim to be there on time."

"Absolutely, I'll be ready." He read the one piece of paper he did have in his cap. "I just remembered something and I wanna look it up while I'm thinking about it."

Clyde sat down at their computer and opened a web browser. He searched for "NATHA treasure hunter" and scrolled through the results. "Ha! North American Treasure Hunters Association. That's the one."

He clicked on a link to their website. In the "Search this Site" box he typed "Paxon Chute" and pressed enter. The search returned several discussion threads and he clicked on the first one. Clyde looked at the member names and the profile pictures beside each comment. The picture for the user "Fame-N-Fortune" caught his eye. He clicked on the name and a larger image came up, along with the profile information.

"Ha! I know you, Nathan with one 'n.' Maybe if you can't find a fortune you're content enough with a little fame."

The profile information included his member name: Bart Milden, from Austin. It also listed an email address.

"Ooh, that's good."

"Clyde, stop talking to yourself and let's get going."

"I'm ready." Clyde wrote down Bart's email and stuck it in his cap.

* * *

Several hours later Clyde walked into The Snorting Bull. A larger than usual crowd filled the establishment with animated conversation. However, discussions quieted and gazes followed Clyde as he walked over to the bar where he joined Tom, Drew, and Wilbur.

Tom raised his glass. "Welcome to the wake."

Clyde sat on a bar stool and sighed.

Drew's eyebrows rose and he scanned the room. "It's packed for early evening, isn't it?"

Wilbur frowned. "Bad news travels quickly."

"And it's as welcome as an outhouse breeze." Clyde wrinkled up his nose.

"It didn't travel to me until I got here, Clyde." Drew scowled. "Nobody told me anything. You could have let me know earlier."

"I came over to tell you, Drew. I knew you'd be here."

Drew tried to dig his hand into his front pocket. "Dang it." He slid off the stool and stood up so he could get the cell phone out. He slapped the phone down on the bar. "I don't know why I even pay for this thing, or carry it around with me for that matter."

"I know what you mean, Drew." Clyde patted him on the back. "Mine barely gets used as well."

Clyde's phone rang, and Drew threw his hands up in the air.

"Clyde's doomsday hotline, who's this?"

"Dad, where are you? I need to talk."

"Hello, son, I'm at the Bull. Why don't you come on down?"

"Argh. Is everyone there?"

"Pretty much. It'd be just as well to get it over with."

"Fine."

Clyde pocketed his phone. "A beer and a bump, please, Eloy."

Both of Eloy's hands were working beer taps. "It will be a minute. People are thirsty tonight."

Drew watched through the big front windows of the bar where a smallish man with a stunted gait walked across the town square. "Hey, isn't that Pastor Brooks coming this way?"

Tom squinted. "Certainly looks like him."

"Holy smokes!" Drew hissed at Clyde. "He's coming in here."

Drew glanced from his beer to Ken and back to his beer again. He quickly set his mug on the bar and sent it sliding past Clyde, where it bumped into a bowl of peanuts. He exhaled into his upheld hand and frowned. Reaching across Clyde, he grabbed a fistful of peanuts, shoved them into his mouth, and chewed frantically.

Clyde leaned back to give his lurching brother more room. "It's a bar, Drew. I expect he won't be too shocked to see you drinking a beer in a bar."

A number of people greeted Ken when he came in.

Clyde stood up and waved Ken over. "Good evening, Pastor Brooks."

"Please, call me Ken."

Drew laughed nervously and a peanut shot out of his mouth and into the air like a signal flare. "As you wisth, Pasthor Ken."

"Really, just Ken will do. I don't call you wastewater engineer Drew, or postman Wilbur, or retired Clyde, or..." Ken looked at Tom and paused.

Clyde laughed. "That's pretty much all Tom does right there, just sit on that bar stool. Whatever you want to call that."

Tom hoisted his glass. "I enlighten the masses."

Drew smiled through his peanutty chewing. "Didja hear that? He called me an engineer. Yes, I like that. I'm an engineer."

"Sure sounds more glamorous than sewage truck operator." Wilbur scratched his chin. "Come to think of it, I do believe I'm a parcel distribution engineer."

Eloy set a mug of beer and a glass of whiskey in front of Clyde. "Hello, Ken. What can I get you?"

"Sweet tea, please, Eloy."

Tom tilted his head. "Is there another kind?"

Drew swallowed his mouthful of peanuts. "This is the kind of enlightenment you share, is it, Tom? The good pastor comes to visit and see how you treat him."

Ken waved Drew off. "I stopped by to see how everyone's doing. I heard about the big news. Eloy, you look overwhelmed. Let me help you wash." Ken went behind the bar and put on an apron.

Tom laughed. "A preachin' bartender. You don't see that every day."

"Oh, no." Ken smiled and stuck his hands in the sink. "I don't think I'll be pouring any drinks, but I can help clean up afterwards."

The front door opened and most of the patrons turned to check out the latest arrival. Peter trotted in, waving to several people on his way to the bar. "Greetings and salutations, everyone. I have just received the most illexplicable news."

Tom took another pull at his beer. "Well, if you've heard about it then it's official: Everyone in town knows at this point."

"Oh, you've already been informed." Peter shook his head. "It is quite the mystery. We must needs appeal to the highest court of detection to resolve this."

The front door opened again and Edgar walked in. Silence

enveloped him as he moved through the crowded room. He looked straight ahead as he walked.

"You come right on over here and don't worry about anything, Edgar." Drew patted the bar stool beside him. "No one blames you."

A voice called out over by the windows. "At least one person does." Several other voices chimed in with their agreement.

Edgar stopped and turned in the direction of the first voice. "Is that you, Bruger?"

A bulky sunburned man in a muscle shirt downed the rest of his beer and smacked the mug onto the table. "Yeah, what's left of me."

Edgar winced. "I can understand everyone's upset. Obviously I'm not happy about it either."

"Upset? Not happy?" Bruger's voice grew louder. "I'm out of business as of an hour ago."

Clyde tossed back his whiskey then wiped the corners of his mouth with the back of his hand. "This affects everyone, not just the river outfitters, Bruger."

Bruger looked at Clyde. "If I were you, I wouldn't be in such a hurry to find more people who're angry with your son."

Edgar shrugged his shoulders. "How is this possibly my fault?"

"Because it was your bright idea to build that tramway." Bruger pointed at Edgar. "That's what got TAGO crawling all around here in the first place."

"Those are two completely different things. Some random treasure hunter found the salamander. It had nothing to do with TAGO."

"So you say. There's some folks who believe they're related."

Clyde pushed up the bill of his cap with his thumb. "How do you figure?"

"What if someone," Bruger folded his arms across his chest, "disliked that project enough to want to put a halt to it any way they could think of, and went and stuck one of those salamanders in our river?"

"That's ridiculous." Edgar shook his head. "No one in our town would do that."

"Maybe. There's some who think it's a possibility."

"Well who are they?" Edgar held out his hands. "Huh? Where are these 'some people'? If you believe it, own up to it and say so. If it's someone else, they can speak for themselves. I've got better things to do than hang around here and be mauled by proxy."

Bruger stared without blinking. "All I know is that everyone was better off around here before you all started whipping up this stuff."

"We presented everything to the Council. Nothing was done that had not been fully approved, and the salamanders have nothing to do with any of that. You're way out of line, Bruger."

Clyde stood up and gently pulled Edgar over to the bar. "Easy, now. You could argue with him until it's slap dark and it wouldn't make a bit of difference."

"It's not my fault." Edgar sat down at the bar between Clyde and Drew. "Nothing has gone right today."

Peter leaned over so he could see around Drew. "Where's Marlon?"

"I wish I knew, Peter. Wherever he is, he's not answering my calls." Edgar flipped his finger across his phone. "I've tried seven times already."

Tom slid his fresh beer towards Edgar. "Here, have one on me."

"No. Thanks just the same, Tom." Edgar stared at the frosty mug then quickly reached out for it. "Oh, why not." He tipped it up and nearly drained the glass.

Drew thumped him on the back, causing Edgar to spill beer down his shirt. "It's all right. This is just a stormy day for you, and it'll blow over."

"Slow down there, son." Clyde held up his hand.

"Well, it looks like it is meat, drink, and be merry for Edgar tonight, eh?" Peter drew in a deep breath. "I can't say that I blame you."

Wilbur frowned. "Peter, you beat all. That's from the Bible, or it was before you got ahold of it, but it ain't talkin' about no good time. It's about someone who thinks he's got plenty of time to party, but he's going to die that night instead."

"That's well said, Wilbur." Ken hollered from the other end of the bar where he was drying glasses. "Perhaps you should preach this week, and I'll deliver the mail."

"Since we're going to die sooner or later," Tom held up his beer, "that's all the more reason to drink while you can."

Clyde gazed into his glass for a moment then pushed it away. "I'd say that's a point well missed, Tom."

Ward Ezell sat at a table next to Bruger. He spoke to the people around him but loud enough to be heard at the bar. "Those two greenhorns thought they'd be able to handle something of this scale. All they've done is pull the pin on a grenade, and now they're just hoping to get out alive."

Clyde looked over at him. "Ward, it seems to me like you want to be the one with all the big ideas."

"They're wrong, Dad." Edgar spoke quietly.

Clyde turned back to his son. "I agree. Facts are stubborn things but they can sure enough be massacred when people want to vent their frustrations."

"Oooh, turn it up, turn it up." Peter pointed at the television on the wall. "We're on the news. This must be from the crew that left a little while ago."

Eloy picked up the remote and the bar quieted down.

A young female reporter with long auburn hair neared the end of her story. "We were contacted today by the man who says he discovered the endangered salamander in the river here behind us." She gestured over her shoulder to the Cobb River in the background. "He prefers to remain anonymous at this time, due to fear of retaliation from the townspeople who are being impacted economically by the river closure. While no actual threats have been made, he is still fearful, and it is easy to see why. Because even though the salamander is the one on the endangered list, it is this town that is fighting," she paused, "for survival. This is Ginger Gillette reporting from Paxon Chute for *Channel 87 News.*"

Moans, groans, and boos drowned out the television.

Clyde laughed. "As if to illustrate my point about massacring the truth. Threats? That's absurd and she knows it."

"Well, that was horrible." Edgar shook his head. "You know, I still don't even know why Strickland shut us down. We didn't find any salamanders in the river. Besides, they never once closed Barton Springs after they were discovered there."

"Well, that was over in Austin. We're just a little Podunk town. Plus, you never know what that rascal Strickland is going to do, or why."

Edgar finished off his beer and waved at Eloy for another. "One more, then I gotta go hear about the haircut I missed."

"It was quite a sight. We got lots of pictures, don't you worry. Oh," Clyde adjusted his cap, "and I'm one step closer to what I'm hoping to track down."

"What is all that, anyway?" Edgar took a long drink.

"I'd rather not say just yet. It's only a hunch I've got and I don't want to get your hopes up."

"No worries there." Edgar downed his second beer and ordered a third.

CHAPTER SIXTEEN

Even though Beth spoke with plenty of volume, the details she shared regarding Junior's first haircut were drowned out by Edgar's retching.

"It was so wonderful, with all of our family there to watch, except for you, of course. Here, smile, I'll get a picture now and paste you in. No one will ever know the difference."

The camera flashed as Edgar leaned over the toilet, his body straining.

"Oopsy, someone might notice the difference, because you'll be the only one vomiting." Her voice oozed cheerfulness. "Oh well, it'll be a good illustration on how any problem can be made worse by getting all sloppy drunk."

Edgar flushed the toilet, then stood up slowly and took very small steps on his way out of the bathroom, his face damp and gray.

"Wasn't avoiding you." He spoke softly. "Just went by the bar to smooth things over, about the river closing." He gagged. "Was stressed out, drank one, then another."

Edgar stood in front of their closet and pulled one of his work shirts off a hanger.

"Your uniform? You must have drowned the poor wee calendar portion of your brain. It's Sunday morning. Remember church?"

"Have to work. Keep people out of river." With his shirt

halfway on, he leaned against the wall and closed his eyes. "Gonna be long day."

"Oooh, yes. Out in the hot sun. I wouldn't want to be you today." Beth filled a cup with water from the bathroom sink. She held it out to Edgar. "Here, you'll be dehydrated from last night. I'm mad, but not so mad I want you to die."

Edgar shook his head, then grimaced. "Not yet." He quickly went back into the bathroom and shut the door.

When Edgar finally made it out of the house the sun immediately shriveled up his eyes and drew beads of sweat out of his forehead. He stopped under the shade of a tree before he even got out of the yard.

The honking of car horns came from the direction of the park. Edgar pulled on his cap and started walking.

Chief Aaron Turner had parked his police car in front of the main entrance to the park. The emergency lights blipped on and off as Aaron waved vehicles along.

"Edgar, I'm glad you're here. You can help me explain to people what's going on. We might need riot gear before this day is done. You just missed some frazzled mom thowin' a walleyed fit 'cuz I wouldn't let her in. Say," Aaron squinted, "are you all right? You look terrible."

Edgar swallowed slowly. "Be okay."

"I've sent another unit to the upstream entrance."

"Oh, yeah." Edgar's eyes widened and he pushed the button on his radio. "Eggman calling River Rat."

The radio squawked back, "River Rat here."

"You upstream?"

"Got it covered. Did you finally show up? Chief Turner was covering for you earlier."

"With him now. Eggman out."

Garth laughed. "That was quite a display last night, watching you single-handedly take on sobriety and defeat it so convincingly. River Rat out."

Chief Turner chuckled. "That Garth, he'll yank your chain any chance he gets."

A black Suburban stopped next to Edgar. The darkly tinted driver's window rolled down quickly with an electric whining sound. The driver slouched back in the seat, his right hand draped loosely over the top of the steering wheel. He spit into a beer can. "Hey! What's the deal here?"

Edgar swallowed again. "The Texas Agency for the Great Outdoors has—"

A very thin and very tan woman with extremely blonde hair screeched from the passenger seat, "What's he sayin', Deke?"

Edgar tried again. "The Texas Agency for the—"

Deke interrupted this time. "What are you talkin' about? We come up to cool off, so just let us in. I'da stayed in Houston if I wanted to sit in traffic."

Aaron gave a sharp blast on his shrill whistle, causing Edgar to wince.

The policeman's voice boomed out. "Get that vehicle out of here or I'll impound it. Park's closed until further notice due to an endangered species in the river. Now move along!"

Deke shook his head and spit in the beer can. He slowly drove off and the window whined again. Just before it rolled all the way up he yelled, "Jack wagon!"

Ginger Gillette and her crew stood off to one side. "And there we have it, more tempers are flaring due to the closing of this favorite local recreation spot." She motioned towards Chief Turner. "Extra law enforcement has been brought in to bolster the regular park security presence." Ginger walked towards Edgar. "Excuse me, sir, could I get a word with you on camera about how things are going here today with the stronger crowd-control tactics being deployed?"

Edgar's face turned gray again and he dashed behind the police car to vomit some more.

Ginger suppressed a smile and turned to face the camera. Her left eyebrow lifted slightly. "As you can see, everyone in this little town is just sick about the whole thing. This is Ginger Gillette reporting from Paxon Chute for *Channel 87 News*." She smiled and held her pose for a moment. "Okay, let's get back to the station. If we can get that last bit in it'll go viral for sure."

The crew snickered as they left.

"They're gone, Edgar." Aaron watched them walk away. "And good riddance."

Edgar leaned against the car for a few minutes then slowly raised his eyes to look at the cloudless sky. He wiped the sweat off his forehead.

An hour later church let out and Ken came jogging over to the park entrance. "Hello, Edgar. I heard you were down here working, and I figured after last night you wouldn't be feeling too well. Is there anything I can do to help?"

"Thanks, Pastor Ken. Feelin' a little better now." Edgar checked his watch. "You must not have eaten yet."

"How 'bout I eat whenever you do? So, what are we telling them?"

"Just that the park is closed until further notice, due to an endangered species."

"That's a mighty short sermon, but I think I can adapt."

Chief Turner finished talking with another carload of disappointed people and walked over to Edgar and Ken. "Howdy, Pastor. You signin' up for this thankless task?"

Ken shook hands with the Chief. "Yes, and I've recruited some more help. They'll be here shortly."

Twenty minutes later ice chests lined the street in front of the park entrance and the townspeople gave away cold drinks to their unhappy guests. Several food vendors set up there as well, including Mavis, Señora Schwertner's, and The Circle on the Square Café.

Karl Schwertner walked up to a minivan and held out a Bramale for each passenger.

The driver scowled at Karl. "Hold on, how much are those?"

Karl held up his hand. "No charge, sir. Just our way of saying we're sorry about the park being closed, and we hope you'll come back when it's open again."

The idea of giving away food caught on and the mood along the park entrance improved considerably.

Chief Turner called in a fire truck, and the firemen set up their water cannon to spray into the middle of the town square. Some of the visitors began to park instead of driving off. Children ran through the water spray shrieking and laughing.

Beth made her way across the square towards Edgar, pushing Junior in his stroller. "There's your daddy." She cooed as she unbuckled Junior and picked him up.

Junior squealed and reached towards Edgar with both arms held out.

"Hello, you two." Edgar took his son and ran his hand over Junior's shortened hair. "Wow, that sure made a big difference, all those long curls gone."

Beth glanced back and forth between them. "Now he looks more like you."

Junior grabbed hold of Edgar's shirt with his right hand and Edgar's ear with his left. His eyelids began to droop and he laid his head on Edgar's shoulder.

"Oh no." Beth stepped closer. "I've got to get him home for his nap. He'll sleep here for five minutes then be a fusspot the rest of the day."

Junior held on to Edgar's shirt and cried when Beth pulled him away.

"I know, I know, I'm sorry for both of you." Beth patted Junior on the back. "See you later." She turned and walked away. After a few steps, she looked back over her shoulder. "I love you, Edgar Rerd."

"Love you both." Edgar waved goodbye and took a long drink from a water bottle.

Ruth stood at one end of the line of ice chests handing out cold drinks. Clyde walked up with a case of water bottles to refill her cooler. "I believe there is one thing missing from this little festivity."

Ruth frowned. "You only know the one song."

"That's not entirely true, I've been expanding my repertoire."

"Expanding as in you've actually learned another song, or did you just find some music that you wish you could play?"

"It's 'The Girl from Ipanema.'"

Ruth stared at him. "Why do you feel the need to stack the deck against yourself like that?"

"You're right, I don't really know it all that well yet. But I'm going to go by the house and retrieve the ol' squeeze box anyway."

Edgar waved at Ruth, gesturing for her to join him. "Where's Dad going?"

"He said we needed some music."

Edgar snorted. "I guess everyone helps in his own way."

"Well, not everyone is helping." Ruth surveyed the crowd. "Your business partner Marlon hasn't even shown up. I'd be mad at him if I were you. But instead, you're frustrated with your father, who loves you and would do anything for you."

"Whenever I can get his attention."

"Well, I don't know. Sometimes it is hard to tell what he's thinking."

* * *

Clyde drove home and fought through his herd of animals. Once inside the house he went straight to the computer where a message from "MildenMan" awaited him in the email inbox.

Bart Milden's reply to Clyde's email contained only two words, "call me," and a phone number. Below it was Clyde's original message:

> Mr. Milden,
> A little bird told me you might be connected with an interesting discovery near Paxon Chute. But there are some people around these parts saying it's all a hoax. Be glad to share with you what I've heard so we can make sure this story gets reported like it should.
> Sincerely,
> Someone Who Cares

Clyde wrote Bart's phone number down and stuck it in his hat.

He drove into town and stopped at Rosa's Mini Mart. After getting change he went back outside to the pay phone. He took the note out from his cap and punched in the number.

A familiar voice and cadence answered. "Bart's the name."

"Hello there, Bart. I'm the feller you sent an email to and said to call you. I think we're both interested in the same thing."

"Yeah? What might that be?"

"Salamanders."

"What do I care about salamanders?"

"I heard you found a very special one in the Cobb River."

"Maybe I did, and maybe I didn't."

"I can appreciate things are a little touchy right now. I wanted to let you know that there's some people here saying you staged the whole thing."

"That's stupid. Why would I do that?"

Clyde smiled. "I completely agree. What you've found is extraordinary and I want to make sure no one tries to manipulate this story for their own interests. Some people don't like what might happen because of your discovery. All I want is for the truth to come out, and for these little salamanders to be protected properly."

"Uh. Yeah, they're rare all right."

"Exactly. Now I understand you happened upon this creature as you were searching for treasure along the riverbank."

"Maybe."

"The mudslinging doubters are saying that you must have remarkable eyesight to spot a well-camouflaged, two-inch-long critter in a flowing river as you're walking past, especially with you being engaged in the complexities of treasure hunting at the time."

"Well I did, and I don't care what anyone says."

"Hey, I'm on your side. I think they just don't want their pocketbooks interrupted by what your find might mean."

"Too bad for them."

"Yes. But unfortunately, they are very powerful. You've got to nip this thing in the bud. Do you have any witnesses, anyone who could verify when and where you made your extraordinary discovery?"

"No. I found it, all by myself. Just me."

"Understood. Well, it really is remarkable what you've done. I imagine you'll go down in history, assuming they don't rewrite it on you."

"You know what? I happen to remember there was a kid there in the river, nearby. Not right there with me, you know, but he was nearby."

"That might help keep things moving, if he could corroborate your story. Do you know who this youngster is?"

"Nope. Just some random boy."

"Oh, that's too bad. He might have turned things in our favor."

"He looked like maybe he was in grade school."

"That doesn't narrow things down too much, does it? Oh well, all we've got is all we've got."

"Wait, if I remember anything else can I call you at this number?"

"Absolutely. You can call this number anytime, day or night. Or send me an email."

Clyde hung up the phone and drove back to the town square. He was watching the children play under the spray of the water cannon when Ruth caught up with him.

"Clyde, where's your accordion?"

"Hmmm? Oh, that's odd. I appear to have forgotten it." He did not turn away from the children.

"You big goober, that's the whole reason you went home in the first place." Ruth squinted. "What are you up to, anyway?"

"Nothing. Just tryin' to figure something out."

* * *

Edgar plodded up his driveway that evening.

Beth startled him when she jumped out of a chair on their tiny front porch. She ran up and hugged him. "I'm sorry I was so mean to you this morning. It's only a haircut." She pulled back to look at Edgar. "It was a really important one, but just a haircut all the same." She held him tight again.

Edgar slowly ran his hand up and down her back. "I apologize. I should have been there, and I feel bad that I missed it."

"Thanks." Beth sniffed. "You won't believe what...no, I'm not even going to tell you who said it. But when I was at Buck Mart getting groceries, someone was talking about the river being closed, and that it was all your fault."

"People will talk."

"Of course they will, I'm one of them. But it was obvious that she was speaking loudly so I could hear, and she was so wrong that I wanted to smack her. She went on and on about what a horrible thing the shutdown's going to be for the town. She kept saying, 'That Edgar Rerd this. That Edgar Rerd that…'" The words caught in Beth's throat. "I walked right over to her and told her my husband's a good man who'll look you in the eye and say what he has to say, not someone who'd pretend they're accidentally being overheard in the grocery store so they can get their pound of flesh." She wiped her eyes.

"I'm sorry that happened, that you had to go through that. What you said to her means a lot to me."

"It was hard growing up hearing people go on and on about my mother, but it's even harder now with you being the one they're talking about. I couldn't stand to hear someone say those hateful things. It's not your fault the river's shut down. I wish none of it had ever happened."

"I know. I'm trying to do everything right, to do what's best for us. I don't know."

Beth kissed Edgar. "Come on, the baby's asleep." She twined her fingers between his and took a step back, pulling him towards the house. "Let's go to bed."

The front door scraped shut and the lock clicked.

CHAPTER SEVENTEEN

The next morning Edgar's phone woke them just before six thirty. Beth groaned.

"Ugh, sorry. I forgot to turn it off." Edgar's hand flopped around on the nightstand until he located the phone. The light from the display added a bluish tint to their darkened, predawn room. "You've got to be kidding me."

"Edgar, lower your voice. You'll wake the baby. He was up three times last night."

"Strickland wants," Edgar paused. "Here, let me read this to you. 'The numbers on park visitors for the last five years in order to ascertain the potential overall future impact of human encroachment on the river.' I don't have those numbers. I don't even know how we're going to come up with them." He tossed his phone back onto the nightstand. "It's going to be another long day."

"What? You're going to work on both your days off? But the park's closed and I thought the three of us could hang out."

"I know, but I've got to do this. It could help us get the river opened up sooner."

"Let Garth look all that stuff up. He works there too, you know."

Edgar drew in a breath between his teeth. "Yeah, but I've been there way longer. I'm the one who would know how to scrounge up something like this. I want to make sure everything's right."

Beth sighed and turned her back to Edgar. "Maybe you could do it better, but Junior hasn't really even seen you in three days. Garth only has his cats to go home to."

"I'll just get a handle on how we're going to deal with those numbers. I won't be gone long." Edgar laid his hand on Beth's shoulder. "We can do something after that. I promise."

Beth kept her back to him. "Try not to wake the baby on your way out."

Edgar dressed quietly and carried his shoes out onto their front porch. The sun broke over the horizon as he tied his laces.

He walked to the park office and pulled a number of dusty boxes off the bookcase. Edgar stacked the boxes on and around the desk, and sat down to sort through papers.

Two hours later, Edgar jumped when his phone rang.

"Hey Edgar, Aaron here. Say, when you goin' to come help turn these people away? We're 'bout as busy today as we were yesterday."

Edgar grimaced. "I'm sorry, Chief, I got buried trying to figure something out to help us get the river back open. I don't know what I was thinking. Of course we're still going to be busy at the park. I'll be right there."

He pushed the button on the radio as he walked to the park entrance. "Eggman to River Rat, you there?"

"River Rat here, as always. Someone's got to keep things from falling apart."

"You at the upstream entrance?"

"Yup, Chief Turner's covering downstream for you, again."

"I just talked with him, we're good. Let me know if you need anything. I think it's going to be another busy day. Eggman out."

"Well I'm here to tell you it's already been a busy day for a good long while now. River Rat out."

Edgar jogged over to the long line of cars at the entrance.

* * *

The sun sat low in the western sky when Edgar got home and kicked off his shoes that evening.

Beth held a spoonful of food in front of Junior's mouth. She did not look at Edgar. "Where were you? You said you were going to be home early."

"Dang it. I completely forgot about that. And I would have called, but it was crazy again today. Listen, I don't know what either of us were thinking. It was just as busy as yesterday. And it's so depressing to see all the river outfitters closed down."

"Well, your son's only another day older, but it's going on a week since he's seen much of you at all. Here," she held the spoon out for Edgar, "you feed him." She went into their bedroom and softly closed the door.

Edgar stared at the door, absently rubbing his thumb across the handle of the spoon.

Junior looked at Edgar and smiled. "Nnnn-blaaah!" Slobbery blobs of white cereal oozed down his chin.

Edgar sat down and smiled back at his son. "How's my little man, eh?" He wiped Junior's chin with a cloth then offered him another spoonful of food.

Junior grasped a red plastic ring and slapped it erratically on the tray of his high chair.

"Best keep that thing away from your mother. She might smack me with it, and I don't think I'd blame her." Edgar scooped another spoonful of the bland cereal. "Your dad is between a rock and a hard place." He paused. "And another even harder place."

Edgar's phone rang and he set the bowl of cereal on the high chair tray. He glanced at the screen before answering it. "There you are, Marlon. Where have you been hiding lately?"

"Not me, Mister. Not hiding. I've been working nonstop to find a way over our latest hurdle."

"Hurdle? The whole town is crippled by the river closing, but to you it's just a hurdle for us?"

"Oh, don't you worry, Gar." Marlon chuckled. "I'll find a way, I always do. I think I may have this nut cracked already."

"Oh yeah?" Edgar set the spoon down in the cereal bowl and leaned back in his chair. "How's that?"

"I found out the TAGO commissioners meet the second Tuesday of each month. That's next week. And, during the public comment section of that meeting we can challenge the closure of the river, get it overturned."

Junior whacked his dish with the red ring and slopped food all over his hands and arms. The bowl clattered onto the floor and came to rest in a glistening aura of cereal.

"Dah-oooh." Junior smiled and rubbed his hands on his head.

Edgar used his shoulder to hold the phone up to his ear, trying to work the gloppy food out of Junior's hair. "How likely is that? Strickland works for TAGO, remember? They'll stick with whatever he says, I would think."

"Nope. Happens all the time. See, you don't waste time with a little worker bee like Mr. Samuel. You go up the ladder, over his head, that's where these things are really decided."

"If you say so. I guess we'll find out."

* * *

On the evening before the TAGO meeting, Edgar walked over to the Ezell's home. A gym bag hung over his shoulder and bounced against his back with each step.

He stood on the porch and rang the bell. Faint voices came from inside the house but no one answered the door. Edgar reached out to push the button again but paused when the shouting voice of Linda, Marlon's mother, came through loud and clear.

"I know you're just pretending, acting the way you think a real man is supposed to act." She drawled out "real man" into "ree-yull may-yunn."

Ward's reply was muffled.

The sound of footsteps came from behind the closed door. Edgar looked at the bell again, then over towards his car, then at the bay windows on the front of the house. When he lifted his foot the porch boards creaked. He eased his foot back down and stood still.

Marlon's voice sounded close to the door. "Why did you even come over? What did you expect?"

"I expected to fight for my marriage." Linda no longer shouted but still sounded agitated. "I'm afraid it's only a matter of time, unless he makes some changes."

Marlon groaned. "I don't know what's weirder, that he's bragging about cheating on you, or that you don't believe him. You two are gonna make my head melt."

"Like I just told him, it's the way he thinks a real man should act. But Trudy has been coming over several times a week doing housework. She knows her business, and she's never seen any sign that any woman has been here. He's living in his own dream world, but it's going to get real lonely for him. They say love is blind, but marriage is a real eye-opener and I've had mine open for some time now. There's still a chance for our marriage, but that chance won't last forever."

After a pause Marlon continued. "Pretending to cheat is even more pathetic than him actually doing it. I gotta go."

Edgar quickly poked his finger at the doorbell, missed, then jabbed at the button furiously as the sound of footsteps drew closer. He succeeded in hitting the button three times before he stopped.

Marlon opened the door and looked at his friend for a moment.

Linda came up behind Marlon. "Hello, Edgar." Her smile appeared tight.

"Yes, Edgar. Great timing, let's hit the road. Catch you later, Mom."

Marlon grabbed his bag and both men got into the old black BMW.

Linda walked by the car on her way down the driveway. "You boys have a good trip."

Marlon drove away, patting the dash of his car. "Ah, I love getting the old girl out on the road again. Plus it'll be good to get away for a night."

Edgar turned his head quickly and looked at Marlon. "Oh yeah? Why's that?"

Marlon fiddled around with the car stereo before he replied. "You know, just something different. Haven't been to Austin in forever."

"I can't say I'm all that excited to go. Beth's not real happy about it."

Marlon didn't say anything.

"I told her we had to stay the night so we could be there for the meeting first thing in the morning. She still doesn't like it though."

"With the traffic in Austin we'd have to leave at like five in the morning and that's no good at all. I've got to be fresh for this little shindig." Marlon smiled and smoothed back his hair.

After a pause, Edgar continued. "This is all taking up so much of my time. Who would've thought we'd be so busy while the park is closed. And it's such a beating trying to come up with those attendance numbers Strickland asked for."

"You make everything so complicated. He wants numbers? Give him some numbers. How about twenty-seven, fifty-one, and one thousand nine? There, all done."

"I can't just make stuff up." Edgar frowned.

Marlon held his fingers like a hand puppet and moved his thumb as if it were the mouth. "Blah blah blah. That all sounds very boring."

"It's a big deal." Edgar rubbed his temples. "They'll want documentation, of course."

Another pause followed.

Edgar took a deep breath. "All of this is stressing me out. So many shops in town are already hurting for business. I'm afraid it's only going to get worse."

Marlon gave no response.

"You know my dad's worked with TAGO over the years. Or worked against, he'd probably say." Edgar shook his head. "He didn't think going to their meeting tomorrow would get us anywhere."

Marlon's half smile slid up his face. "Ah, no offense to your old man, but I've rolled through many a meeting like this before, Gar. Just watch and learn. It'll be great."

* * *

The two men arrived outside the chambers of the TAGO commissioners at eight o'clock sharp the following morning.

The sergeant at arms requested their cell phones before they entered. "Agency meeting rules. If you want to go in there, your phone stays out here." He pointed to the sign above the door that read "Absolutely No Cell Phones Permitted in the Chambers of the Texas Agency for the Great Outdoors."

Marlon smiled. "No need, my good man. We'll set them to mute."

The man did not return Marlon's smile. "Everyone says that. The commissioners got tired of the ongoing distraction and banned them from the meetings."

Marlon scowled. "I may miss some extremely important communications."

The sergeant at arms did not flinch. "You can come back outside the chambers and check them whenever you like."

"Draconian," Marlon muttered and set his phone on the padded tray.

The sergeant at arms applied a sticker to the phone and gave Marlon a token with a number matching the sticker.

Edgar set his phone down as well and pocketed his token.

"Thank you, gentlemen." The sergeant at arms pointed towards the entrance to the chamber. "Agendas are on the table to your left, just past the door."

Inside the chamber, dark oak paneling went from floor to ceiling and the thick burgundy carpet muffled Marlon's and Edgar's footsteps. Black leather executive chairs sat behind a curved dais along the far side of the room. The TAGO seal hung on the wall behind the dais, flanked by the flags of Texas and the United States.

Edgar and Marlon were the first people in the room. They sat down and waited for the meeting to start. Marlon sorted through papers in his briefcase and Edgar squinted at the shiny brass nameplates on the dais, trying to read the names of the commissioners. About a dozen people came and took their seats in the audience during the next half hour.

At eight thirty, right on schedule, the commissioners filed into the chamber and sat down. The chairperson, Dr. Wainwright, adjusted the microphone in front of her and called the meeting to order.

Edgar read through the agenda. The discussion for item one, "Monthly Enforcement Report," went on for forty minutes.

Marlon leaned towards Edgar. "We've got to sit through all this because there's no telling when they'll get to public comment. If we're not here when they do, we're toast and have to wait another month, if that makes sense."

Edgar let his jaw hang open and halfway closed his left eyelid. He stared cross-eyed in the vicinity of Marlon's ear. "Uhhh, that's pretty komplikated, but I guess I kin foller all that there fancy talk of yers."

"Cool." Marlon glanced at his watch. "I'm gonna go check my phone. Come get me if anything happens."

Item two, "Consideration of Revision to the Texas Agency for the Great Outdoors *Field Agents' Manual Labor Operations Manual*, as directed by the Gender Neutrality Commission," took a bit longer. The commissioners had trouble getting past the new title, *Personnel Physical Exertions Operations Suggestions*. After an hour and a half they tabled item two.

Marlon rejoined the proceedings for a few minutes then ducked back out to the lobby to reunite with his phone.

Item three, "Discussion of Public Awareness Campaign Regarding Air Quality Issues in Texas," produced such a firestorm that contentious debate flowed freely until they broke for lunch at eleven thirty. The conflict regarding item three continued at twelve thirty when the meeting reconvened.

Marlon checked his watch at one fifteen. "You know what they're really arguing about? They all want to be in charge so they can put themselves in the commercials for the campaign. Everyone wants to star in their own movie. I'll be right back."

At three o'clock they were only on item four, "Waste Permits Prioritization Issues – Sewage Treatment vs. Radioactive Materials."

Marlon fidgeted constantly, his knee bouncing. "This is insane," he hissed. "They should use these meetings instead of waterboarding. Gonna check my phone."

"Seven." Edgar spoke in a low voice.

Marlon stopped. "What?"

"You've checked your phone seven times now. Not that I care, but counting your excursions gives me something to do."

Marlon came back twenty minutes later. He took the last bite of a granola bar then crinkled up the noisy wrapper and stuck it in his pocket.

Edgar leaned towards him. "Dude, I'm starving. Did you bring me one of those?"

"Huh? Oh yeah, there's tons of them out there in the machine." Marlon nodded towards the door. "Go help yourself."

At four thirty the chairperson rapped her gavel. "The Commission will now receive comments from the public on any matters within the jurisdiction of TAGO. In the interest of time, speakers will be limited to three minutes. Action items will not be taken during this discussion-only session."

Marlon jumped up and walked over to the microphone provided for audience members to speak at the meeting.

The chairperson watched Marlon. "For the record, please state your name and the nature of your comment."

"Yes, hello everyone. Marlon Ezell, from Paxon Chute."

The Agency members seemed to perk at the mention of the small town.

"I am here today to request the rescinding of a prohibition on the use of the Cobb River. I think everyone here would agree with me—"

The chairperson cut him off. "One moment please, Mr. Ezell. You are proposing an action item during the discussion session. Did you not understand the ground rules I just explained?"

"Oh, yes. Of course. I wanted to discuss that, at this time."

Dr. Wainwright stared at Marlon over her glasses for a moment before continuing. "Then we can discuss your matter in order to help you understand the proper procedures, which you can then pursue at your discretion. Now, what is your basis for the item we are discussing?"

"Well, the whole reason it's shut down is because someone supposedly, allegedly, found an endangered salamander in the river. There has been no following discovery that supports this claim and the impact on the town has been tremendous. I am personally overwhelmed by the hardship my good friends and neighbors—"

Dr. Wainwright interrupted again. "We are well aware of the situation in Paxon Chute and are sensitive to the effect this discovery has had on the community. We are trying to move forward as quickly as possible with our investigation. Have you brought your concerns up with our field agent working on the investigation? That would be Mr. Strickland Samuel."

"Yes, of course, and I am in no way trying to paint Mr. Samuel in a bad light. I just don't know if he fully appreciates the economic impact, the revenues that are being lost during this critical peak tourist time of year. I'm certain everyone here can appreciate the importance of generating tax revenue so we can all continue—"

Dr. Wainwright removed her glasses and set them down on the dais. "What everyone in the Agency can appreciate is the need for cooperation from the community so we can move forward. In Mr. Samuel's latest daily report he noted that he is still waiting for information regarding the level of human interaction in the river. Has this information been provided to Mr. Samuel?"

Marlon turned to Edgar, whose face glistened with sweat. Edgar shook his head.

"Not exactly, but—"

"Mr. Ezell, I do not understand why you have come here trying to do an end run on Mr. Samuel when his most reasonable request for required information has not yet been accommodated. You would have been better served exerting your efforts to produce the information we have requested. Your three minutes are up." She banged the gavel. "Next."

* * *

Marlon drove them back to Paxon Chute that evening after the TAGO meeting. Neither man spoke much. The phone in Edgar's shirt pocket beeped and he pulled it out to read the message.

"Beth says Junior is asleep, so just drop me off at the end of my street."

Edgar took his shoes off on the front porch and quietly entered the house. He found Beth reading in their bed with her back propped up against the headboard.

She set down her book and looked at Edgar. "So that was a big bust, huh?"

"Yup. I'm so mad at Marlon, thinking he could just stroll in there and do whatever." Edgar sat on the edge of the bed next to Beth. "But he was so sure. Now he's mad at me, saying it's my fault because I haven't gotten that stuff over to TAGO."

"Edgar, I'm sorry Marlon took you on a total time-waster trip. But I have to ask, why is it you don't have those numbers yet?"

"There's more to it than that and if you're not there working with the stuff it's difficult to explain."

After a pause Beth asked, "Can you try? To help me understand."

Edgar sighed. "There's gaps in the information over several periods of time because some of the boxes are missing. There's no details for most of the receipts we do have, they only show the total. How do I know how many people were there without the details? There's different admission prices for adults and children and different prices for weekdays, weekends, and holidays. It's harder than you think and working all the possible calculations trying to figure out each one is absolutely mind-numbing."

"All the more reason you should let someone help you."

"I told you I know all this stuff way better than Garth."

Beth frowned. "There are plenty of other people on the planet besides Garth. I'm not just a pretty face, I'm an accountant, remember? I deal with numbers, that's my strength. My dad, he's an auditor, he knows how to work these kinds of things. And you said you're doing manual calculations on each transaction? I can probably write a function that will figure it all out for you."

"But this isn't in a computer. It's boxes and boxes and boxes of receipts."

"Even if we have to key the numbers in, that's less work than what you're doing now, running calculations over and over trying to figure each one out."

Edgar stared at his feet. "That makes sense. I guess I didn't think it through too well, just thrashing, trying to get it done."

"I know." Beth took his hand in hers. "We're a team, and I think I can help you with this."

"Deal. I'll show you the stuff tomorrow." Edgar's phone rang and he answered it. "Hey Dad, what's up?"

"How'd it go?"

"It was a typical Marlon venture."

Clyde laughed. "That bad, huh?"

"You don't sound surprised."

"Well, Marlon does tend to be all thrust and no vector." Clyde paused. "TAGO's not likely to work with you when you've not yet done their bidding."

"Oh yeah, they made that perfectly clear, even to Marlon. Beth and I were just talking though, and I think she can help get me out of the weeds and get that stuff over to them."

"That's a good start, son. Make sure you get that done, and I'd recommend doing a little bit more."

Edgar lay down on the bed. "What do you mean?"

"Tell TAGO you want to educate the folks around here about the salamanders and the risks they face."

"That sounds slightly odd to me."

"It's a big river and it's impossible to police all of it all the time. You're a park ranger, you know that better than anyone."

"Oh my gosh." Edgar scratched his head. "Yeah, no doubt about that."

"Things will go better for us if we cooperate and do all we can to make sure everyone stays out of the river until TAGO reopens it. We've really got to focus on the youngsters. They're the most likely to sneak in and cause a big ruckus."

"And you think that will help?"

"I don't believe those salamanders are in our river, but I can't say why just yet. But you won't get anywhere fighting with Strickland about whether they're in there or not. He's always expecting a big tug-of-war with everyone about everything. So don't fight him. The easiest way to knock him off balance is to let go of your end of the rope."

CHAPTER EIGHTEEN

Two weeks later Edgar was sitting in his living room when his father called. "Hey, Dad."

"Howdy. What's Strickland's mood like lately?"

"Better than most everyone in town. A bunch of the river outfitters are hanging out in front of the park office. Bruger just sits there staring at me, smoking like a chimney."

"They're stressed out, being shut down and all." Clyde paused. "So Strickland's settled down a bit?"

"Once we got all the numbers over to him he seemed more agreeable. Now he's all fired up because we're going to promote awareness of the salamanders."

Clyde chuckled. "I thought he might be. So we're all set with the school, right?"

"Yeah, I double-checked with them this afternoon. They were pretty busy with it being the first day back, but Mr. Kopf confirmed we're on for tomorrow."

"Outstanding. I'll meet you there bright and early."

"Uh, do you have a note to remind you?"

"Don't you worry, son, I'm all over this one."

* * *

Edgar spoke with his father as they stood outside a classroom the next morning. "What grade are we on now?"

"Second. We'll keep working our way up. Now don't be afraid to lay it on real thick this time."

"What do you mean?" Edgar frowned.

"Put the fear of the law in them. That'll get their attention."

"You think?"

"Hey, it's not my first time in a classroom, you know." Clyde opened the door. "Excuse me, Mrs. Forte, is now a good time?"

Mrs. Forte stood at the chalkboard. "Yes, please come in. Class, I'm sure you all remember—"

A number of students interrupted Mrs. Forte with yells of "Mr. Clyde!"

Clyde smiled. "Hello there, hope for tomorrow."

Mrs. Forte cleared her throat and smoothed out the front of her dress with her plump hands. "Yes, Mr. Rerd has been a substitute teacher for us before, hasn't he?"

A sandy-haired boy in the back laughed. "Oh yeah. He's the best."

The boy next to him raised his hand. "Mr. Clyde, didja bring the possum with you again?"

"Oh good gracious me." Mrs. Forte muttered. She shook her head vigorously and her face turned red. "No no no no, Javier! We discussed that incident at length. And remember," her gaze swept across the classroom, "the school board made a new rule after what happened the last time." She turned towards Edgar. "Today we have two Mr. Rerds visiting with us. You all probably recognize the younger Mr. Rerd from the park. Welcome, gentlemen, and please proceed."

"Uh, good morning, everyone." Edgar closed the door and walked over to Mrs. Forte's desk at the front of the room. "We're visiting with all of the classes today to make sure everyone understands the importance of what has been found in the river."

A girl with a long ponytail in the front row raised her hand. "My dad says those stupid sala-danders are just a pigment of someone's imagination and our whole town is going broke for nothing."

"Priscilla, that will do." Mrs. Forte wagged her finger at the girl. "Please proceed, Mr. Rerd."

"Yes. Okay. Well, that's what they're trying to figure out, whether or not they're really here. And until we know for sure, we have to stay out of the river. I know everyone wants it open again. I sure do. But the more we cooperate the sooner this can all be over."

Clyde cleared his throat and raised his eyebrows.

Edgar took a deep breath. "Because these salamanders are endangered, it would be really, really bad if you interfered with them by getting into the river."

"That's right, ladies and gentlemen." Clyde watched the children as he spoke. "Now we know for sure that these salamanders do exist over in Barton Springs. Some people may not be aware that it's illegal to take them home with you. I'm sure nobody wants to get arrested and go to jail over one little old salamander."

Javier stared at Clyde, his eyes wide.

Clyde turned quickly to the teacher. "Could we speak with you in the hall, Mrs. Forte?"

She looked at Clyde for a moment then addressed the class. "Everyone get out your *Penny and Jimmy* books and start reading our story for today, "Jimmy Finds a Bunny." I'll be right on the other side of the door."

The three adults went into the hall.

Clyde held up his hand and spoke in a quiet voice. "Now this might sound a bit odd, but we'd like to speak with young Javier for a moment."

"We would?" Edgar frowned.

Mrs. Forte glanced back and forth between the two men,

tapping her fingers on her chin. "Well, I can see that one of you wants to talk with him anyway. But whatever for?"

"I think he might be able to clear up this whole salamander fiasco for us."

"You'll have to clear it with the principal first. I've got to get back to my class, gentlemen."

Edgar turned towards Clyde as they walked to the principal's office. "What's this all about, Dad?"

"Just throwing out a net. I may have caught something."

"Why didn't you tell me what you were really up to? Between you and Marlon I never know what's going on."

"I have lots of ideas but I'm not always right. And like I said before, I didn't want to get your hopes up. But we'll find out soon enough now."

* * *

Principal Kopf sat behind the desk in his office. Edgar and Clyde sat on either side of young Javier, facing the desk.

Clyde offered the boy some licorice. Javier shook his head and stared at the floor, his lower lip trembling occasionally.

"Now, Javier," Clyde laid his hand on the boy's shoulder, "you're not in any trouble. All we're trying to do is uncover the truth about the salamander, and I think you can help us."

The boy shrugged his shoulders.

"Let me tell you what I think, and you can tell me if I'm wrong. I think gum-smackin' Nathan stole your salamander. Did he?"

"I don't have one."

"Did you borrow one from Barton Springs?"

Javier cried as the words quickly spilled out of him. "I didn't know I wasn't s'posed to take her. We went there and I found one under a rock and she was so awesome and I wanted to keep her and I took her home in my water cup."

"And she died, didn't she?" Clyde spoke quietly.

Javier wiped his nose with the back of his hand then slowly nodded.

"I'm sure you didn't know, but those salamanders need just the right amount of oxygen in their water, or they won't survive."

"I named her Sally."

Clyde leaned in a little closer to the boy. "That's a fine name."

"I thought she was sick and needed to go home. But I couldn't get her home so I took her to our river but she didn't get no better. Then that man saw me."

"The man wearing black leather gloves, and chompin' on gum?" Clyde worked his jaw on an imaginary piece of gum.

"Yeah. He was lookin' for treasure. He said, 'What are you doing?' and he said I done a bad, bad thing and he took Sally from me. He said if anyone asked me just tell them he was the one who finded her in the river. He said he'd take the blame for me."

"I bet he did. I bet he did." Clyde exchanged glances with Edgar and Principal Kopf.

Javier wailed, "I done a bad thing and she died and now I'm gonna go to jail!"

"Now now, easy there, son." Clyde knelt down beside Javier. "I can tell you really care about critters. If I remember right it was you who wanted to set the possum loose because he looked so sad, hissing and gnawing on the bars of his cage. I bet you'll be a park ranger yourself someday."

Edgar smiled. "Oh yeah, I can totally see that. You'd be great, Javier."

Javier took a deep breath and tried to suppress the little smile that crept across his face.

Principal Kopf clasped his hands and set them on the desk. "I'm very proud of you, Javier. You've done a brave thing today."

"Yes indeed. A brave young man. Now," Clyde held up his

finger, "all we need is for you to tell what happened to one other person and I think we can put this all behind us. I'm going to make a quick phone call."

Clyde stepped out of the office and scrolled through the contact list on his phone. He pushed the call button and held the phone to his ear. "Strickland? This is Clyde. Listen, I accidentally discovered what's up with the whole salamander thing over here. I think you'll agree it all makes sense when you hear it. But there's one thing. It involves a young boy who made a mistake, and we need to protect him in this. He had no idea he was doing anything wrong, then he got bullied and manipulated by that cheesy, fame-grabbing treasure hunter."

Strickland's voice sounded tight. "Why does that not surprise me."

* * *

The next day Edgar and Beth sat on their sofa. Junior giggled as Edgar bounced him on his knee. "It's one meeting, for one afternoon. Strickland got us on the agenda for the Waterway Impact Assessment session tomorrow. He and Dad were able to work out some understanding. Turns out they don't really hate each other, they just like to argue. Although it still seems like Dad doesn't trust him completely. Anyway, it's a big deal, Strickland doing that for us. I can't not show up after he's gone out of his way to help us. But even more importantly, we should be able to get the river open, and approval for the cofferdam. This is huge, Beth. I have to go."

"I know it's a big deal." Beth sighed. "But I thought we'd see more of you with school back but now you're going off somewhere again."

"It's an afternoon meeting so I won't have to stay overnight again. I do have to drive this time, Marlon said it's my turn. But I'm taking my dad's truck, so you'll still have the car. I'll go to Austin tomorrow morning and be back in the evening. Then I'll be done with all this TAGO stuff."

Beth frowned. "Oh all right. I guess I'm getting used to you being gone, and I don't think I like that, or it seems like I shouldn't like it. I'm just tired of all this."

"I know, me too. But, like I said, this is the last meeting. I promise."

* * *

The next afternoon Edgar and Marlon sat in the TAGO chambers again as the hours ticked away. They were the last item on the agenda.

At five thirty Dr. Wainwright closed the current item and looked over the agenda. "We will break at this point for the evening and reconvene at eight thirty tomorrow morning." She banged her gavel and the TAGO commissioners pushed their chairs back, stood up, and left the chambers.

Edgar collapsed back into his seat. "Great."

"Buck up, little camper." Marlon patted him on the head. "We'll be rolling along tomorrow."

Edgar and Marlon walked out and collected their phones from the sergeant at arms.

Edgar pushed the redial button on his phone. "Beth, ah, glad you're there this time. Listen, we've been waiting around all afternoon and they didn't even get to our item yet. I have to be back first thing in the morning, and I won't have time to drive over from Paxon Chute. I'm afraid I'm going to have to stay overnight, but then I should be back home early tomorrow afternoon."

"How can you know that? They might not get to you tomorrow, either." Beth's voice sounded flat.

"I'm sure they will. We're coming up real quick on the agenda."

"I miss you. Junior misses you. Plus, I think he's cutting a tooth, he's been real cranky all day. I'm beat. I really need a break, Edgar."

"I'm doing everything I can. I'll get this over as soon as possible and then I'll be back there to help you with whatever you need."

"He's crying again." She sighed. "I gotta go. Love you."

* * *

Beth hung up. She looked at the kitchen counter where Edgar's park ranger gear lay in a jumble. "I've told him a million times not to leave this stuff here." With a quick motion of her hand she swept it all into the trash can.

She picked up the crying baby and walked around the living room, patting him on the back. Her phone rang and she checked the caller ID before answering. "Hello, Dad."

"Hello, sweetie." Clyde's voice came through loud and clear. "Whoa there, I can hear someone's not happy. What's wrong with the little feller?"

"I think he's cutting a tooth. He's been fussing all day."

"Well now, it seems like he needs some Paw-Paw time, and you sound like you could use a break. Where's Edgar?"

"TAGO didn't get to their item, and now he's stuck in Austin overnight."

"Ah, the wheels of justice are so easily encumbered by the wagging of tongues. I'll be there in a few minutes to rest you a spell."

Clyde rang the doorbell not long afterwards. As soon as Beth opened the door Shimei bolted into the house and went straight over to where Junior lay on the floor. The baby smiled and giggled when he saw the dog.

Clyde laughed. "I thought old Shimmy would cheer him up."

Beth grabbed her keys. "Let's get the baby carrier out of my car, in case you need to go somewhere."

It took them a while to figure out how to lock the seat belt in Clyde's car. Once they had the carrier secured, Beth led the way back to the house.

"Ack!" she yelled when she had gone through the door. "The dog knocked over the trash." She looked at Junior. "And he's brought a bunch of garbage over for Junior to play with."

"Oh dear, I'm so sorry." Clyde followed her into the house. "I'll take care of this mess."

Beth quickly picked Junior up from his ring of trash. Shimei wagged his tail and barked, his long black doggy snout covered in orange cheese ball dust.

Beth looked at Junior. "What have you got in your mouth?" She pressed down on his chin then stuck her finger in his mouth and swept it all around. "I can't find anything but I could have sworn he was chewing on something. Let's see if we can figure out what it might have been." Her eyes darted around the spilled garbage.

Clyde got down on his hands and knees. "There's a park ranger flashlight, and radio. They're all covered in coffee grounds. And look, Junior's got Edgar's name badge in his pudgy little fist."

"That's weird." Beth's face reddened. "I wonder how all that stuff wound up in the trash."

"Do you, now? That is most peculiar, isn't it?"

Beth did not look up. She pried the name badge away from Junior and tossed it onto the counter. "Well, I don't see anything particularly scary in there." Beth sighed. "I'm torn between going over to the café to see Abbie or just staying home and taking a nap."

"You know Abbie and her pies have great rejuvenating powers." Clyde ushered her towards the door. "Go on, let someone wait on you for a bit. We'll be fine."

"Thanks, Dad." Beth kissed Clyde on the cheek. "Call me and let me know if you need anything. I won't be gone long."

Two hours later Beth returned to a dog-trampled house and an unhappy baby.

Clyde smiled at her. "We've been playing fetch with Shimmy. Junior's been a little grumpy, but not too bad."

Later that evening Junior lost all interest in teething rings and would not stop crying. The numbing gel brought him no relief either.

Beth called Ruth. "I don't know, he's so fussy all of the sudden. I thought it was a tooth, or at least that's what the nurse said this morning. But he's acting different now, like something else is bothering him. I'm worried because he got into the trash earlier."

Ruth groaned. "Or had it delivered by that fool of a dog. I heard all about that."

"Well, if he's not better in the morning, I'll take him to the doctor."

"Call me if you need anything."

Junior kept Beth up most of the night. As dawn broke, mother and son finally fell asleep, but the baby woke up crying just after eight o'clock.

Beth called Edgar. "There's something wrong with our baby."

"What? Oh no, what's the matter with him?"

"He hardly slept all night. I thought it was a tooth, but now I don't know. There's definitely something wrong with him."

"Oh man. Well, we're going into the meeting right now so I should be headed back that way real soon."

"Edgar Allan Rerd! Our baby is sick and I've been up all night. I need you."

"It won't take long, really, but I have to get in there right now or I might miss our item."

"So you're not coming home now?"

"How much difference would it make at this point even if I did leave—"

Beth hung up on Edgar.

* * *

Edgar stood at the door of the TAGO chambers for a moment then finally set his phone down in front of the sergeant at arms and walked into the room.

The meeting dragged on for several hours while the commissioners discussed the next to the last item on the agenda, "Zebra Mussel Infestation."

Marlon leaned over to the woman sitting next to him. "What's the big deal, anyway? Live and let live, I say."

The woman turned and glared at Marlon. "They've only been here a few years and have already cost us hundreds of millions of dollars. I'd say that's worth our time to discuss."

Marlon raised his eyebrows and settled back into his chair.

Edgar looked at the clock on the wall. "I'd go check in with Beth, but I know they're going to get to our item any minute now."

As noon approached, Dr. Wainwright banged her gavel. "We only have one item remaining on the agenda. If there are no objections let's press on so we can close out this session."

Dr. Wainwright flipped through some papers. "This item concerns the discovery of a Barton Springs salamander in the Cobb River. I received Mr. Strickland's latest report, which was a last-minute submission for this session. Have all the commissioners had time to review the report?"

They all nodded.

"This seems very cut and dried to me. I see no evidence that this was anything other than the innocent mistake of a young child. A mistake that was then seized upon for shameless self-promotion by an opportunistic man. Are there any objections to closing out this investigation, and allowing the resumption of regular activities in the Cobb River?"

No objections were raised.

"Then this investigation is closed."

"Yesssss," Edgar whispered.

Marlon did a fist pump. "Boo-yah!"

Dr. Wainwright stared at Marlon until he settled down. She flipped over another sheet of paper. "Related to that investigation, we have the request for a cofferdam in the Cobb River. The impact-assessment study can now proceed. When that study has been completed we will rule on the cofferdam permit request."

"What?" Marlon stood up. "Wait!"

Dr. Wainwright banged her gavel. "That concludes this Waterway Impact Assessment session."

Marlon's face turned red. "This is ridiculous."

"Aw, come on Marlon, one step at a time, eh?" Edgar stood up. "At least the river is back open again. That's a huge relief, anyway. Ooh, I better call and see how Junior is doing." He hurried out of the chambers.

When he retrieved his phone from the sergeant at arms there were thirteen new text messages from Beth.

> 8:07 a.m.   Dr office still thinks it's tooth. Dunno bout that.
>
> 8:31 a.m.   He's getting worse. Taking him to Dr. right now.
>
> 9:16 a.m.   Told Dr about Junior getting into trash, she still thinks it's a tooth.

"Trash?" Edgar took a deep breath and kept reading.

> 9:22 a.m.   He won't stop crying.

9:25 a.m.   I asked Dr to take xray just in case.

9:40 a.m.   They're sending us to hospital for xray. Scared. Pls call.

10:33 a.m.   Waiting at hospital, arrrgh! He's crying constantly.

11:01 a.m.   They're taking x-rays.

11:09 a.m.   He swallowed those tiny magnets off your name badge!

11:18 a.m.   Waiting for Dr. again. They said those super strong magnets can be fatal if they're in different parts of intestine. I'm freaking out!

11:29 a.m.   Emergency surgery! Where are you?

11:32 a.m.   Can't do surgery here, or in Peyton either.

11:35 a.m.   Careflight to specialist in San Antonio. Where are you???

Edgar's face went pale. He opened the last text message.

11:44 a.m.   This is from your father. I know they won't let you have your phone there. Tried to get a message to you but can't get through to anyone at TAGO. I'm sending Garth over to get word to you. Don't worry, we're with Beth and praying for Junior.

Edgar ran down the hall and yelled over his shoulder at Marlon, "My son is having emergency surgery. Garth is coming here so he can give you a ride back."

He called Beth as he drove through Austin but she did not answer. Merging onto the interstate towards San Antonio he pressed the accelerator to the floorboard. The speedometer fluttered around ninety.

CHAPTER NINETEEN

Edgar rushed through the door to the surgery waiting area, trying to catch his breath.

"Where have you been?" Beth shouted at Edgar then ran over to him. She pulled him into her arms and started to cry. "I'm so scared and I had to sign these horrible forms about how he might die. I kept trying to call you."

"I'm so sorry." Edgar spoke quietly in her ear. "My battery gave out on the way here and I couldn't find the charger."

Beth sobbed on his shoulder. "It's all my fault!"

"What do you mean?"

Clyde got up from his seat next to Ruth and walked over to them. He looked ten years older than he did the day before. "It's okay, Beth." He laid his hand on her shoulder. "We all agreed you're not to blame, remember?"

Beth took a deep breath. "I know."

"How's he doing? Where is he?" Edgar's eyes darted around the room.

"Still in surgery." Clyde pointed to the doors at the back of the waiting room.

Penelope Anne sat bolt upright near the doors and stared at Edgar, mascara smeared down her face and her lips compressed. Richard slouched in the chair beside her, his head resting on his hand.

A doctor came through the back doors and motioned for

the family to join him at one of the circular tables. He shook hands with Edgar. "We've not met, I'm Dr. Jimenez. So we're all done. He's in recovery and doing great. We were able to scope him and use a Roth net to remove both the magnets."

Beth reached out for Edgar's hand and a tear rolled down her cheek.

The doctor continued. "Everything looks good and there doesn't appear to be any damage."

"What a relief." Ruth dabbed at her eyes with a tissue and gave Beth a hug.

Dr. Jimenez pulled the surgical cap off his head. "It's an interesting case. It's likely all the changes in behavior you noticed were caused by that tooth coming in. There's usually no symptoms for a day or two when magnets like this are ingested. We caught it at the earliest stage because your instincts were right about him swallowing something."

"I don't understand." Edgar frowned. "What kind of damage could have been done?"

The doctor nodded. "Good question. When these rare earth magnets are swallowed, the magnetic attraction can pin the bowel walls together and result in a blockage or tearing, which can be life-threatening."

"Oh my goodness," Penelope Anne held up her hand, "none of that happened so let's not talk about all that. Please."

"Uh, so she's right," Edgar gestured towards Penelope Ann, "he didn't have any of that?"

"Nothing that I can see. The magnets never separated, they were still stuck together and had not even moved out of the stomach. If we hadn't gone in to get them, he might have passed them without any issue. But that's not a risk we take once we know they're in there."

"How long for him to heal? Does he have stitches?" Edgar laid his hand on his stomach.

"Oh no, there's no incision because we didn't have to do

surgery. We inserted an endoscopic camera down the throat and into the stomach. It's a very low-risk procedure. He's only in recovery because of the sedation. If everything continues to look good today and through the night we can discharge him tomorrow, which is what I'm expecting."

"This is such wonderful news." Ruth pulled her phone out of her purse. "I'm going to call Mavis and she can pass it along. There's lots of folks praying for Junior."

The doctor allowed them to visit Junior in the recovery room two at a time. Beth and Edgar were led to a small hospital bed where their baby lay on his back.

"Ooh, there's my baby." Beth kissed him on the forehead. Several of her tears fell onto Junior's face, and she wiped them away.

Edgar, fingers shaking, took his son's hand and gently squeezed it. "That's my little man. You hang in there, okay?" Edgar hooked the leg of a chair with his foot and pulled it closer. He sat down and rested his head on the rail of the hospital bed, still holding their baby's tiny hand.

Junior slowly looked back and forth between his parents. A faint smile appeared on his face before his eyes closed.

Beth sat in a chair on the other side of the bed. She stroked his cheek with the back of her hand. "He's a little sluggish but other than that he looks good."

Edgar and Beth both said a prayer over their son. Afterwards they were silent for several minutes.

Edgar stood up. "I'm going to let someone else come back and see him, but you go ahead and stay here."

The grandparents each took a turn, and Penelope Anne went last. When Edgar returned to the recovery room, mother and daughter were talking quietly, their backs to him.

"I think it's irresponsible. Your son could have died. And where was Edgar?"

"Mother, we'll handle this ourselves." Beth spoke quickly.

"If you and the baby ever need a place to stay, you can always come back home."

"Thank you, Mother, but no. No thank you. That won't be necessary. Or helpful."

Edgar stood right behind the women. "How is he?" His voice startled them both.

Penelope Anne sniffed and walked around Edgar. "Well I'm glad the baby is all right. That's the most important thing, of the many things that are so very important right now."

Edgar watched his mother-in-law walk out the door, then turned to Beth. "What was that all about?"

"Just Mother being Mother."

Edgar looked back towards the door. "Hmm. That's what I thought."

"She's always suggesting things I'd never do." Beth stared blankly at Junior's bed.

* * *

Late the next afternoon Edgar drove his family back towards Paxon Chute. Silence enveloped the car as Beth and Junior slept most of the way. At the edge of town Edgar's phone beeped and woke up Beth.

"That's a text, would you see who it's from?" Edgar handed his phone to Beth.

She rubbed her eyes. "It's from Orville."

"Ah, that's really nice of the mayor to check on us. What does he say?"

"How do you open a message on your phone? Oh, there it is. Okay, he says, 'Got the good news about Junior, so relieved for you and your family. And you all sure do move fast, getting ready in the river.'"

Edgar leaned over so he could see the phone. "Ready for what?"

Beth pointed his chin back towards the windshield. "Eyes forward, Mister. I don't know. That's all he says."

"Oh, I forgot all about the TAGO meeting. I haven't even told anyone. Marlon must have gone back and shared the good news. I bet Garth's got everything organized and has the park open again. What a relief to have people you can count on when you need them."

They turned onto Station Street and Edgar slammed on the brakes. The car skidded to a stop.

"Edgar! Be careful." Beth twisted around in her seat to check on Junior. "What's wrong with you?"

"Oh. My. Gosh."

"What?"

"Look at the river."

Beth's eyes followed Edgar's pointing finger.

Giant blue tubes formed a perimeter around Nickel Rock. The flowing river caused minor undulations to pulse through the tubes. No water was visible inside the structure that surrounded Nickel Rock.

"Gah! What is that?" Beth frowned.

"That is a cofferdam. Marlon's gone ahead and put it up without a permit." Edgar thumped his head on the steering wheel. "I am so fired."

They drove home and Beth carried the sleeping Junior to his crib.

Edgar sat on the couch, his hands shaking. "What was I thinking, that Marlon would actually be doing something to help me out and get the river back open? But I never imagined he'd pull something like this."

Beth stood by the kitchen. "It is pretty unbelievable, even for him."

"I've got to find out what's going on."

"Seriously?"

"I'm seriously going to lose my job. So yes, I have to go

over there and see if there's any way I can salvage our only means of economic survival."

"Why would you lose your job over something Marlon did?"

"Because I'm the head park ranger and it's my responsibility, what we're doing in the park, or what we're supposed to be doing."

"Well okay then. I'll just stay here and keep continuous watch over our son who is recovering from yesterday's near-death experience, which I handled all by myself, thank you very much, while you were out tending to the latest thing that was more important to you than your family."

"Beth, that's not fair."

"Fair? Fair is where pigs win ribbons. This is life, Edgar. I suggest you join us."

"But he's sleeping right now anyway."

"I need to sleep but someone has to watch the baby for the next couple of hours. The doctor said so."

"I'll be right back, and then you can sleep all night."

Beth put her hands on her hips. "I've had about enough of this, Edgar."

"I swear I won't be gone long."

Edgar went out the door and walked to the park. Several of the barflies stood outside The Snorting Bull.

"Hey, Edgar! Edgar!" Uncle Drew waved his arms wildly. "Over here."

"Yes, I see you." Edgar shouted back across the square. "I'm already looking right at you and walking in your direction."

Edgar stepped up onto the sidewalk and joined the group of men.

"I'm so glad Junior's okay." Wilbur whistled through his teeth.

"Absolutely." "Oh yes." Tom and Drew agreed.

"Thanks, guys." Edgar shook hands with each of the men.

Drew bobbed his head. "Didja see, Edgar? They put up the coffee dam."

"Kinda hard to miss something like that, isn't it, Uncle Drew?"

Tom laughed. "Even harder to miss with your uncle around to point it out for you."

Drew's head kept bobbing. "They were real fast with it, too. They had it up early this morning before anyone really knew it was happening."

Edgar turned towards the parking lot for Nickel Rock Park. "I don't see any cars. So the park didn't open today?"

"Of course not, TAGO's got it shut down, remember? I thought you'd know that better than anyone." Drew laughed at Tom. "See, Mister Smarty Pants, he does need me to point these things out after all."

"Obviously I know that, it's just that something's come up and I didn't know if..." Edgar paused. "Never mind, I'll explain later. I've got to go check this out, guys."

Edgar walked towards the river. He saw Marlon's car in the far corner of the parking lot but there was no sign of anyone around the cofferdam.

Edgar unlocked one of the small wooden ferries along the riverbank and stepped onto it. He pulled on the rope anchored from the riverbank over to Nickel Rock and the flat-bottomed craft glided across the river until it bumped into the blue water bag of the cofferdam.

The exposed base changed the appearance of the entire structure of the park's namesake. A plank lay across the top of the cofferdam and spanned the gap to Nickel Rock. Edgar walked across it and onto the off-white limestone.

At the upstream end the cofferdam extended quite a way past the end of Nickel Rock. He peered over the edge and the reason became evident. Another massive limestone formation lay in the riverbed, nearly butted up against the base of Nickel Rock but about five feet lower.

"And there's what makes the big wave."

He dropped down onto the lower rock. Edgar pulled out his phone and took some pictures from a vantage point normally underwater. Then he called Marlon, who answered after five rings.

"Gar! Are you back yet? 'Cause I've got a big surprise for you."

"I'm staring right at your big surprise. Have you lost your mind? What do you think you're doing, Marlon? We don't have a permit."

"Permit schmer-mit. It's easier to ask for forgiveness than to get permission with this kind of thing. Right now is the best time, while the park is still closed. We'll finish it up and get out of the way without disrupting a single valued park visitor. I know how important that is. That's why I pressed on."

"Marlon, you idiot! You're going to get me fired."

"Relax, it'll all be okay. Trust me."

"Trust you? After this stunt? Where are you, anyway?"

"Got some loose ends to tidy up, should be back there most soonest. Gotta go."

"Marlon!"

But Marlon had already hung up.

Edgar climbed back up to Nickel Rock and crossed the plank over to the ferry. He pulled on the rope, muttering. "What is he thinking? No, what's he up to?" When he got back to the riverbank he snapped his fingers and pointed at Marlon's car.

The evening skies were darkening when Edgar went to the park's maintenance building and grabbed a six foot pry bar. As he approached Marlon's car, the security system's blinking red light on the dashboard caught his attention. Edgar looked around the empty parking lot. He hesitated, staring at the blinking light. The smell of burned motor oil and MAgNITUDE swirled about the car. He caught sight of the cofferdam again and scowled.

"He deserves it."

Edgar shoved the pry bar into the gap in the trunk below the keyhole. He strained at the bar but the latch would not release. Edgar slid the bar to one side of the trunk and with a mighty upwards heave that rocked the entire car, he peeled up a corner of the trunk a few inches. As the sheet metal shrieked, groaned, and finally gave way, the alarm chirped twice and went silent.

Edgar smiled. He attacked the car in a silent, sweaty-faced rage, opening the trunk lid like a can of tuna. The black paint cracked and flaked off in long slivers.

"That sure is a big key you've got there, Edgar, and it doesn't seem to fit very well."

Edgar whirled around. Tom smiled at him.

Drew shook his head. "Yeah, Edgar, what are you doing to Marlon's car? He's gonna have a fit when he sees this."

"Stand back, please, gentlemen." Edgar held his hand up. "We've got a bit of an emergency regarding that cofferdam over there. The information I need is in Marlon's trunk and he's not available."

"Emergency?" Drew's eyes widened.

Edgar peered inside the hole he'd created. "Sorry, I can't say any more than that right now." In a corner of the trunk sat the gray metal file box. Edgar imitated the way his friend's smile slid up one side of his face. "The road warrior's mobile office."

Tom laughed. "You sound just like Marlon."

Edgar snatched the box out of the car. "Excuse me, I've got some things to do." He picked up the pry bar and trotted back to his house. In the backyard he set the box on its side in the grass with the lock facing up. He stood on it and crashed the pry bar against the latch. The lid popped open.

A few seconds later Beth came out the back door. "Edgar! You scared me so bad. Quit it, or you'll wake up the baby."

Edgar set the pry bar down and picked up the mangled box. "Sorry, I didn't think about that. But I'm done, no more noise." He followed Beth into the house.

"I couldn't find out anything down at the river. It's really weird, there's no one there. I managed to get Marlon on the phone but he was evasive, as usual. However, I've got his files." Edgar sat down on the couch with the box in his lap. "I had to tear his car apart, so hopefully there's some answers in here." He pulled out a stack of manila folders.

"Okay, this is all just 'River in the Sky' propaganda, I've seen this stuff before. Town Council minutes, seen that. Sorrentino and Sons Investments, that's where my paycheck came from. This looks like a bunch of contract stuff, maybe you could read through it?" He held the folder out towards Beth.

She leaned against the wall, arms folded. "I don't feel right about this, and even if I did, I'm too tired right now."

Edgar shrugged and stuck the file back in the box. "Okay, maybe later. Wow! What's this?" He pulled out another file and opened it. "It's a printout of an old newspaper. *The Daily Graphic*, dated March 22, 1883. It's the obituary for Molly Hardwick Paxon."

"Really?" Beth came and sat down next to Edgar. "She was George Paxon's wife, right?"

"Yup. I've never seen this before. Check out the photo. The caption says, 'Molly Hardwick partaking of the view from Ship Rock, located along the Texas river where she lived.' Someone's circled 'Ship Rock' and written 'idiots.'"

Beth pointed. "That's Marlon's handwriting."

In the photo a woman sat on a stool in a cleft in the rock. Marlon had also drawn a circle around the woman and written next to her "Whoever that is ha ha!"

Beth looked at Edgar. "So that's not really Molly?"

"I don't know who it is, but I've never heard of anything around here called Ship Rock. Somebody probably screwed up somewhere." Edgar held the page closer to his face. The upstream end of the rock came to a point and sliced through the river like the bow of a ship. "Definitely resembles a ship, though."

Beth ran her finger down to the "Survivors" section of the obituary. "It doesn't say anything about George, just her family from back East. That's sad."

"Well, it's a New York newspaper, so maybe that's why they focused on her family. She was from there."

"Hmm." She frowned. "Still seems weird to me."

Edgar flipped through more papers in the folder. "Check this out, it's a photo of Nickel Rock."

The writing at the bottom of the photo read "June 1892."

Beth took it from Edgar. "Wow, that's really old."

"Look, there's writing on the back." Edgar reached for the photo and turned it over. He read aloud the words written in scratchy pencil. "'Front edge of Nickel Rock. Molly's treasure sealed into the rock on this end, which is now under the water.'" Edgar collapsed back into the couch. "Marlon, you dirty, rotten, liar…" His voice trailed off. "He thought he'd found out where the treasure was hidden. But I crawled all over that area and there's nothing on the front end of Nickel Rock, except some more rock. He's done all this for nothing."

Beth shook her head. "That's quite a risk he's taken, for himself and for us. Well, you also took the risk, but you didn't know everything the way he did."

"Wait a minute." Edgar sat up on the edge of the couch and examined the obituary printout again. He stared at the photo, covering up the front of the rock formation with his hand. "That sorta looks familiar." He went into the bathroom and held the page up in front of the mirror. "Beth, come check this out. It's Nickel Rock! The image is reversed. There's the ferries that run across the same places they do today. And the bow shape in this picture, the part that looks like the front of a ship, I think I saw that today. It's lying at the bottom of the river on the upstream end of Nickel Rock." He tapped on the screen of his phone, opening up a picture. "See the resemblance? I bet that crevice where the woman is sitting, that's where the treasure was sealed into the rock. Then somehow, before," Edgar picked up the photo of Nickel Rock again, "before June of 1892 that whole big piece fell into the river. That's why it's underwater in 1892. Marlon got within twenty feet of finding it, but he was looking in the wrong place."

Beth stared at the woman in the picture. The sun shone brightly on her white bonnet, her hands clasped in her lap. "Then this might actually be Molly."

"It's possible." Edgar held up his phone and took a picture of Ship Rock from the obituary printout, then got up and grabbed his flashlight.

"Where are you going?"

"I think I know where the treasure is, Beth, and I'm going to get it."

"No, Edgar. It can wait." Beth's voice grew louder.

"No, it can't. What if Marlon figures it out? I have to go now. I'm gonna lose my job, and we'll need any spare change we can find."

"Edgar! Stop! I don't care about some stupid treasure. All I want is you. If you walk out that door right now," she paused and took a shuddering breath, "I can't guarantee that I'll...that we'll be here when you get back."

"Don't you get it?" Edgar pulled on the knob of the front door but it didn't open. He leaned towards the door and heaved backwards, finally jerking it open and swinging it into the wall where the knob punched a hole. "Marlon's taken this too far and now we'll be financially ruined. I have to go see if it's there. It'll change everything."

"I agree." Beth's voice choked with emotion. "It will change everything." She stood up and went into their bedroom.

CHAPTER TWENTY

Edgar retrieved the pry bar from the backyard and made another trip to the maintenance building at the park. He added some tie-down straps, a pickaxe, and a shovel to his arsenal of tools, which he placed in the cargo box of a park utility vehicle. A reddish glow from the setting sun filled the sky as he drove down to the river. Marlon's car, with its gaping trunk hole, sat in the same place. The park was still deserted.

Edgar set the tools on a ferry raft and quickly pulled himself across the river. He stumbled when stepping onto the plank between the cofferdam and Nickel Rock. The pry bar slipped out of his sweaty hands and fell nearly fifteen feet onto the rocky riverbed. The prolonged, intense ringing of the bar pierced the quiet evening air. A flock of birds in the trees along the riverbank erupted into flight and headed upstream.

Edgar crouched low, his eyes scanning the area. Other than the fluttering and squawking of the startled birds, everything remained quiet. After several seconds he stood and walked across the plank and over to the upstream end of Nickel Rock where he hopped down onto the fallen limestone formation. From there an incline down the spine of the rock gave Edgar easy access to the riverbed. He set the shovel and pickaxe down and went to get the pry bar. Edgar brushed up against the long horizontal layers of water bags that made up the walls of the cofferdam. He poked gently at one of the bags and gazed up at the top. The height of the wall made him shudder.

He picked up the pry bar and went back to the upstream end and took out his phone. The glow from the screen lit up his face as he studied the picture he'd taken of Ship Rock. The crevice where Molly sat was on the left side in the photo. Since the photo had been reversed, Edgar explored the right side of the fallen rock. An overhanging ledge near the bottom caught his attention. In the recession below the ledge lay an accumulation of mud and gravel. After he shoveled away several loads of wet debris, an area appeared with a darker color and smoother texture than the surrounding limestone.

"Mortar," Edgar whispered.

He grabbed the pickaxe and poked at the cracked mortar. The area remained intact so he took a hefty swing at it. He cringed at the resulting sound and paused to listen. A large piece of mortar fell away and a quick check with the flashlight showed something brown in the newly exposed area. For the next twenty minutes Edgar swung the pickaxe over and over, knocking away more pieces. When only a few patches remained the brown object suddenly slid out of the rock and fell to the riverbed with a thud.

Edgar sat down and tried to slow his breathing. Crickets chirped and the river gurgled past him on the other side of the cofferdam. He picked up the flashlight again to shine it on whatever had fallen. The intensity of the light in the darkening skies made the whole cofferdam glow so he quickly shut it off.

Even in the fading light the shape was visible: A rectangular box about three feet long and two feet tall. Edgar ran his hand along the top and it came away with a layer of brown mud. He hoisted the box up onto his right shoulder, leaving streaks of mud on the front of his clothes.

The walk back up to Nickel Rock went slowly. Edgar checked his footing with each step and paused to look around when his head came up above the level of the cofferdam. He leaned over and reached across the gap to Nickel Rock, resting his weight on his left hand. He slid the box off his shoulder and onto the top of Nickel Rock, then pulled himself up. Once back across the plank he set the box on the raft and secured it with a cargo strap.

Edgar pulled on the ferry rope, his arms, legs, and back straining. The raft scooted along and ran aground hard on the riverbank. He unstrapped the box and carried it to the back of the utility vehicle where he strapped it down again.

Edgar got behind the wheel. Even though he'd ratcheted the strap tight over the box he reached around behind and kept one hand on it as he drove.

He coasted through the open bay door of the maintenance building and parked inside. Edgar rushed out and dragged in a garden hose before pulling down the bay door, locking it about an inch before it closed all the way. Leaning against the door, he wiped the sweat from his forehead and took a deep breath.

He turned on the lights, unstrapped the box, and set it down on the concrete floor. As he washed off the chest, coffee-colored water slowly flowed across the room and under the barely opened door. Black areas with a faint pattern, like woven fabric, began to show through on the box where the mud dissolved away. The box appeared to have been wrapped in burlap and coated with tar.

Edgar suddenly pointed the hose away from the box and stuck his fingernail into a hairline crack in the tar. Closer examination revealed a network of cracks laced all over the surface. He shrugged and resumed washing away the mud. "Not gonna be any wetter than the river," he muttered.

At that moment someone tried to open the locked bay door, which made the metal panels rattle and clang. Edgar startled so badly he dropped the hose and got his clothes soaked trying to grab the spray nozzle to shut off the water flow.

The person outside pounded on the door. "Let me in, Edgar. I know you're in there, and what you're up to."

Edgar tripped on the hose and finally got the water shut off. "Marlon?"

"You got that right. Lemme in."

"Why?" Edgar shouted through the door. "You got some new big fat lie to tell me?"

"Maybe I should rip this door open the way you did my car? I assume I have you to thank for that."

"Turns out it's much easier to get answers out of the car than you. Be quiet and come around to the side door." Edgar unlocked the door and opened it.

Marlon pointed at Edgar's muddy clothes. "I think you've been playing in the river. Did you find it?" He tried to look past Edgar.

"It?"

"Come on, Edgar, you know what I'm talking about."

"Why should I tell you anything?"

"It'll make sense when I explain it all to you. But for right now I think we can agree," Marlon smiled, "neither of us could have done this without the other. Am I right?"

"I could have done it within the law, and without jeopardizing my job." Edgar shook his head. "I did come across something, but I don't know what's inside yet."

"Where was it? I searched all over that stupid rock today and couldn't find anything."

"That's because you were looking in the wrong place. It was hidden in that giant formation lying on the upstream end."

"You're a genius, Edgar." Marlon laughed and patted him on the shoulder. "So, let me see it."

Edgar pulled his shoulder away from Marlon. "You've got a lot to answer for, but first I really want to find out what's inside."

Marlon let out a whoop. "You and me both, brother."

Edgar stood aside to let Marlon pass then closed the door and locked it. They walked around behind the utility vehicle where the box sat on the floor.

"And theeeeere it is." Marlon examined it closely. "It just looks like a box. I thought it would be a big pirate chest. So," he rubbed his hands together, "what are we doing here?"

"The covering makes it hard to tell what's under there, or how to get it open. But see this lump?" Edgar pointed to a raised area the size of a deck of cards located on one of the long sides, in the center and near the top. "I'm thinking that's a latch mechanism for a lid."

"Sounds good to me."

"I hope there's no lock to mess with." Edgar frowned.

"That did not appear to have been a problem with my car. I'm sure a Houdini like you can figure it out." Marlon glanced around the room. "Plus, there's plenty of stuff here to help us get it open."

Edgar held a utility knife. "I'm going to cut through the wrappings directly above that lump, and hopefully there'll be a seam where the lid opens."

When the blade touched the box, Edgar hesitated. "It seems sacrilegious to just start hacking into it. Maybe we should leave this to an archaeologist or someone who knows how to preserve historical artifacts. We have no idea what we're doing. What if we accidentally destroy what's inside?"

"Come on, Gar, you worry too much. We worked hard to find it, we've got it now, and I want to know what's in there."

"Okay. I guess." Edgar slowly guided the blade into one of the cracks in the covering and pushed. The tar had hardened into a formidable barrier and the blade did not go in very far. Edgar exerted more and more effort until his hand shook. "That tar is like a rock now, or I could be trying to cut through the container itself, for all I know. But I've got an idea."

Edgar went to a shelf on the wall and came back with a propane torch that he lit with a flint striker.

Marlon whistled. "Oh yeah."

Edgar turned the flame down low and moved it around the area near the lump.

"Crank it up, Gar."

"I don't wanna set it on fire. This thing might go up in a big ball of flame if we're not careful."

"Oh. Good point, I guess you're right."

A puff of smoke rose up from the box and Edgar pulled the torch back. "That's exactly what I was talking about."

"Okay, okay. I already agreed with you." Marlon pushed on the covering with his finger. "It's getting softer. Try cutting it again."

Edgar shut off the torch and wiped the sweat from his face onto his shirt. This time the blade cut through several layers of burlap. "It's working."

Edgar kept at it with the cutter, working down to a layer of fabric that did not have any tar.

Marlon peered over his shoulder. "Looks dry. That's a good sign."

The blade hit something solid and stuck.

"Grab me that screwdriver on the bench." Edgar pointed behind Marlon. He stuck the screwdriver into the cut and wiggled it around to make it wider, exposing pale wood. Prying back the burlap cover revealed a seam in the box. The screwdriver left scratches and dents in the wood. "Dang it," Edgar grimaced, "I'm scratching it all up."

"Come on, the inside's what counts. Not the stupid box. Think about what you did to my car."

"Still, I hate to tear it up for no reason."

Marlon picked up the torch and lit it. "I'll work the torch. You keep cutting."

"Okay," Edgar turned the knob on the torch, "but keep

the flame down low. Let's work all the way around the seam first, before we do the lump. If there's a lock it's going to bum me out."

It took almost an hour to extend the cut around to the back side where they came across a metal hinge.

"Hold on, Gar. We may not even need to cut this side open if it's hinged. Let's get the other three sides done and come back to this if we have to."

Edgar agreed and they started working on the other short side.

Thirty minutes later the seam lay exposed on three sides and they started in on the lump. Edgar cut around the perimeter and pulled away the covering, revealing a black metal latch with a keyhole.

"I was afraid of that." Edgar dropped the cutter and groaned.

"What's that button, below the keyhole? Try that."

Edgar shook his head and pushed on the button, which moved easily and let out a crisp click.

"Yes!" Marlon slapped the top of the box.

Edgar's arms trembled as he pulled up on the lid. It opened with a muted scraping sound. Inside a fitted oilskin pouch filled the entire chest, its flap buckled down snugly. The rich aroma of oiled leather hung in the air.

Edgar unfastened the buckles and lifted up the flap, which opened towards him and draped over the front of the chest. Underneath the flap lay a fur pelt. "That's beaver, and George Paxon was a trapper. This is incredible." Edgar pulled on the fur. "Feel this, it's like cream."

The fur turned out to be another fitted pouch that opened the same way. Lying inside were an assortment of boxes, small containers, and some photos. On top of it all sat a thin book covered in cloth.

"Well, I don't see any coins or jewels yet." Marlon pulled

out one of the boxes and turned it over in his hands then shook it. "There better be something of value in here."

Edgar picked up the book. "I think we should start with this, since it was on top. It looks like a journal."

He opened the cover. Written on the first page with black ink in a masculine hand was the name George Paxon. "This is George's!" Edgar flipped through the pages and they fell open to a section near the end. He read the entry aloud to Marlon:

> 16 May, 1883
>
> My time left on Earth I cannot say, as none of us can, but now is the time for me to lay these things aside. Packaged herein are the treasures of my dear departed wife, Molly. She held to them so firmly that she was unable to move on. Most notable is a lock of hair from our daughter Emma, bound with the purple ribbon she wore the day she drowned.
>
> Molly faulted herself in mistaking frantic cries for joyful shouts. I assured her she could not have known Emma had struck her head against Ship Rock, but she would have none of it and blamed herself.
>
> My dear Molly never recovered. She would sit upon her stool in the crevice of Ship Rock and stare at the river for hours, worrying that lock of hair with her fingers...

Marlon took a photo from the box he held and tossed it to Edgar. "So that really is old Molly, sitting at the river. There was a copy of this picture in her obituary."

"Yeah, I know." Edgar glanced at the photo. "I've seen it." He went back to the beginning of the last sentence he'd been reading:

> She would sit upon her stool in the crevice of Ship Rock and stare at the river for hours, worrying that lock of hair

with her fingers, unable to reconcile herself to the loss of our daughter.

I have no doubt this was all the more difficult to bear having lost so much family already. Her father disowned and disinherited her when she married me. Her mother and sisters were dear to her, and she loved and missed them all, even her contentious father.

Molly lost her past and her future, the bookends of her life removed against her will, and she could not stand in the present without them. She died of grief this past winter, five years after our dear Emma.

I have walked by this chest all winter, a continual reminder to me of Molly's heartache, and now of my own. I have come to realize what she valued is not in this box. The real treasure has been sent ahead, and it is time for me to move on.

My two greatest treasures on Earth have passed beyond my reach. The loss of them both has inflicted great pain which I often feared might undo me. That pain is very real, but I also know what is even more real - all this life is but a blink of an eye in eternity, and I will see them both again when I join them there. So it won't break my heart to leave this place when I die, and I won't let it break me while I'm still here. I walk through the darkness of today in faith that God will make all things perfect in the end.

I cannot bring myself to destroy these things, but I cannot keep them either. So I aim to put to rest both Molly's treasure and that infernal rock. This box is to be sealed into the very spot where Molly would sit and watch the river. I have hired quarrymen to blast away that section of Ship Rock so the leading edge will drop into the stream. If it falls straight and true, which the men say can be done, I believe it will cause a great wave to form for the approach to Ship Rock.

Edgar looked up from the letter. "He was right. You couldn't hurt yourself there now if you tried." He continued reading.

I drew people to these parts and I believe it my duty to do what I can to make it safe for those who follow. Some folks are upset that the appearance of the rock will become unrecognizable. That fool newcomer Ezell wrings his hands and asks "But whatever are we to call it now?" Frankly, that is not my concern. It does not make a nickel's bit of difference to me what it is called.

There is not much holding me here now. I have set aside my life earnings to start an orphanage in town. I desire no recognition for this, though I am compelled to name it after Emma.

Edgar paused again. "Emma's House? I'd say he kept that a pretty good secret. I know the building used for the children's home goes back to the early days of the town but nobody knows how it got started."

"Whatever." Marlon held up a cigar box. "This is worthless. Full of rocks and shells and junk." He dropped it on the floor.

"Hey! Don't do that." Edgar picked up the box and set it on his lap, then resumed reading.

I want to do what I can to help because I have endured the pain of losing a child, and I cannot imagine a child losing their parents.

So I say goodbye now to these reminders of my treasures. When I see them again there will be no more sorrow, no more pain.

Signed,

George Paxon

When he finished reading the entry, Edgar sat staring at the journal.

"Hair?" Marlon held up a mason jar. "A jar of hair, seriously?"

Edgar snatched the jar from Marlon. His mouth hung open as he gazed at the lock of blonde hair tied with a frayed purple ribbon. "This is unbelievable."

Marlon kicked the box. "I haven't found one single thing of any value." He rifled through the contents. "There's a blanket, an old Bible, a doll, a book of pressed flowers, some little dress thing."

The white christening gown fell onto the wet, muddy floor.

"Marlon! You self-absorbed clot." Edgar picked up the gown. "You know what? Beth has a lock of hair from my son's first haircut, which I was not there to see because I was jacking around with this stupid scheme of yours! George Paxon lost his family through tragedy. Beth's right, I'm losing mine because I'm not even showing up."

Edgar quickly set everything back in the box, closed the lid, and jumped to his feet. He pulled Marlon to the side door and yanked it open.

"Get out." Edgar shoved Marlon. "Get out!" He pushed Marlon again, sending him stumbling through the doorway.

Marlon turned and faced Edgar. "What's wrong with you?"

Edgar followed him outside and dead bolted the door. "I have to go home." He ran off into the darkness.

CHAPTER TWENTY-ONE

Edgar ran through the empty town. Turning onto his street he saw the truck parked in front of his darkened house. As he got closer the empty driveway came into view. Edgar ran faster.

Inside the house he found an empty bed, an empty crib, and a note taped to the refrigerator. It read:

> This is not what I want but I can't stay here right now.
> I've taken Junior with me. Please don't call.

Edgar called her immediately and it went straight to her voicemail. He tried to catch his breath before the beep. "Beth. I've been an idiot. I'm so sorry. I don't want to lose you. I love you, I love Junior, and I want our family."

He hung up and grabbed the keys to the truck. The clock on the stove read 11:42 PM when he ran outside. Edgar sped out of town, headed to Peyton.

Edgar rolled into Peyton at ten after midnight. The lights were off at Richard and Penelope Anne's home and Beth's car was not there. He stopped the truck and banged his fist on the steering wheel. "Dang it!"

He drove back to Paxon Chute and went by his parent's home but her car wasn't there either. Arriving back at the town square around one o'clock, he went to Emily's Place. There, parked in front of the picket fence, sat their old dingy car. Edgar came to a stop, took a deep breath, and whispered, "Thank you, God."

Edgar got out of the truck and felt the hood of the car. "Been here a while," he muttered.

No sounds came from within the bed and breakfast and all the lights were off. Edgar slowly wandered down Short Chute Street and over to the square. The stained glass windows of the church were brightly lit and Edgar went to peek through one of the front windows. Inside, Pastor Ken sat working at a small desk in the foyer. Edgar tapped lightly on the glass.

Ken smiled at Edgar and got up to open the door. "Good evening, Edgar." He looked at his watch. "Or rather, good morning, I suppose. Come on in."

Edgar stood at the doorway. "Uh, I didn't mean to disturb you. I just happened to be out and saw the lights on."

"Not at all, not at all." Ken motioned for Edgar to come inside. "I couldn't sleep so I came here to pray and work on my sermon for tomorrow." Ken closed the door behind Edgar. "You look distressed. Is everything okay?"

"No, not really. Beth's left and she's taken Junior."

"I'm sorry to hear that, Edgar. Let's have a seat in here." Ken led the way into the sanctuary and pointed to a row of chairs against the back wall.

Edgar dropped his weight onto one of the chairs. "I drove all over the place trying to find them and just now found her car at Emily's."

"Why did she leave? If you don't mind me asking." Ken turned a chair around so he could sit facing Edgar.

"She said I wasn't there when she needed me."

"Hmm…were you?"

"I've been busy, you know, working a lot, for sure. But I was doing it all for them, for Beth and the baby. We're barely getting by." Edgar shook his head. "Beth doesn't seem to understand that."

Ken pursed his lips and looked towards the ceiling. "Now Beth, she's an accountant, isn't she?"

"Well, yeah. I mean, she knows all the numbers and all that. But all she ever says is 'It'll all work out.'"

"There's a verse in the Bible, in Matthew chapter six, and I wonder if that's what Beth has in mind." Ken flipped through the pages of a Bible on the seat next to him and handed it to Edgar. "Here, read verses twenty-five and twenty-six."

Edgar took a deep breath and read it aloud. "'For this reason I say to you, do not be worried about your life, as to what you will eat or what you will drink; nor for your body, as to what you will put on. Is not life more than food, and the body more than clothing? Look at the birds of the air, that they do not sow, nor reap nor gather into barns, and yet your heavenly Father feeds them. Are you not worth much more than they?'" Edgar stared at the page. "But I was doing it all to provide for them."

"Were you? From what you told me it didn't seem like Beth was worried about it."

"I guess she wasn't." Edgar frowned.

"So who was all that work for, if she wasn't concerned?"

Edgar shrugged his shoulders. "I dunno."

"I wonder if you were doing it for you."

"What? No way. I hate working so much."

Ken nodded. "I'm sure you do, and I may be wrong. But, it sounds to me like you couldn't tolerate the discomfort and anxiety of not knowing what would happen, how God would provide." He paused. "Or, could it be you don't trust that God is good? All of our fathers here on earth disappoint us to some degree. Maybe you think God will let you down the way your own father might have let you down."

"Hmm. Maybe. There's definitely been some of that."

"When we doubt God it creates a hole in us, and fear rushes in to fill it. Fear, as a guide, is a ruthless tyrant. Instead of working to love them you were serving yourself. You thought you were meeting Beth's needs, but the whole time she was telling you what she really needed. Look back a few verses, at twenty-one."

"'For where your treasure is…'" Edgar faltered then started over. "'For where your treasure is, there your heart will be also.'" He stared at his feet, shaking his head. "What have I done?"

"The same thing a couple billion other people have done. You made a good thing, providing for your family, the most important thing."

Edgar glanced back at the Bible. "It's like this was written for me. And this whole thing, meeting you here now, in the middle of the night…" His voice trailed off.

"Ah, yes. Sometimes God does things like that, when we show up. I'm glad I showed up tonight."

"You and me both. I've been so stupid."

Ken shook his head slowly. "Well, I wouldn't put it that way, but it is an opportunity to grow."

Edgar stood. "There's one thing that symbolizes all of this. That stupid cofferdam. I'm gonna go tie up one loose end and then figure out how to dismantle it."

"I see. And the cofferdam," Ken raised his eyebrows, "you think it's really important to Beth right now?"

"No. I guess not."

"Then maybe it can wait?"

"Hmmm." Edgar walked over to the door. "Maybe. Thanks, I wish we'd talked months ago."

Ken held the door open and smiled. "I'm available most days, and many nights."

Edgar went back out onto the square. The lights along the park cast a faint glow on the blue cofferdam. He looked down the end of Short Chute Street where Beth's car sat in front of Emily's Place. Edgar stood still, glancing back and forth from the river to the car. He finally walked over to the bed and breakfast, went under the wrought iron arbor at the front and stepped up onto the porch. He sat down in one of the rocking chairs and fell asleep almost immediately.

* * *

Early the next morning when Beth came downstairs with Junior, Emily told her she had a visitor on the porch. Beth went out the front door and found Edgar asleep in the rocking chair.

Junior gurgled and reached his arms out for Edgar, who woke up at the sound of his son.

"Beth," he quickly sat up straight in the chair, "I've got to tell you something—"

"Hello, Edgar. Here, he wants to see you." Beth handed Junior over to him. "Whatever is going on with us, he needs you around."

"Of course." Edgar blew on Junior's belly, who squealed with delight. "I'm not going anywhere. But I've really got to tell you—"

"I'm not ready to talk about anything."

"All right." Edgar exhaled slowly and stretched out his legs.

Beth walked to the door. "I'm going to check on breakfast."

Edgar blurted out, "I went all the way to Peyton in the middle of the night, as if you'd be there. Not sure what I was thinking."

She kept her back to him and spoke softly. "I actually did drive about halfway then the thought hit me, 'What am I doing? Going back home to Mother? *My* mother?'" She shuddered then turned to face Edgar. "So I came back to town, and knocked on the door here. Emily said maybe it's no coincidence she's next door to Emma's House. They take the children and she takes the adults." Beth paused. "Thanks for finding us, but I'm not ready to talk. Not yet."

"Why don't Junior and I hang out somewhere for a while, and then go to church. Maybe we'll see you there?"

"Yes, I'm planning on going. I need it today." She turned away again and paused at the door. "That would be nice, for you to spend some time with him, plus I can have a break. I'll go get his bag." She went inside.

Edgar held Junior's arms so he could stand on the wooden porch. "Well, she didn't smile, but one step at a time, eh, little man?"

Beth returned with the bag. "He seems fine. None of the symptoms they told us to watch for have shown up at all. The list is in the side pocket. There's a couple tubes of numbing gel in there if he gets fussy. All right then, I'll see you at church." She turned and headed back inside.

"I love you." Edgar picked up Junior then slung the bag over his shoulder.

Beth gave no reply but did wave as she went through the doorway.

Edgar walked over to the playground at Nickel Rock Park. He and Junior were spinning slowly on a tire swing when Marlon stumbled out of The Snorting Bull. Edgar called out to Marlon, who squinted and looked around.

"Over here!" Edgar waved one hand and held Junior tight in his lap with the other, dragging his feet through the mulch to stop the swing.

Marlon walked slowly towards the playground.

"What happened to you, Marlon? You're all rumpled."

"Went by the Bull last night." Even from several feet away his breath smelled of whiskey.

"I can tell that, but it's morning."

Marlon licked his lips. "Woke up this morning on the courtesy cot."

"So we both did some porch sleepin' last night. Is everything all better for you now, after getting blind drunk?"

"What's it matter? I sat there yesterday," Marlon pointed at the river, "all fired up watching them pump the water out, or 'dewatering,' as they called it." Marlon held up his fingers in air quotes. "I was all Eager McBeaver to get in there and find my fortune. And now, nothing."

"Exactly. You dragged me and the whole town through all of this for nothing."

Marlon slowly blinked his bleary eyes and sat down in the swing next to Edgar and Junior. "You have no idea what I've lost."

"What you've lost? Do you know what I may have lost? All because you lied to me, Marlon."

"Lied? I only held back certain details, and that was to protect you. You would've had a fat share in whatever we found. It wasn't like I was going to cheat you out of anything."

"Well, nothing except for my time, my family, my dignity, my job, my trust." Edgar took in a deep breath then exhaled. "What got you going on this crazy idea anyway? You always said those treasure hunters were idiots."

"Last time I was in town I found an old photo of Nickel Rock in the attic," Marlon gestured in the direction of George's Goods. "I needed a frame for a picture I have of me skydiving. So when I took the photo out of the frame—"

"You saw the note on the back about Molly's treasure being underwater at Nickel Rock."

"Oh yeah, I forgot you violated my car and stole my files."

"If you'd just told me in the first place," Edgar pointed at him, "I wouldn't have had to do that to find out what you were really up to."

"My car's the least of my worries, right now anyway. All

the money to make this happen, I got it from my girlfriend's dad, in Chicago."

"Girlfriend? Let me guess, a Miss Sorrentino?"

"Yeah, Mary. I couldn't believe how lucky I was to find her, and that she actually stuck around. She and her whole family think the River in the Sky is real. All the money is gone and there's no treasure to pay them back, so I'm sunk. You remember that diver, Fritz Yunger? He got the crew to set up the cofferdam but went all psycho on me when he figured out we didn't have a permit. He started shouting at me about wanting payment in cash, immediately. That's where I was yesterday afternoon. He collared me," Marlon ran his fingers across a red abrasion on his neck, "and personally chauffeured me to Peyton for a wire transfer. I had to beg Mary for more money. She'll dump me when she finds out I blew it all on a failed treasure hunt."

"Wait, you really have a girlfriend? What about that hot date you told me about a month or so ago?"

"Ah, well, it wasn't really a romantic date, you know. Just friends."

"Hmm. Seemed like you were really, really good friends the way you described it." Edgar paused. "What's your dad going to say about all this?"

"I can't talk about it anymore." Marlon rested his head in his hands.

Edgar lowered his voice. "What are we going to do with the box? I think we should put it back where it came from."

"Whatever." Marlon shook his head. "I gotta go." He slid out of the swing and left.

* * *

Clyde and Edgar walked out of the church together after the service. Down at Nickel Rock, workers were winching the last of the empty cofferdam bags out of the river. The water flowed around Nickel Rock once again.

"Hey!" Edgar pointed at the river. "Someone's taken it down."

Clyde pulled Edgar aside and looked him in the eye. "I called Strickland and told him about the cofferdam."

"Why'd you do that? I thought you didn't trust him."

"I trust he'd find out about it very quickly, one way or another. It's best to have him as close to your side as you can, if at all possible. Having him report it to TAGO is better than it coming out the other way around."

Edgar turned to the river. "I won't be able to put it back."

"Put what back?"

"I, um, left some tools down there and I wonder if I'll get them back. What exactly did you tell Strickland?"

"I'll explain it, but not here. I'm hungry. Let's grab some Brammies and go for a ride. Your mom, Beth, and Junior are having lunch at the café."

They stopped by Señora Schwertner's butcher shop then walked over to the truck in front of Emily's Place. Clyde held his hand out. "Keys, please. I know where we're going."

They got in and Clyde drove off. "I told Strickland you'd gotten tangled up with a loose cannon. He said he'd worked that out by himself right off the bat. I let him know about that Yunger character and his outfit, he's an interesting piece of work. Anyway, Strickland made them come out straight away and take down the cofferdam." Clyde drove up into the hills that ran along the west side of town.

"Oh man oh man oh man." Edgar leaned back on the headrest. "What's going to happen now? Will TAGO fine us?"

"They might. Strickland said he's going to include in his report that Mr. Rerd tipped him off and provided assistance in getting things resolved, so that might help you and the town both. Ambiguity can be a powerful tool in the right hands."

"Do you think he should do that? And why would he?"

"He knows all about Junior's emergency and how you were tied up because of that. I did not mention that there were other family issues you were dealing with."

"Family issues? What do you mean?"

"What do you mean, what do I mean? You've lived here your whole life and don't know word's gonna spread about Beth staying at Emily's last night and you sleeping on the porch? Didn't seem like a portent of ongoing marital bliss between you two. So did you boys find what you were looking for?"

"What do you mean?"

"This conversation's gonna get tiresome if you keep asking that."

"Well, that was an abrupt change of subject. It caught me off guard."

"And the answer to my question is?"

"How did you know we were looking for something?"

"Come on, son, all the smartest people in town suspected something was up."

"What?"

"Of course, I'm the only smartest person in town I know, so I'm not sure if anyone else suspected anything. Except Eloy, he's always on top of things." Clyde turned onto a narrow dirt road where the trees formed a canopy overhead.

Edgar stared at his father. "Why didn't you say something?"

"Because I'm not always right and I didn't want to be raining all over your parade in case I was wrong. Early on I figured it was one of two bad ideas: Either Marlon was after the treasure or that aerial monstrosity was for real. But lots of my good ideas turn out to be bad, so I thought maybe whichever bad idea this was might turn out to be good. After a while it became clear to me Marlon's endgame was the treasure."

"How was that clear to you? He caught me by surprise."

"I knew for sure at the town meeting where he showed the pictures about drilling into Nickel Rock. That was a red herring if I've ever seen one. So you found something, right? And it's not the economic bonanza you thought it would be, is it?"

"How...? Maybe it would be faster if you shared with me everything you already know. You're as bad as Marlon."

Clyde smiled. "Even if what you found had been filled with some kind of financial instruments of the day, like bonds or banknotes, it's highly unlikely they'd be worth anything now. Unless it was overflowing with gold coins and giant rubies, but come on. There was a low probability that any real riches were waiting to be discovered, and the odds are diminished even further by what I'm about to show you."

"Where are you taking me? This road only goes to the old Chibitty place, and the gate's always locked."

Clyde stopped at a rusty stock gate with a large "No Trespassing" sign on it. He dangled a key chain from his finger. "That must be what this key is for. If you'd do the honors."

Edgar got out and unfastened the lock that secured a thick chain around the gate. He swung the gate open.

Clyde pulled up next to his son. "Close that and lock it, if you would, please."

"Seriously, Dad? No one ever comes up here."

"Yes, seriously. Recognize this fence? You helped me build it."

"Oh yeah, sloggin' around in the mud, diggin' in the rain. Longest spring break of my life."

"That's the one. Still looks solid, huh?" Clyde drove past the gate, which Edgar shut and locked.

When Edgar got back in the truck he started in with another question. "Why did we—"

Clyde held up his hand. "You'll find out soon enough."

The dirt road wound around among the trees. An abandoned house came into view on their right.

Edgar looked out his window at the ruins of the house. "That must be the old homestead. I've never been up here."

"Not many have, for many generations now." Clyde drove past the house.

Tree branches scraped against both sides of the truck as the road narrowed and went up an incline.

A limb smacked into the windshield, making Edgar flinch. "Sure is overgrown."

The branches encroached farther and farther until the road came to an end in front of a heavily wooded area.

Clyde shut off the engine. "This is where we get out."

The doors of the truck would not open very wide because of all the scrubby brush. Both men had to squeeze through to get out.

The distinctive sounds of cicadas filled the air. A group of buzzards circled above, gliding effortlessly on a thermal. The hot afternoon air felt thick in the still woods.

Clyde worked his way around the truck and over to Edgar. "Let's go." He ducked his head and went into the dense foliage.

Their feet sunk through the deep layer of leaves on the ground and stirred up smells of dust, mold, and earth. After making their way along for about ten minutes the trees thinned out and they came to a clearing bordered by a low iron fence. There were several headstones in the clearing.

"Wow." Edgar stopped. "I didn't know there was a cemetery here."

"It's kept secret." Clyde pushed on the rusted metal gate and it screeched open. "There's only a few laid to rest here."

Three headstones sat in a row, side by side. Edgar spoke the name on the rightmost stone, "Molly Paxon."

The full inscription read:

Molly Hardwick Paxon
Born December 21 1851
Died November 3 1882
Lord haste the day
When the faith shall be sight

Edgar kneeled down. "This is incredible."

"Now read that one." Clyde pointed to the stone on the left:

George Paxon
Born June 22 1839
Died December 21 1898
Thou hast taught me to say
It is well with my soul

In between them a smaller headstone read:

Emma Marie Paxon
Born August 1 1871
Died July 17 1877
Our treasure

Edgar sat down facing the graves. "Amazing. Dad, I've got to show you what I found, it makes all of this so clear." He turned to Clyde. "But you already knew, didn't you? You knew Emma was their treasure. Why didn't you just tell everyone the real story? Then all the hunting nonsense would go away."

Clyde sat on the ground beside Edgar. "I don't think it would have worked out that way. George didn't go crazy and bankrupt like the stories about him say. He gave away all he had to help others. When he died, George's Goods was auctioned off, but not because he was in debt. It all went to Emma's House. At the time everyone around here knew what he'd done with his money, they knew what Molly's treasure really was, and they knew it was Emma's keepsakes hidden in the submerged section of what used to be called Ship Rock. They knew but they kept quiet, out of respect for George and what he wanted."

"How do you know all of this?"

"Eloy. The Chibitty family was around these parts back then, and they were good friends with George. The family has passed down the true story through the generations. But over time things get distorted by other people because they believe what they want to believe. That's where all the tall tales came from. So now, even if we revealed poor little Emma's grave here, it wouldn't convince them otherwise. It'd only get her dug up over and over. Nothing is more mulish than misguided public opinion. The way to keep this place safe is to keep it hidden, which is what the Chibitty family has done. That's the reason they keep this property locked up."

Edgar leaned over, reached out his hand, and traced his fingers across the lettering on Emma's headstone. "Why were they buried here, instead of the town cemetery?"

"Molly wanted Emma tucked away up here, far from the river. The Chibittys gave this plot to the Paxon family."

"Okay, you've got to see what's in the box we found, Dad. It'll make the hair on the back of your neck stand up. Oh my gosh." Edgar jumped to his feet. "I locked it in the maintenance building at the park. I've had so much on my mind I forgot about it. We've got to go get it."

"We will, but hold on a minute. The cofferdam's gone, you can't put the box back where it came from."

Edgar drew in a breath past his clenched teeth. "I know. I feel terrible about that. I wanted to seal it back up in the rock, but I don't know what to do now."

"You can't un-happen what's happened, but what you can do is the next right thing. And I think the next right thing is to lay that box to rest right here with them. That will keep it secret and honor George's intent."

"Seems right." Edgar stared at the headstones. "I want Beth to know about all this. I haven't had a chance to tell her."

"I spoke with Eloy and he agreed it was good for you to let Beth know. Your mother is the only one I've ever shared this with, until today."

"So everyone who knows should be here, when we bury it."

"Yes, our wives should be here." Clyde nodded. "No one else knows."

Edgar looked at him. "What about Eloy?"

"He said to go ahead without him. Eloy connects with the past through stories, not things."

"Were you ever going to tell me about all this?"

"The deal is that we each pass it on to one person. I knew you were the one a long time ago because of how you love this land. You always seemed at home here, like me. That's why I had you help me with the fence."

"And we built it to help keep this secret."

"Yup."

"Wow. All those years ago when I was just a kid, and I had no idea. I always wondered why we did that for Eloy. I figured you'd run up a big bar tab."

"That was an honest guess." Clyde stood up. "Let's go fetch that box. I'll tell your mother to give us a couple of hours and then she can head up this way with Beth and Junior."

* * *

Clyde and Edgar waited for the women at the gate of the Chibitty homestead. The men were sweaty and dirty from hauling in the box and the tools, and then digging a hole at the foot of the three graves.

Ruth's car pulled up, bringing a cloud of dust with it. Clyde waved her through the gate, which Edgar shut and locked behind them. The men got in Clyde's truck and led the way up to the wooded area.

They stopped a little ways before the dirt road ended. Edgar picked Junior up out of the car seat and the four adults made their way through the woods to the clearing. Clyde and Edgar took turns sharing parts of the story with Beth and Ruth as they walked.

"Edgar!" Beth thumped him on the arm. "You found the treasure? What was in it?"

"I think it would be best if you experienced it for yourself. We're almost there."

When they came to the clearing Beth stopped at the sight of the headstones and gasped when she read them.

Ruth dabbed at her eyes with a tissue. "I still tear up sometimes when we come here." She handed a tissue to Beth.

They spread a blanket on the ground for Junior.

Edgar sat down in front of the box. He opened the lid, folded down the two flaps, and picked up the journal. "Dad hasn't heard this yet either, so I'll read it aloud." He read George's last entry, stopping several times to take a deep breath.

When Edgar finished, Clyde pulled out his hanky and blew his nose. "That's a fine thing, that is."

Beth and Ruth both needed another tissue when Edgar held up the jar with the lock of Emma's hair.

Edgar moved over beside Beth and took her hand in his. "I want to say that I know I've screwed everything up. When I read about how George lost his family, all I could think was that I didn't want to lose mine. Can you forgive me for not listening, for not being there, for letting everything else be more important?"

Beth pulled him in and hugged him tight. "Yes." Her tears dropped onto Edgar's neck, leaving streaks across his dusty skin. "I forgive you, Edgar Rerd."

He held her close and whispered in her ear, "I'll never be the same, after this."

"I know." She sniffed. "Me either."

Junior looked up at his parents, smiled, and kicked his legs. "Doo-woo!"

CHAPTER TWENTY-TWO

Clyde and Edgar were smoothing out the dirt over the box when Edgar stopped and leaned on his shovel. "Are we sure about not keeping the journal, or even reading the rest of it?"

Beth sighed. "I am. We've seen enough to know what George wanted. Seems like anything beyond that would be a violation of some kind."

Ruth set three yellow roses tied together with a pink ribbon on top of Emma's headstone.

Clyde took Edgar's shovel. "There's one more thing I want to show you, and it's back at the house. Why don't you and Beth and Junior come over for supper?"

They made their way out of the trees and back to the vehicles then drove to the elder Rerds' home. Clyde stopped the truck in front of the barn. "Let's step into my office."

The dogs, and Luther the goose, wove around Clyde's feet as he walked to the barn. Shimei stopped suddenly and sniffed the air. He barked and raced over to Ruth's car. Junior giggled when the big Labrador leaned in through the open door and licked his bare foot.

Clyde went to the back of the barn where his model railroad layout took up most of the far corner. He swapped his feed store cap for a train engineer's hat. "All aboard." Clyde smiled and handed a hat to Edgar.

Edgar pulled it down on his head and looked over the

layout, which depicted Paxon Chute and the railway lines in the surrounding area. "I haven't seen this in a while. Any changes lately?"

"Funny you should ask. I've opened up the old loop again."

"The one that goes through town, past the square? I thought you only ran on track that's actually open in real life."

Clyde adjusted his hat. "Maybe real life needs to run where I'm running, instead."

"Why?"

"See if this gives you any ideas." Clyde turned a knob on the control panel and a model train emerged from the enclosed maintenance depot. He pushed a button and the whistle came to life.

Luther squawked in reply.

"Good dog." Clyde picked out a piece of deer corn from a bag hanging beside him and threw the corn to the goose. Luther pecked at the corn and wagged his stubby, feathered behind.

The black and red locomotive cleared the depot and three open-air passenger cars were in tow behind it.

"What's that all about?"

"Marlon was right about one thing: The buses are a pestilence we'd love to be rid of and that's how he got the town to go along with all of his monkey business. This is an alternative that's for real. The loop runs right through town and around the upstream end of the park."

The model train headed down along the river towards Paxon Chute.

"Yeah, but if buses are expensive I can't imagine what a train would cost."

"That's a valid point. However, I still have lots of good contacts at Texas and Pacific and they want to donate some equipment. It's good PR for them."

"Who would run them?"

"There's a bunch of us old-timers trying to find something to do. This would be way more interesting than puttering around on speeders once every other blue moon."

Edgar pointed at the south end of the town square. "Where's the old A. L. Cooke engine that used to be in front of the museum?"

Clyde laughed. "You're not paying much attention, are you? Look at the train."

"That's it?"

"Yup. It's one more reason T&P is interested. They want to work with us to get that old steam engine operating again, and another one like it. It'll take a lot of volunteers to keep it going, but people always come out in droves to bring this kind of history alive."

"Two trains? We could haul a lot of people. And with steam engines, that would be so awesome."

"It'd be a great attraction in itself, even for people who aren't interested in floating the river."

"Wow. So what would you call it? Texas and Pacific?"

"They'll put their name on it as a sponsor. But I've something else in mind." Clyde stopped the train in front of Edgar.

Red letters ran along a lightning bolt on the side of the engine. Edgar read aloud, "Rail Rerd? You've got to be kidding."

"What? I like the play on words."

"Dad, you've gotta admit you don't have the best track record when it comes to naming things."

Clyde turned the knob again, sending the train on its way. "I have no idea what you're talking about."

* * *

The next Wednesday Mayor Orville called an emergency Town Council meeting to discuss the cofferdam incident. It set the all-time record for attendance and everyone had something to say.

Orville rapped his gavel. "All right, there's too many mouths in here for everyone to mumble their comments to their neighbor. You can either quiet down or take a lap around the square. What's it gonna be?" He glared at them with his bulging eye.

The crowd quieted immediately.

"That's better. Now, I have here a letter given to me by Mr. Marlon Ezell and I would like to share it with y'all." Orville read it aloud.

> To the town of Paxon Chute,
> I, Marlon Ezell, tricked the town in general, and Edgar Rerd specifically, into going along with my River in the Sky proposal. It was never my intent to actually develop the aerial tramway. It was all a cover story so I could look for Molly's treasure...

Gasps and voices among the attendees interrupted Orville, who paused and swept the room with his gaze until they settled down.

Orville cleared his throat and continued.

> ...which I believed to be hidden within Nickel Rock below the waterline. When we set up the cofferdam I found no treasure. My information was flawed. I take full responsibility for any consequences of my actions. I apologize to the town and to Edgar. He did not know about any of this.
> Sincerely,
> Marlon Ezell

Edgar turned to Clyde. "Just once I'd like to have some idea what's going to happen at one of these meetings."

"At least this is a good surprise, eh?"

"Yeah, that's rare from Marlon."

"And you already know what I'm going to bring up next." Clyde winked at him.

Edgar tugged at the collar of his park uniform. "I guess knowing doesn't always help."

Mavis raised her hand. "Is Marlon here? I've not seen him."

"No. He left me this," Orville displayed the piece of paper, "on his way out of town earlier this week."

Someone at the back of the room called out, "Full responsibility indeed!"

Orville shook his gavel at the commentator. "That's enough of that! Now, TAGO has agreed to not assess any fines against the town. They may go after Marlon, but that's their business. As for poor Edgar here, I find no fault with him. He was duped like the rest of us. If anyone has anything else to say, now is the time."

Tom Walker raised his hand. "I'm in agreement. Let's move on."

Audience members chimed in with calls of "yes," "hear, hear," and "amen."

Orville nodded his big round head. "Okay. That's the end of that. But it still leaves us with a bus problem. Mr. Clyde Rerd has asked to speak to this issue. Mr. Rerd?"

Clyde went to the podium. "I don't have any fancy charts or anything to show you all, but my son and I do have an idea for you to consider. Texas and Pacific wants to donate a bunch of rolling stock for us to use in hauling people back upstream. And they also want to help us get two old steam engines operating. One of them is sitting in front of the museum right now. It would become a living, breathing museum instead."

The crowd erupted into lively discussion as people fought over the chance to voice their approval.

Orville stood and banged his gavel repeatedly with a slow cadence. "All right, all right. I think I can discern the overall mood of the attendees."

From the councilor table, Ward held up his hand, index finger pointing to the ceiling. "I have one question. Who is going to manage this operation?"

Clyde waved Edgar up to the podium. "I think it should be run as part of the park. That's what makes the most sense to me."

Ward tapped his fingertips together and stared as Edgar walked towards Clyde. "Need I remind everyone how Edgar's last endeavor turned out?"

Clyde leaned in close to the microphone and turned so he could lock eyes with Ward. "Yes, but your son is not involved in this one so I think we're good." The crowd broke out in laughter and applause. Clyde smiled. "I propose we call it Rail Rerd."

The room went silent.

"Ward," Orville fixed his bulging eye on him, "we've moved on. I suggest you catch up. Mr. Chibitty," Orville pointed the handle of his gavel, "you had something to say?"

Eloy stood. "A good name is not as important as a good idea. The tramway was a bad idea. The train is a good idea. When my great-great-grandfather first saw a train come through here, it was an unnatural beast that never looked right to him because he had nothing to compare it to. He grew up in a society that did not even use the wheel. It is funny what you get used to. But I would never have got used to that ugly thing Marlon wanted to build. I think we should do what Clyde and Edgar are talking about."

The Town Council voted approval to conduct a financial analysis and a safety review of the railroad concept but tabled Clyde's motion to name it Rail Rerd.

After the meeting, Edgar pulled Clyde away from the

crowd in the parking lot. "Dad, I don't know how to run a train." Edgar watched people stream out of the Town Council meeting. "What am I getting myself into?"

Clyde grinned. "We'll get there. Life is a one step at a time venture. Just take the next step."

"I know. I guess I'm still a little rattled after Marlon's deal, afraid my next step will take me off another cliff."

"I hope this doesn't seem quite as perilous as trying to navigate through Marlon's mysteries."

"No. Definitely not. And," Edgar paused, "I don't intend on standing in this parking lot the rest of my life for fear of cliffs." He took a deep breath and looked up at the late-summer sky. "I love this time of year."

Peter walked up to them. "Clyde! Edgar here has informed me of your fine detective work in ferreting out the dark forces behind the salamander issue. To think a man of your generation using modern technology to track down the truth being obscurified by the duplicitous Mr. Milden."

"You make it sound so miraculous. I'm not a complete troglodyte."

Peter shook his head. "No no no, that is not my point at all. Exactly the opposite. You single-handedly sleuthed it all out, and now you've come up with this fantastically new idea, rescuing us from the River in the Sky and returning us safely to the ground once again, bringing the romance and adventure of train travel from a bygone era back to our lovely hamlet. That's a fine performance delivered by you, sir, act after act."

Clyde smiled. "Why thank you, Peter."

"Come along, you two," Peter clapped them both on the back, "I'll buy you gentlemen a drink."

Clyde did not move. "Thank you kindly, Peter, but I'm going to take a pass."

"Now that I think of it," Peter stopped and turned to Clyde, "I haven't seen you around the Bull very much lately."

"Is that so?" Edgar raised an eyebrow.

"Well now, I always intend to go have one drink and just enjoy everyone's company. But too many times I wind up drinkin' until I can't even remember who was there. Seems to defeat the purpose. I try to have Eloy cut me off but that's no real solution. He's too short to be my mother and too smart to pretend he's my conscience."

* * *

The next spring, Beth and Edgar stood near the gazebo on the town square after the ribbon-cutting ceremony for the new train service. Junior tottered around at their feet taking stiff-legged steps.

At the south end of the square in front of the railroad museum the old A. L. Cooke engine sat in nearly the same position it had occupied for the last fifty years. Fresh paint sparkled on the locomotive and the three cars behind it. Smoke rose steadily from the stack. Steam hissed near the wheels and dissipated as it swirled up the sides, revealing bright red lettering that spelled out "Rail Rerd."

The train whistle blew at the top of the hour and Edgar glanced at the clock tower. "Time for our first run. I half expected Dad to be late. It still makes me a little nervous, relying on him."

Junior held up his arms towards Edgar and laughed. "Daa!"

Edgar picked up his son and hugged him. "But, I have to say he's really seen this through." Edgar watched his dad climb up the steps of the locomotive.

Beth held Edgar's hand. "You okay?"

"Yeah, I am. I'm okay. Supper at five-thirty, right?"

She took Junior from Edgar. "Yes, but I thought you'd be busy today."

"I'm sure I will. See you at suppertime." Edgar kissed each of them on the cheek then ran off to catch his own train.

THE END

CAST OF CHARACTERS

Aaron – see Turner, Aaron

Abbie – Waitress at the Circle on the Square Café

Beth – see Rerd, Beth

Brooks, Kendall – Pastor of Cornerstone Church located on the town square

Chibitty, Eloy – Owner of The Snorting Bull, also the head bartender

Clyde – see Rerd, Clyde

Drew – see Rerd, Drew

Drew, Mavis – Owner and operator of the Kettle Corn Cart

Dunlop, Wilbur – Local postman, one of the barflies at The Snorting Bull

Edgar – see Rerd, Edgar

Eloy – see Chibitty, Eloy

Emily – see Wright, Emily

Ezell, Linda – Marlon's mother, Ward's estranged wife

Ezell, Marlon – Childhood friend of Edgar

Ezell, Ward – Marlon's father, owner of George's Goods

Fritz – see Yunger, Fritz

Gardner, Orville – Principal of Creekside Junior High and part-time mayor of Paxon Chute

Garth – Works for Edgar in the park

George – see Paxon, George

Kendall – see Brooks, Kendall

Linda – see Ezell, Linda

Marlon – see Ezell, Marlon

Martel, Peter – Drama and history teacher at the high school and leader of local community theater group The Interpretarians

Mavis – see Drew, Mavis

Molly – see Paxon, Molly

Orville – see Gardner, Orville

Owens, Richard – Beth's father

Paine-Owens, Penelope Anne – Beth's mother

Paxon, George – Frontiersman and trapper, founded Paxon Chute in 1869

Paxon, Molly (Hardwick) – Eastern socialite heiress, married town founder George Paxon

Peter – see Martel, Peter

Penelope Anne – see Owens, Penelope Anne

Peyton – Larger, neighboring town of Paxon Chute

Rerd, Beth (Owens) – Married to Edgar

Rerd, Clyde – Edgar's father

Rerd, Drew – Clyde's younger brother and Edgar's uncle, one of the barflies at The Snorting Bull

Rerd, Edgar Allan – Married to Beth, head park ranger at the local Nickel Rock Park

Rerd, Ruth – Edgar's mother

Richard – see Owens, Richard

Ruth – see Rerd, Ruth

Tom – see Walker, Tom

Turner, Aaron – Police Chief for Paxon Chute

Walker, Tom – One of the barflies at The Snorting Bull

Ward – see Ezell, Ward

Wilbur – see Dunlop, Wilbur

Wright, Emily – Owns and operates Emily's Place, a bed and breakfast right off the town square

Yunger, Fritz – Engineering diver hired by Marlon Ezell

ACKNOWLEDGEMENTS

My thanks to...

Jesus.

Stacey, my love, best friend, wife, best editor, and biggest believer.

Justin for awesome book conversations, and your edits, and proofreading once again.

Kevin for theater workings and terminology, and ongoing enthusiasm regarding my efforts.

Julie for being so excited about my writing, and how you inspire me with your lovely imagination and stellar writing skills.

Sarah, Linda, Mike, and Patrice from The Inklings, who gave me such great feedback and encouragement.

Bonnie for being so awesome, asking so many questions, and reading every chapter, every time.

Camille at An Eye for Editing for such top-shelf editing. Any mistakes are mine and undoubtedly instances where I choose to go my own way.

Percy for asking me lots of questions, for reading, for sharing your thoughts, and for your friendship.

Ada for reading the whole thing... twice, and for so much prayer and affirmation.

Ellen for taking the time to share her labor and delivery nursing expertise.

Lee for sharing the words and scripture references he uses during baby dedication ceremonies.

The other Keith for urging me to attend my first writer's group, and for Lois who joined us and graciously hosted our meetings.

The Keller Writer's Association for always helping me to improve.

Everyone who asked to read my manuscript (or agreed when asked), read what I gave them, and shared their thoughts with me: Tammy, Odessa, Deon, Mark, the other Julie, Allison, Charlotte, Amos, Tom, Denise, Clover, and Teri.

The following public domain works were quoted directly: "Under The Round Tower" by William Butler Yeats, 1918; *As You Like It* by William Shakespeare, 1623; *Great Expectations* by Charles Dickens, 1861; "It is Well With My Soul" by Horatio G. Spafford, 1873.

Clyde's use of "endeavoring to persevere" was inspired by the movie *The Outlaw Josey Wales*.

Peter's "appeal to the highest court of detection" was inspired by Sir Arthur Conan Doyle's book *The Sign of the Four*.

The line in George's letter, "So it won't break my heart to leave this place when I die," was inspired by the song "Elijah," by Rich Mullins.

ABOUT THE AUTHOR

For years people have been telling Keith Cartlidge he should write a novel. He finally believed them and poured his vision of small town life into *Paxon Chute: A Novel about Life and Other Funny Things in the Texas Hill Country*, the first offering in the Paxon Chute series. Keith lives in Texas with his wife and three children.

www.keithcartlidge.com

Find out more about the town of Paxon Chute at
www.paxonchute.com
and search for the Paxon Chute community and its residents
on Facebook.

This book is available in ebook format at most online retailers, where you can also leave a review. Thanks for reading!